SCHOOLED
IN
DEATH

A Thea Kozak Mystery

Book Nine

Kate Flora

Book and cover design by eBook Prep
www.ebookprep.com

January, 2019
ISBN: 978-1-947833-99-9

ePublishing Works!
www.epublishingworks.com

CHAPTER 1

$\blacklozenge$

It was Monday. Always the worst day of the week in the working world. So when my phone rang before I'd showered, brushed my teeth, or even opened my eyes, I knew I was about to be the recipient of bad news and a summons to someone else's troubles.

I was not wrong.

"Is that Thea, then?" a man's voice asked.

Reluctantly, I agreed that it was.

He didn't need to give his name. His gentle Welsh lilt announced my caller was Gareth Wilson, headmaster of The Simmons School. Gareth was the most optimistic person I knew. Usually, just hearing his voice improved my mood. Today, his tones were shot with pain at the situation he found himself in, a situation he rapidly described. One of their young boarding students, a girl no one knew was pregnant, had given birth in her dorm bathroom during the night and left her baby in the trash. It was only because another student had heard the faint sounds of crying that the tiny infant had been found and saved. Now the baby was in a neonatal ICU and the terrified mother, only a child herself, was facing potential criminal charges.

Gareth needed my help—or rather the help of my business, EDGE Consulting—to manage the situation on his campus and in the wider world. Immediately if not sooner. That was the problem with being a private school trouble-shooter—when people called me, their emergencies were usually already underway and they were rarely something I could handle over the phone. Today was no exception. Gareth needed me on campus now. He was two hours away in the crawl of morning traffic and my calendar was already full.

"It's complicated, Thea," Gareth said. "The girl insists that she has never had sex, never mind been pregnant, and the baby can't possibly be hers, even though she has obviously just given birth. And she seems, as much as one can judge under these circumstances, to be utterly sincere."

In the background, I could hear the soothing music of a Palestrina mass. Gareth definitely needed soothing.

A million questions immediately presented themselves about the girl and her situation. Questions of drugs and date rape, or of mental illness, among others. But those would wait until Gareth and I were face to face.

On the other side of the bed, my husband Andre gave up trying to sleep and grimaced at a clock that said five forty-five. He tossed off the covers and stood. Naked. Gorgeous. The outline of his little red Speedo the only untanned part of his body. A wonderful sight to start the day. It's not just me, though I readily admit to being prejudiced in his favor. Perfect strangers of the female persuasion stare and sigh softly when he passes. He mouthed, "Shower. Join me?"

I nodded as he headed for the bathroom, throwing off my own covers so I could cross to the desk and make some notes on what Gareth was saying. Damage control was my specialty. I was the girl in the white hat, the word-slinger who rode into town and made things right again. He needed me there as soon as possible. I would have to do some rearranging if I was going to be able to help.

"She's not been arrested, which is something," Gareth said. "They took her to hospital and she's now in our infirmary. But the investigation's on-going, and the police are considering charges."

"What's our girl's name?"

"Heidi," he said. "Heidi Basham."

That name, Heidi, conjured up images of blond pigtails and the Swiss Alps and Grandfather feeding some goats. My mother had been a great fan of the book.

"What year is she?"

"Sophomore. But this is her first year at the school."

So yes, I thought, *the girl is awfully young.* "You've called her parents?"

"Of course. And they're on their way. Her mother and stepfather, at least. Flying into Boston from the West Coast," he said. "It's a divorce situation. The mother said she'd let the father know."

I wasn't comfortable with his decision to let the mother control the notification, but discussing that could wait until I was showered, dressed, and on the road. I preferred to handle important details when my eyes were open and my brain was fully operating.

As if he'd read my mind, he said, "We've tried to reach the father. This time and others. He's…uh…difficult to reach. I gather he travels a lot."

The traveling parent. Another reason kids got sent to private school. No one at home had time for them. I felt a spike of sympathy for this girl, wondering if this pregnancy might have been a grab for attention that went horribly wrong.

Anticipating my next question, he said, "And yes, I was on the phone to our lawyer as soon as ever it happened. Once he'd established that she hadn't been arrested, I got a quick paragraph of instructions and a 'call me back in the morning,' which I took to mean at a more civilized hour. We'll for sure get him in later this morning, but I'm expecting he'll be telling me that the poor girl will need her own lawyer. I'll get some suggestions from him so we'll be prepared when her mother arrives. Obviously, Heidi being a minor, we'll need mother's consent for that."

The clock was ticking. I had calls to make to free up my day if I was going to drive to Simmons, so I said, "I'll be there as soon as I can, Gareth. I'll call you from the road."

"I'm beyond relieved to know you're coming," he said. "I'm afraid I'm a bit thrown by all this."

"All this" had happened in the night, but the facts would soon spread across the campus. Boarding schools were like small towns. Everyone—students and faculty alike—lived in each other's pockets and news and gossip traveled at the speed of light. Gareth was already reeling from the implications of the event for his school and anticipating the sorrow and confusion his students would feel over such shocking behavior by one of their own. Any headmaster would be struggling with this. Heidi's unusual situation, and assessing her denial of the facts and getting at the truth, was a significant complication.

The other complications were the kind that occurred whenever there was a crisis involving a student on a boarding school campus: managing the disclosure of information to the media, to the involved student's parents, the student body, and their parents, in a manner least damaging to the school. Divorced parents made things even more difficult, as often the divorces were so bitter the parents couldn't even be in the same room together, despite the fact that the matter concerned their child. Far too often, when EDGE came into these situations, part of our job ended up being to babysit, or verbally control, a set of warring parents. Also complicating things, of course, would be dealing with the police.

Our business, EDGE Consulting, works with independent, meaning private, schools. We work with schools on their image, on "branding" their special niche in the education world and helping them to promote and protect those brands. Simmons's brand was particularly vulnerable in this situation. It was a small, elite, non-denominational private school north of Boston with a reputation for educational excellence. Their special niche was nurturing a responsible, caring, community-oriented student body with particular attention to environmental science, social justice, and global awareness.

The Simmons campus was so green and vegan it was practically a sin to wear leather shoes. Students worked in the greenhouses and campus gardens and helped run a day-care center for low-income children. They valued diversity of culture and opinion. It was a self-selected community of budding activists, humanistic citizens, and locovores. The last place on earth, in short, to have a pregnant student fly under the radar, never mind surreptitiously deliver a baby and abandon her newborn to almost certain death. The situation would have been bad anywhere, but the value the school placed on personal responsibility and open and honest communication made it a particularly bad place for someone to deny responsibility for endangering a vulnerable life.

Mostly, EDGE worked on promoting positive images. Branding was the buzz word. Gareth had called me at such an uncivilized hour because of the importance of *protecting* an image. He needed immediate help with public relations and damage control. My job was shaping the message to the student body, parents, and public in a way least damaging to the school. Not that this situation would ever be all right, but the timing was terrible. Acceptance letters had recently gone out and prospective students were choosing their schools for next fall.

In this case, the school's unusual character would be a double-edged sword. Gareth would have better control of his students, and what they communicated, because they believed in discussion and consensus within the student body, and a more difficult job explaining to his students how one of their own had veered so far from the school's core values.

In most school populations, information control was difficult. Between cell phones and social media, students were so connected to the world that keeping the story under wraps was impossible. Still, Simmons was a community, with shared values, and a sense of responsibility to that community and the wider world. Students chose to go there because of that. It was a better place for shaping the message than most.

I wanted to disconnect and get dressed so I could get on the road, but there were a few more issues we needed to discuss.

I urged Gareth to email his students, explain the dilemma they faced, and ask them to hold off discussing it until the administration could explore the details of what had happened. His message should be that the situation was complicated, called for open minds and compassion, and that when he had the facts, he would bring them together as a student body to explore the implications. That was how they worked at Simmons. Community. Open communication. Respect for a diversity of opinions.

As I stumbled across the cold floor to grab some clothes, I ached for the pain they would be feeling. For a student body who felt their values had been betrayed, and for the student whose situation—about which we knew so little—had led her to betray them.

I knew how the world would judge them. I feared for how the parents would react, even though they'd chosen this special community for their children. But I hoped, a hope Gareth echoed, that within their community they could come to understand what had happened, offer forgiveness and support, and emerge stronger.

We both knew he had other things to worry about: the impact on applicants for next year's class, on skittish parents who might consider withdrawing their children, and damage to the school's reputation as a close and caring community if something like this could happen under their noses. Schools acting in loco parentis were always vulnerable to the charge that they had failed.

I was about to disconnect, but as I pulled out underwear and tights, I had another thought. "You said the girl denies that she was pregnant?"

"She does."

"And her denial seems genuine?"

"She wasn't in the best of shape to answer questions, in the circumstances, but I'd say yes. She seemed credible."

These were critical issues—the age of the young mother, the events leading to the pregnancy, the mother's mental state, the reaction of her family. It was all part of building the story, of translating Heidi from heartless monster to someone deserving of compassion. From someone indifferent to the welfare of an innocent baby to a desperate child herself, possibly even unaware of her pregnancy, with few options and impaired judgment. Perhaps a victim herself.

I was not being a weasel. Truth mattered. But there were often many versions of the truth, depending on whose point of view you told the story from. There is a Rashomon element to most stories that involve more than one person. "So have you...or will you...get a good psychiatrist involved?"

"We will. I agree that it's essential. It's not a good time of day to try and reach anyone."

An embarrassed silence as we both shared the thought that he hadn't hesitated to reach me.

"We have some good prospects in hand," he said, "and as soon as the hour's more civilized, we'll be making those calls." He hesitated again. "I'll ring off now, Thea, and let you get ready. But do, please, call me when you're under way."

He didn't say, "And hurry!" but that was what he meant.

I would hurry. Of course. But first, despite the urgency of my client's situation, I needed a shower, and the world's best inducement awaited me.

I carried my clothes into the bathroom, pulled off my nightgown, and stepped into the shower.

CHAPTER 2

L ess than half an hour later, I stumbled down the stairs and headed out into the cold, dark morning. I wore stretchy black pants that felt too tight and a loose black knit tunic. The combo seemed too informal for the work that lay ahead, but most of my clothes didn't fit anymore. I had no time for shopping, and I wasn't going to wear anything bright or colorful to deal with a crisis like this. I had tried to counter the informality with a hand-painted silk scarf in shades of gray, black, and navy. It helped a little.

As I unlocked the car, I could hear birds twittering in the fat pine trees across the lawn. At least the birds were in a good mood. Me, not so much. I was still very tired. I need more sleep these days.

I was getting better at taking care of myself. I used to throw myself headlong into everything. I used to go hours without eating while I focused on my work and then ravenously devour food that was bad for me. Now I had Kind bars and almonds in my briefcase and carried a go-cup of coffee. I was clean, dressed, and utterly unenthusiastic about the task ahead.

Don't get me wrong—I love my work. I love helping clients out of difficult situations, bringing order out of chaos, and calming people who are thrown by campus mishaps of all sorts. I've been doing it for quite a while now and I'm good at my job. Given the number of times I've had to go up against recalcitrant, or downright dishonest headmasters, stubborn boards of trustees, careless or indifferent faculty, hostile families, and even armed bad guys, I have dubbed myself "Thea the Great and Terrible." I'm a trouble-shooter. I am not someone to tangle with. I don't back down from hard work and serious challenges.

This case, though, presented a unique challenge. Pregnancy and babies are kind of a tender subject for me. Finally pregnant myself after a traumatic miscarriage, I worried that I might not be able to muster the detachment and compassion that Heidi Basham, Gareth, and Simmons would need to get through this. I'd briefly considered sending my partner, Suzanne, instead. But Suzanne was nursing an infant, and had temporarily stepped back from any work that involved travel. It would have been quite a picture, though—the mother of a newborn defending a mother who'd abandoned hers.

But that was unfair. The shorthand version might include the word "abandon," but it sounded like there was a whole lot to Heidi Basham's story that we didn't know yet. Until I had the details, I couldn't make a judgment about her decisions. And I had to remember that we were dealing with a young teenager's brain.

I spent the first twenty minutes of the drive making calls to rearrange my day, and freed up the next day as well, in case I was still needed at Simmons. Luckily, our EDGE staff is incredible, and Lisa and Bobby quickly stepped in to pick up what they could. We needed to hire new people, but with Suzanne's limited availability, everyone was moving so fast there had been no time for that. As soon as things slowed down, one of us would start the process of hiring. Meanwhile, we all lurched from task to task and tried to remain good humored.

I called Gareth and told him I was on the way. The good news was that they'd located a psychiatrist, a woman with a strong local reputation, and she would be seeing Heidi later in the morning.

We made some plans about meeting with his deans and the trustees. I gave him some basic advice about keeping his staff and teachers on message, and assembling a list of parents' names and phone numbers. Then I went back to driving and he returned to damage control.

Driving in rush hour traffic anywhere south of Portland, Maine, took a lot of concentration. Increasingly, people are finishing their personal grooming in their cars, and some of the things they're doing are truly astonishing. Shaving? Check. Squinting into the rearview mirror to put on mascara at seventy miles an hour? Check. Eating a bowl of noodles, which required one hand to hold the bowl and the other the spoon? Check. But every time I think I've seen it all, something new and more shocking comes along. Among the oddest? The man using scissors to clip his nose hair. I couldn't help but wonder what they'd say in the ER if he was rear-ended and the scissors cut into his brain. The lawyer's daughter in me wondered if that would be contributory negligence?

My current candidate for Gross Act of the Year was not on the highway, thank goodness, but on a local street. It was the guy who was brushing his teeth. Seriously. At first I didn't know what I was watching as that moving arm went scrub, scrub, scrub. Until he came to a stoplight, opened the driver's door, leaned out, and spat into the street. Then he drove to the next light and did it again. Too horrid to imagine, if I hadn't seen it done.

I'm not that old, in calendar years. Only heading into my mid-thirties. But in terms of being judgmental I'm suffering from premature old fart syndrome. Maybe it's because so much of my work involves helping people out of messes caused by bad behavior or bad choices. And I might be a little influenced by being married to a Maine state police detective whose work involves homicide, child abuse, and other nasty things. If I deal with the difficult and uncivilized, he deals with the inhuman, and the ripples caused by crime in the lives of others. I guess we're entitled to be a bit cynical.

The Simmons campus pretty much matched its values. Much of the landscape was open and green, or densely treed. Green lawns ran down to a winding, bucolic river that disappeared into a copse of trees. The buildings were modern, painted brown, and built to blend into the landscape. The architect's object, I'd been told, was to create a design where the land dominated the buildings rather than the reverse. I knew that nestled into the trees behind the administration building were some larger, modern classroom buildings and a state-of-the-art gym.

As I wound my way through the campus, admiring the fresh spring greens of grass and new leaves, I lamented, for a moment, a life that never seemed to give me time to be outside. Perhaps little Mason or Oliver or Claudine—MOC or Mock—would change all that.

As I got out of the car, I could smell spring in the air— that strange combination of wet and muddy and green and hopeful. A hope that might be dashed as a freak late-season snow was predicted for this afternoon. But there was no time to linger. I grabbed my briefcase and hurried inside to Gareth's office.

Normally, Gareth was the epitome of calm, the kind of person whose affect calms those around him. Today he looked like someone who has taken a severe emotional beating but has to keep on functioning. His gaze fixed on me like a drowning man hoping to be tossed a life ring. I often worry that people put too much faith in me. It's a burden that I volunteer for, yet feel the weight of.

Gareth was an import from across the pond, with an English accent (he would correct me and say Welsh) and a charming, rather un-UK openness. He had unruly sandy brown hair, a neatly trimmed beard, and the kind of dark-framed glasses male models wore in ads to make them look smart. A few seconds of conversation with him, though, left no question that this man *was* smart. Smart and decent.

Dedicated to his school and the well-being of his students. I've spent years in the independent school world, and I can vouch that this is not always the case.

I'd never seen him off his game before, but the way he grabbed my hand told me he was close to the edge. We sat down on a pair of matching sofas, and I got out my pad to take notes.

"Dr. Elaine Purcell will be joining us shortly," he said. "She was able to rearrange her schedule and come earlier. We are so lucky she's available. Dr. Richard Alvin, one of our trustees...you've met him, I think...says she's very good at this."

I was about to say that I still had only the vaguest idea what "this" was, when Gareth did his mind-reading trick. "I know. I know. You've little idea what this whole business is about, and yet I've dragged you into the middle of it. We truly do need your help, so let me fill you in a bit more."

I waited while he rang his assistant and asked if we could get some tea and perhaps a plate of scones, while I smiled politely and wished I'd eaten a dozen Kind bars in the car. Or a small cow. Some days, it didn't so much feel like I was eating for two as that I was eating for a pack of wolves. MOC obviously took after daddy.

Politeness—and food—having been taken care of, he settled back and began to describe the situation in more detail. The young woman who'd been pregnant and delivered her baby in the bathroom, Heidi Basham, was a sophomore, just turned sixteen. Heidi was a shy, quiet girl who tended to keep to herself, new to the school this year. It had been winter. Heidi was tallish, big-boned, full-figured. She'd favored oversized flannel shirts and bulky sweaters, and although they'd been attentive and made a point of spending time with her, neither her advisor nor her dorm mother had noticed her condition. Even though the Simmons food was very healthy, when Heidi grew rounder, they had assumed it was the weight gain common to students new to eating institutional food. The famous freshman, or in this case, sophomore, fifteen.

The hand he rested on his knee was shaking. I put mine over it. "Gareth, obviously this situation is serious, but it is not the end of the world. We'll handle it."

"I'm supposed to be in charge here, Thea, and I'm struggling to wrap my mind around this. Around any of it. It breaks my heart to think of the hurt the students feel, their sense of betrayal, never mind the damage to the school, and yet I can't blame that poor child and I need to see that they don't, either. At the same time, I keep thinking how could she? I have to keep reminding myself she's only a child herself."

He broke off. "Let me finish filling you in, instead of this pathetic whingeing."

Heidi had been home for two weeks for March break, only six weeks ago, yet, as far as he could ascertain, neither her mother nor her stepfather had noticed her condition, unless the squawks of shock and dismay during his phone call were simply well disguised lies. Communication with them had been spotty and difficult even before things became an emergency. Neither parent had taken an active interest in their child's progress and despite several attempts to update it, the father's information in the file was so scanty as to render him unreachable.

"Quite frankly, I have no idea what their reaction is," he said. "There's been the phone call I made to report the situation, and another from Mrs. Norris about their travel plans. In neither have I been able to get any read on their feelings."

His eloquent shrug conveyed his disbelief more clearly than words. "They, well actually only the mother, though I could hear the stepfather in the background, didn't ask any questions about Heidi's health or emotional state, not whether she was in hospital or distressed, never mind her legal situation." His wide shoulders rose and fell. "What parent doesn't express concern or ask questions in a situation like this?"

A smaller shrug, and a sad smile. "And there was no mention of the baby. I fear it's what we see far too often at boarding schools. The parents divorce, the custodial parent forms a new relationship, one in which the child becomes an inconvenience, and the child is shipped off to school and effectively forgotten." He sighed. "Though you know, we see less of that here. We're not a school most parents would choose. Our Simmons students are pretty much a self-selected population. Heidi had to affirmatively want to come here."

I wondered whether, if a parent was eager to be rid of the girl, it didn't matter what Heidi chose so long as she went somewhere. But we didn't have enough information at this point to assess that.

He pulled his hand back and ran both of them through his hair. "But to choose us, and then do this?"

I had to interrupt. "We really don't know what she's done, Gareth, or what may have been done to her. What if she's telling the truth? What if she never knew that she'd had sex? What if she had no reason to suspect she was pregnant?"

"Is that possible, in this day and age, in a girl of fifteen?"

I wasn't sure of my facts, just of my instincts, when I said, "I think it's possible. Let's see what the psychiatrist says."

I switched back to our immediate problems—what to do about Heidi's parents and what to tell the students, faculty, and the rest of the parents. "When does her mother get here?"

"Mrs. Norris, and the husband she refers to as 'the General,' are arriving from California this afternoon. I've arranged for a car service to pick them up and they'll be staying with us at the headmaster's residence."

I was pleased they would be staying at his house, as his guests. Keeping them on campus, away from reporters, would be better for damage control while still showing concern and compassion. I wished more of my clients were as far-sighted. And then I remembered that this was a divorce, and there was a father, and that there were questions I needed to ask about him.

But Gareth was talking.

"About Heidi," he said, and continued to share what he knew. She had had a friendly relationship with her roommate, but had not confided about her condition, and her roommate, Bella, reported that Heidi was very private—almost secretive—about dressing and undressing, so that she had rarely seen Heidi undressed, especially since they'd come back from Christmas break. It was odd, but Simmons was the kind of place that attracted odder students because of its culture of accepting, even celebrating, individual differences. Bella said she assumed, from things Heidi had said, that this was because Heidi was self-conscious about her weight.

Heidi's passion was working in the greenhouses, and she seemed to have a real green thumb. She sang in chorus. She played the guitar. She was a strong science student. Her advisor found her pleasant, if somewhat quiet, and a good citizen of the Simmons community. She did not have a boyfriend or a girlfriend, though Jaden, a boy who also liked to work in the greenhouses, was described as a good friend, and another sophomore transfer, a boy named Ronnie, was also a friend. No one who knew her at all thought what she had done was consistent with the person they knew. Simmons as a community was big on personal responsibility, and the students Gareth had spoken with couldn't understand how Heidi could have done what she did. The consensus was this wasn't like her at all.

I admired how much Gareth had gotten done while I was driving and most of the world was just waking up. He'd learned—or knew—a great deal about her, information that would be valuable to me in helping to understand, and shape, the story. Another mark in his favor.

"Where is Heidi now?" I asked. "Still in the infirmary?"

He nodded. "She went to hospital earlier to be checked out, but they saw no need to admit her. We just wanted her someplace safe, where we could keep an eye on her. Harder to do that in the dorm, with everyone else so agitated, so I suggested the infirmary. The police, and Heidi, agreed. I think, to give them credit, that the police are handling this as sensitively as they can. They've no interest in demonizing her. It's going to be the media and the public. And the police chief warned me that unfortunately we've got a grandstanding DA."

He ran a hand over his face and I heard his calluses grate against stubble. He had earned those calluses from working with the students in the greenhouse and the gardens. From chopping and stacking wood. The stubble was from having been called out to handle this before he'd had a chance to shave. Headmasters tended to be a tweedy bunch, but Gareth looked like someone who should be wearing hiking boots and a backpack and heading off to climb something challenging in the Brecon Beacons in South Wales. Tall, broad-shouldered, lean, and lanky, he looked like, and was, a good man to have your back. I hoped he and I would have Heidi's. Despite my earlier reservations, I was feeling strangely protective of this girl I'd never met.

He'd bucked up while sharing the details. Now his big shoulders slumped. "This is not a case for blame, Thea. It's a situation that calls for compassion for that baby and for Heidi. But it's going to be hard to get people to see it that way."

He had that right. The public is always looking for someplace to put blame, a focus for all their own anger and frustration with their lives and with the people around them. They loved stories of people behaving badly, especially mothers. The press understood this only too well. They would pump this one dry, demonizing Heidi as sexually promiscuous and heartless, and Simmons as a place that encouraged teenagers to be radical and irresponsible. Few, if any, would read the school's mission statement, or, if they did, would claim the students cared more about plants than people. In their thirst for sensation and scandal, few would consider what Heidi's true situation might be.

Not that I knew that yet myself.

"What about the baby?" I realized I didn't know. "Boy or girl?"

"Little girl. She's doing okay. A premie. She's a bit under four pounds."

"So this wasn't a full-term pregnancy?"

He shrugged. "The doctors say it doesn't look like it was."

"What does Heidi say?"

He looked at the ceiling, down at his hands, and finally, at me. "She says that she's a virgin. That she has never had sex, never mind been pregnant. That the baby isn't hers and this is all a big mistake. She doesn't understand why anyone would accuse her of this awful thing and is terrified about what the other students must think."

The door opened and his assistant, Peggy, came in with a tray that she slid onto the coffee table in front of us. A teapot. A carafe of coffee. Two cups. Cream and sugar. A plate of scones and another plate with bagels, little pots of cream cheese, and smoked salmon. That last was inspired. Far too often, despite my intent to reform, I left home without breakfast and struggled through a client day with nothing that resembled food. I could get by on Kind bars, kinder to myself than I used to be. But they really didn't count as food. I could tell Gareth shared my views by the way he had to still his hand from grabbing a bagel before he'd thanked her. He probably hadn't had time to eat, either.

When Peggy had gone, he smiled. "The bagels are her idea. She worries that I forget to eat or that I don't eat well. Not that bagels really count as eating well."

At least they counted as eating. *Thank you, Peggy*, I thought. I wanted a Peggy to look after me. I'd had the perfect assistant but she was left behind when we moved the business from Massachusetts to Maine. I organized a cup of cream and sugar with a little coffee. The advice on coffee and pregnancy was conflicting. I like it a lot and I need it to function. I limited it as much as I could.

I snagged a bagel, and asked, "But this *is* her baby, right? She *was* pregnant? She has recently given birth? There's no question about any of that?"

"Absolutely. But what she said was that she woke in the night because she'd gotten her period. It had been irregular and she was worried. When it came, it was very heavy and she was having terrible cramps, so she went into the bathroom and she dealt with it. She cleaned herself up and went back to bed."

He shook his head. "She didn't act like someone who was lying to protect herself. She genuinely seemed to believe what she was saying."

It was possible. Sometimes teenage girls could be in serious denial about an unwanted pregnancy. "Sounds like you're really going to need Dr. Purcell, if Heidi will talk to her."

He nodded.

I could almost feel the ticking of the clock. "Your lawyer," I began.

"We've talked by phone again. Someone is coming around eleven. I think," he looked a little embarrassed, "I think they're sending a woman because it will look better. As though this is a game and not about real human lives." Another big shrug. "I hope we'll have some information for them by then."

He was right. It shouldn't be a game and it was about humans. But managing the parents and the media? Shaping the story? In some ways, that *was* a game. A big stakes game where winning was important. Maybe I *was* becoming too hardened. Because this was mostly a tragedy, perhaps a tragedy averted for the tiny little girl, but a big tragedy for another girl. For her mother.

In this context, the word "mother" seemed so out-of-place. I hoped, when Heidi's mother arrived, Heidi would get some mothering, and there would be someone to make thoughtful decisions about the baby.

Gareth cleared his throat, a subtle call back to the matters at hand. If I was a human checklist, then Gareth was a big black pen crossing things off. So often, when I give advice over the phone, I show up at a school to find they'd done nothing but wait for my arrival. It's hard to get out in front of things if you don't take immediate action.

Before I could move down the list, and ask about Heidi's father, Peggy knocked on the door and entered without waiting. "Dr. Purcell is here," she said. "Shall I bring her in?"

Elaine Purcell was tallish, slim, and had the kind of thick, sleek, gray chin-length bob I've always admired. My hair, when it reached that stage, would just be a wild gray mass. She was head-to-toe shades of gray, with a paisley gray scarf so perfectly arranged her stylist might have just stepped out of the picture. I didn't have a stylist and the best I could do with a scarf was drape it around my neck and tie a knot, as I had done this morning. Suzanne, who despairs about me, was, until recently, my personal shopper, and Andre likes me without clothes, so I've never come to terms with sartorial challenges. Dr. Purcell had.

She looked smart and pleasant, and when she spoke, her voice had the rich resonance of someone who sang plaintive folk songs in her spare time. A pleasing voice to listen to, though in my limited experience shrinks didn't talk all that much. Also a commanding voice, one that could compel a response.

She crossed the room in three quick strides, took Gareth's hand between hers, and said, "Dr. Wilson. I was so sorry to hear about your situation from Dick. I hope I'll be able to help."

As Gareth introduced us, she shifted her gaze to me. She had eerily penetrating eyes, the odd light blue of a husky, and I felt like she could see through my skin. Maybe she could, because she took my hand between both of hers and repeated, "I hope I'll be able to help." A quick glance at my midriff told me she hadn't missed my condition, either. A clever and observant woman. Exactly what we needed right now.

I didn't know how Heidi would react to Dr. Purcell, but *I* wanted to confide in her. Some of the situations I've been called in on have left plenty of bad stuff going on in my head that she might have helped with. But she wasn't here for me. I wasn't here for me, either.

Gareth explained that I was there as a specialist in managing campus crises.

"I hope it won't come to that," she said. "But we all know what the press is like." She dropped onto the couch across from me, took a scone, and smiled at Gareth. "If you could rustle up another cup, I would love some coffee. And then you can fill me in about your student."

If I'm fairly confident, she took it to a whole new level. I finished my bagel, moved on to a scone—orange-cranberry and delish even if it did cover me in crumbs—and drank my coffee while he filled her in with the little we knew. Then I went to meet with the deans and the school's communications staff while he took Dr. Purcell to the infirmary to meet Heidi. We really couldn't do much without the results of her assessment. What she learned would help us to craft the school's public message as well as help the administration prep for the student meeting to be held later that afternoon.

In the meantime, I could work with them on the basics— get family contact lists generated and designate the staff members who would be calling all of the parents with a prepared message about the campus situation. Help them with an outline of what would be told to the students at the all-school meeting. Begin working on a draft press release for distribution and to be posted on the school's website that would represent the school's official position on the situation to the world at large. Perhaps most important, having the Dean of Faculty send a reminder to all staff about not discussing the situation with anyone outside of school, and noting that discretion about discussing school business was part of their contract. It's sad but true— sometimes the faculty can be more childish than the students.

I also spoke with the Dean of Students and the Head of Residential Life about ways they could support the rest of the students. A situation like this, where a student breaks the rules in a manner that's shocking to her peers, can have all kinds of ripple effects through a school community. The students would need their advisors and their faculty (often one and the same) to be available and understanding. They would also need that universal staple of teen life—snack food—available in places they tended to congregate. They would need to know, and frequently be reminded, that counselors were available if they needed to talk. They would also need to be reminded that, if possible, they were not to discuss the matter outside the community except with their parents. That last was a long shot, but we had to try.

As I talked, I suppressed visions of the story exploding on social media before we even had an idea of what "the story" really was. With so little known and such an explosive event, I was walking around with what felt like ten pound weights pressing on my shoulders, with a sense of impending doom I needed to shake off in order to work.

It was wonderful news that the baby had been found in time and that she had survived and was doing well, but the threat of criminal prosecution still hung over us—a whole range of potential charges from neglect to attempted murder. I was disappointed that the school's attorney was scheduled for so late in the morning, even though Gareth said they had spoken earlier, and concerned about when she would meet with Heidi. I'm a lawyer's daughter, and while I know how unpleasant lawyers can be, in this case, both Heidi and the school were seriously in need of a lawyer's protection.

That was something I could deal with when Gareth and Dr. Purcell returned. I needed to meet their lawyer myself. Another item on my checklist for protecting the school. It seemed unlikely, given the maturity of the baby, that she had been conceived at Simmons. Heidi had started the school year late, arriving in mid-September. Still, the fact that the pregnancy had gone undetected *was* a problem we had to anticipate. It could be seen as evidence that the school hadn't taken proper care of Heidi, and, by implication, wasn't caring for their other students. We were in an awkward position here—we had to protect the school while also protecting Heidi. At some point, the school's interests and hers might diverge, and there would be choices to make. We would know more after Dr. Purcell had spoken with Heidi.

Though Gareth had been diligent and I'd gotten a good response to my preliminary advice, much of the situation was still very murky. And more murk lay ahead. None of us knew how the situation would develop when Heidi's mother and stepfather arrived. And I still didn't know whether Heidi's father had been informed about the situation. I had seen noncustodial parents go ballistic when they felt they'd been slighted, however indifferent their behavior toward their children had been. Gareth said the mother was going to notify the father, but that was not something it was wise to count on in a divorce situation. Depending on the parents' relationship, she might have deliberately neglected to tell her ex.

Gareth had noted that the father was hard to reach, but that didn't let Simmons off the hook. I was going to have to get on top of this.

I made more notes about things to do on my pad, with "Heidi's father?" at the top of the list.

Meanwhile, my vibrating phone had been rustling in my purse like a restless mouse. Gareth hadn't come back yet, so I wouldn't upset anyone by dealing with my own business instead of his. I pulled it out and scanned my messages. Crap! The easy immediacy of texting and phone calls, coupled with the way it feeds into peoples' entitlement and impatience, means no one is willing to be put off any more. I had canceled, rescheduled, or postponed all of my other clients for today and tomorrow, but several people who still had questions weren't waiting. Whoever advised us to "be here now" obviously hadn't had a life that demanded being in several places at once. Maybe I'll retire soon and write my own book: Be Everywhere Now.

Worse yet, in the course of efficiently postponing my business responsibilities, I had forgotten about my own mother despite the fact that my focus was all about mothers and children. More specifically, I'd forgotten to cancel dinner with my mother. We were supposed to meet half way between my place in Maine and her home south of Boston. Now the screen said she had called and left a voicemail.

We'd arranged to have dinner because my mother wanted my help planning a baby shower for my brother Michael's toxic wife Sonia, a task somewhat akin to agreeing to rub myself all over with sandpaper and then letting my skin be salted. Michael and Sonia carry such a miasma of dissatisfaction, arrogance, and entitlement that two meetings a year are about all I can handle. Helping my perfectionist, never-satisfied mother plan the perfect party for them fell somewhere below cleaning up after raccoons that have been into the sunbaked remains of a lobster dinner on my list of favorite activities.

Today's dinner would have had one positive aspect: I'd planned to surprise my mother by telling her she was going to have two grandchildren. She'd be sure to find something wrong with how I was going about it, but at least news of my pregnancy would temporarily suspend her infuriating inquiries about my reproductive progress.

I would have to cancel. I had no idea when I would be done here, and didn't need any more pressure on my day. I had time to cancel, it was still morning, but I would have to make actual voice contact. My mother doesn't believe in texting. Or short messages. Nor does she read, or pay attention to, most texts or email messages sent to her. Before I called her back, I checked voicemail to see what she had to say. Maybe she had called to cancel. My stomach clenched as I listened through a series of complaints, problems, and slights before she finally got to the point. A point that drew an immediate sigh of relief. We would have to reschedule dinner.

My relief lasted exactly one inhale and one exhale before she delivered her reason for canceling. There was an emergency. She'd call me later to give me an update.

CHAPTER 3

The word "emergency" clicked me into panic mode—a panic mixed with extreme irritation. What sane person leaves the message that there's an emergency, but fails to say what the emergency is? I tried her cell phone. She didn't answer. She's pretty good about answering, so that cranked my anxiety up a few more notches. Then I tried my brother. He wasn't answering. Neither was Sonia. I tried Aunt Rita and Uncle Henry. No answer. Either the whole world was avoiding me, or, more likely, the whole world was busy helping her deal with her emergency, and none of them had thought to keep me in the loop.

I could hear my mother's voice as clearly as if she was in the room. "Well, I tried to call Thea to let her know, but she's always too busy to bother with me."

I *was* busy. I have a demanding job. She doesn't respect what I do because I don't have an MBA or make a high six-figure salary, like the daughters of some of her friends. And of course, while she had all the time in the world to natter on with her complaints, she had not told me what her emergency was. My mother is organized in the extreme. She runs her volunteer organizations with an iron hand, so her failure to include relevant information scared me even more. Complaining was her MO, being evasive was not.

There wasn't much I could do about it, though. I left a message I didn't expect she would listen to. Then I left texts and messages for everyone else. If no one called back, I would try again in a while.

Meanwhile, I called Magda, our office manager, gave her everyone's numbers, and put her on the case. Magda is the epitome of efficiency and she intimidates everyone, including my mother. If anyone could get me the information I needed, it would be Magda.

The message had rattled me, though. As we all know, our imaginations fill these voids with the worst possible scenarios. And I needed all my concentration here. I pushed my own concerns to a back burner, trying to stay calm as I refocused on Simmons. Gareth and Dr. Purcell should be back soon, and the lawyer was due soon, too. I wanted to make one more call while I was still alone. To my partner, Suzanne. I wanted to run the situation—the one here at Simmons, not my mother's mysterious emergency—past her, in case there were things I was missing.

"What about the student?" she said. "Have you met her yet? Got any idea what's going on?"

"The psychiatrist is meeting with her right now. I expect we'll know more once that's done."

"If the psychiatrist can talk to you."

That raised an alarming possibility. I'd been naively assuming that since the school had contacted her, Dr. Purcell worked for us. What if Dr. Purcell came back and said she was sorry, but even though we'd contacted her and arranged for her to meet with Heidi, she could repeat nothing about what had transpired between them? What if we had no more information to work with than we had right now? That would complicate everything.

"I'm sure she will. She and Heidi must both understand that part of the purpose of this meeting is to help the Simmons community understand what's going on."

"We can hope," Suzanne said. She didn't sound optimistic.

I was still trying to be an optimist. Not easy, given what life keeps dishing out. We agreed to talk again in a few hours, and I went back to damage control. I was supposed to be the cool-headed professional, here to meet my client's needs. I took my worries about my mother's emergency and tried to shove them into one of those lock-boxes that Andre always tells me I need to use. Cops are good at that, but I'm a civilian. The door wouldn't quite close.

Then Dr. Purcell and Gareth were back, and we sat down to discuss what they'd learned. It wasn't good. Heidi had talked freely enough, but instead of providing concrete information that might help her fellow students understand the situation, what she'd said was pretty mysterious.

Affirming what she'd told her housemother, Gareth, and the police earlier in the day, Heidi insisted that she had never had sex and so she couldn't possibly have been pregnant. Dr. Purcell talked about psychological reactions common to young teenage girls that led to denial and an ability to suppress reality to the point where their own truth became their reality. She also talked about fear and trauma and the resulting possibility of repressed memories if the pregnancy had resulted from an assault, and stressed the importance of trying to get more background on Heidi's life before she came to Simmons.

"It is genuinely possible," she said, "for Heidi to have not known she was pregnant, even to have delivered that baby and thrown it away, honestly believing she was just cleaning up a mess. Possible, in other words, if she was suffering some kind of traumatic amnesia, for Heidi to believe she was telling the truth when she denied being pregnant or delivering a baby."

She fixed those penetrating blue eyes on both of us. "If there are traumatic circumstances involved in the events surrounding Heidi's pregnancy, then we will need her parents' help in figuring out what happened to her." She hesitated. "Her parents and depending on what you learn, her local police as well."

She sighed, like what she'd learned in her conversation colored her next question. "Gareth, what kind of a relationship do you have with her parents?"

"Sadly, not a strong one," he said. "She's new. This is her first year. And our contacts have been brief and infrequent. With one exception, those contacts have been exclusively with her mother."

"Yet she indicated to me that she's closer to her father," Purcell said.

I made a note about that, which reminded me of my earlier question about whether Heidi's biological father had actually been notified about the situation.

Before I explored that, because of what I'd seen in other campus populations, I had another question for Dr. Purcell about Heidi's denial that she'd ever had sex. She was thinking about trauma and repression. My mind was running in a different direction. Along with the possibility of traumatic amnesia, I was wondering not about repressed knowledge but a genuine lack of knowledge—whether it was possible that Heidi had been a victim of date rape. She could have been drugged and assaulted and because of the memory distorting effects of the drug, not known that she had had sex. If she'd never knowingly had sex, of course she wouldn't have suspected she was pregnant and of course she wouldn't have understood what was happening to her in the night.

I asked about that.

"It's possible," Dr. Purcell agreed. "Certainly, she's absolutely credible when she says she hasn't had sex and couldn't possibly be pregnant. But repression could produce that effect as well."

She turned to Gareth. "What do you know about her situation before she came here?"

"Too little, I'm afraid. She wasn't happy at her school in California. And it seems she also was unhappy with her home situation. Her mother recently remarried and she appears to actively dislike her stepfather. Beyond that?" He shrugged. "We really don't know much. With a transfer student, we're usually looking at their academic record and potential, and whether they'll be a good fit in our community. Heidi was a strong student whose interests and politics—to the extent they have them at her age—seemed to mesh very well with the values at Simmons."

He spread his hands and looked from one of us to the other, as if he wasn't sure if either of us would have any answers for him. "So now what do we do? What are we going to say at our school meeting? It's supposed to start in..." He looked at the clock on the wall and flinched. "...just a few hours."

He looked at Dr. Purcell.

"Heidi wants you to tell them the truth," she said.

"But we don't know what the truth is," he said.

It might be a long while before we had a clear view of the facts, and we had to make some decisions now. "Well, what do we know?" I said. "We know what Heidi's truth is. She believes she has never had sex and couldn't have been pregnant. We know that she has no conscious memory of delivering a baby, never mind having some intention to harm it. She doesn't believe there was a baby."

I realized that Heidi had probably never even seen her baby, except as something strange and bloody and painful happening to her in the dark. I pictured a child in pain, the mysterious behavior of her body and the sudden onset of a massive period, an embarrassed effort to clean things up, and a confused and uncomfortable retreat to her bed. All that followed by a bewildering explosion of medical and public safety personnel, people asking intrusive questions, and the threat of criminal action.

The world would censure her enough. From this community, she needed sympathy and support.

"We know that in general, Heidi is not known to be a liar," I continued. "She's considered a good person and has been a good citizen of this community. And we know that this is a complicated situation, one that is going to take further investigation to understand. We know that such further investigation is essential, and that by the rules of this community, she is entitled to the benefit of all doubt until the full facts are known."

Gareth looked like what I had just said wasn't helpful. Under stress, people often fail to hear what is said, and need the information broken down into smaller bites.

"Okay," I said. I tried to put it in context for him. "If a student were accused of cheating, or of lying, or stealing from another student, or some unacceptable act of violence, how would you proceed?"

I watched him consider.

"We'd withhold judgment until we conducted a full and fair investigation," he said. "We'd remind the student body of that policy, and of the fact that we're conducting that investigation, and urge them not to rush to judgment. When the facts were ascertained, we would present the situation to our discipline committee, which is made up of both faculty and students. It would be up to them to decide whether an infraction had taken place, and what the penalty would be. We've got a rule book. The standards are pretty clear."

I watched him nod as he understood my point.

Elaine Purcell smiled wryly. "But there's nothing in your rule book about child abuse or attempted murder?"

Who was the abused child, I wondered, as my lawyer's daughter's tendencies surfaced again. Probably there were two—Heidi and her little girl.

"Isn't the critical issue here, from the point of view of her fellow students, intention?" I said. "Intention and state of mind? Doesn't it matter what she believed? What her reality was at the time, not some external reality that assumes a person can't be pregnant without being aware of it? Or that a person can't have sex and not know it?"

I look at Dr. Purcell. "She could be telling the truth, couldn't she? She could have been unaware of her pregnancy?"

"Absolutely. Girls her age can have pretty irregular periods. Pregnant women sometimes do bleed. It is entirely possible that she didn't know. I'm not sure how likely, but it's possible. And of course, if there's trauma involved, in her life and particularly with respect to the events of the conception, if she was deeply in denial, she could have ignored the evidence of her own body."

"And if she didn't know she'd had sex?"

"Then it's even more possible."

"So whether it's the result of psychological trauma, or physical trauma, Heidi's version of what happened could be a genuine truth for her?"

"It could."

Gareth looked helplessly from one of us to the other. "But I still don't know what to tell them."

I thought I'd just laid it out for him, but maybe he was uncomfortable with so much uncertainty. His population did like comforting certainties—teenagers did—even though the goal of their education was to teach them to question, analyze, and evaluate. They were learning to keep open minds and weigh different points of view until they reached their own conclusions. And, in matters pertaining to the community, to strive for consensus, even if it meant their side didn't always win. They were also still teenagers without fully developed adult brains.

Before I could take another stab at laying things out, Dr. Purcell stood and reached for her coat. "I'll need to continue to work with her, Gareth," she said, "if that's what she wants. I'll need to get a much clearer sense of her before I have a good read on what this is. Whether her story is self-delusion, some form of traumatic amnesia, or, as Thea suggests, some kind of truth—a pregnancy as the result of drugs or alcohol, perhaps from sex she genuinely didn't know she'd had. You'll need a lot more information from her family. And Gareth, I know you aren't going to like this, but I think you should share all of this with the police investigators. Whatever the circumstances under which she had sex, she was too young to consent. They've got resources for getting information that none of us have."

She had that right. Once we got over the hump of convincing the police to consider the possibility that Heidi had not known she was pregnant, or was suffering from some significant trauma that had caused her to repress the knowledge, everything was cast in a different light and forced a different look at her behavior. And frankly, whether she had knowingly had sex or not, she was still a victim. They would have a lot more resources to put into finding out what might have happened and who the baby's father was. Obviously there would be DNA, but DNA was only useful when there was someone to match it to.

Who knew how forthcoming her custodial family would be?

I was already anticipatorily pissed off at her family. At her mother. How could Heidi have spent two weeks at home and no one noticed her condition? True, folks here at Simmons had missed it. But this was her mother, a woman who had watched her daughter grow from a newborn. She should have been deeply familiar with her daughter's body, her appearance, the way she carried herself. Pregnancy changed those things. I was already changing. And didn't mothers take their daughters shopping for spring clothes during spring break? I wasn't supposed to prejudge, but I already thought I didn't like Mrs. General Norris.

Poor Heidi.

Gareth wanted to know if Dr. Purcell could attend the assembly, in case the students had questions, but she shook her head. "I cleared enough of my schedule to meet with Heidi, and to meet with you, but now I've got to get back to work. My time, you know, is not my own. Like you, Dr. Wilson, I have a lot of people depending on me."

He looked stricken, and she put a comforting hand on his arm. "I think you're in good shape for your meeting, and you've got Thea. I'll plan on coming back tomorrow to see Heidi again. It will likely be in the afternoon. As I told you, this is not a simple thing. She'll need some kind of therapeutic relationship, possibly for a long time, to help her deal with this. For that, of course, we'll need parental consent."

She checked her phone, tapped a few times, and named a time.

Gareth nodded.

She rose and headed for the door. Then she paused, and turned. "You should know that she's very anxious about seeing her parents. She says she'd like to see her mother, but is adamant that she doesn't want to see her stepfather. She says he openly dislikes her and that he frightens her. Right now, she doesn't feel like she can handle that."

After another pause, she said, "If it appears that he's likely to insist on seeing her, you can use the old 'against doctor's orders' line, and back him down. I'm no expert, but I expect he doesn't have any legal rights with respect to her. He's not her biological father."

She wanted badly to be gone, and I understood the pressures of a demanding job, but I had one question before she left. "Dr. Purcell, did she say anything about her biological father?"

Again, she hesitated. "Just that she hoped he'd come, but usually he was too busy for her. Then she seemed to regret having said that and said he wasn't really too busy, just that he traveled a lot and that anyway he would be no help. I didn't get a chance to probe that any further. The impression I got was that 'too busy for her' was a phrase someone had imposed on her, not something she really felt. Maybe by her mother and stepfather? And it was wistful, like she wished things were different and really wanted him here."

She shook herself a bit, like she was frustrated at not having said this earlier. "You know that I am only telling you this because Heidi gave me permission to talk to you. Otherwise, everything she said would be confidential. If I continue to work with her, you may need to get the school an expert of its own. I can suggest someone. And one more thing. You can share what I've told you with the investigators, if necessary, but she's not to be questioned by the police. Not today. Not in the state she's in right now. And that is also 'doctor's orders.' I've given her a sedative, in any case, and instructed the nurse that they're to keep her sedated at least until tomorrow, so that, in my professional opinion, at present she isn't competent to be interviewed. I'll send you a list of expert psychiatrists the school might want to consult."

In a quick, economical motion, she crossed to the door and was gone.

Gareth and I looked at each other. "Whew!" he said. "She sure saved it up for that last blast, didn't she? It's as though she didn't want us asking any more questions."

"Busy woman," I said, shaking my head. "And very impressive."

Changing the subject, I said, "What about keeping the police away from Heidi? Will you be able to do that?"

He shrugged. "They spoke to her very briefly yesterday. Otherwise we have so far been able to protect her to give her some time to recover. I'm glad that Dr. Purcell left instructions with the staff that she's not to be disturbed. The sedative was an interesting touch, though."

It was indeed. And clever, if her goal was to keep the police away. No police officer wants to take the chance on questioning a vulnerable young woman under those circumstances. Not if he or she wants it to hold up in court. Not a good cop, anyway. Bad cops will do anything they can get away with. I had no idea which we were dealing with here, though Gareth seemed to believe they were sympathetic.

Uncertainty about my mother's emergency bothered me like an itch I couldn't scratch. I needed to try to contact her again. Call the office and see if Magda had reached anybody and if there was an update on what the emergency was. I needed to know so I could stop filling the information void with dire stuff.

But it was time to meet with the school's attorney, and Gareth wanted me with him. Like a knight readying for a joust, I slammed my helmet shut, raised my lance, and rode forth to meet our next challenge.

CHAPTER 4

The law firm had sent a no-nonsense woman who looked like she ate nails for breakfast and styled her hair with a chainsaw. Not the comforting and reassuring person we'd want for talking to Heidi. But as someone to protect the school? A few minutes of conversation showed that she was perfect. It was undoubtedly sexist of me, but I'd been afraid that they would send us an attractive young associate who would provide good visuals if we needed to hold a press conference, but wouldn't have the gravitas or experience to lead us through the complexities of the civil and criminal issues Simmons and Heidi faced.

Janet Connor knew her stuff. Her questions regarding the school's role, knowledge, timeline of the events, and issues of possible negligence, were focused and precise. She wasn't warm and fuzzy, but the school had other people for that. Still, at the end of her billable hour, Gareth and I were both ready for the grilling to be over. MOC and I, at least, were ready for a short nap. It's a fact of the business, though, that naps are never on the agenda.

She left us with a list of items she needed—names and contact information for Heidi's housemother, advisor, teachers and close friends. Names, contact, and employment information for her mother, father, and stepfather, as well as friends, teachers, neighbors, or others we could identify as having been close to Heidi back home. She wanted Heidi's medical records and school records from back home as well as here. She wanted to find a time, sooner rather than later, to interview Heidi.

"I know it's a lot," she said, "but the cops will want this stuff, and we'd like to get out ahead of them, if possible. Cops have a tendency to tell the people they interview not to talk to anyone else, which makes it a lot more difficult for us to provide an adequate defense." She waved a hand to ward off Gareth's questions. "Of course we don't know if there will be charges. We hope to avoid that. But we absolutely know there will be an investigation. If what you've said about the situation—and her version of events—is true, or we can persuade them it's true, they'll be looking to charge whoever is the father of that baby."

She shoved her notes into her briefcase, and then asked a question we'd both been wondering about, too. "What about the baby? Any idea what will happen with her? Is there a family member who will be looking for custody?"

"We don't know," Gareth said. "Social services has taken temporary custody. Her parents haven't arrived yet. There's been no opportunity to discuss it."

"Any likelihood that the mother will want to keep her baby?"

"She's been in no shape for that conversation," Gareth sounded like he was running out of patience. "Anyway, she's barely sixteen, almost a baby herself."

"But she's the mother. You need to at least keep that question on the table. She wouldn't be the first sixteen-year-old to raise a baby."

We both thought she was done, and were heaving inward sighs of relief, when she delivered her final thought. "And of course, assuming that the father is identified, there will be questions about his paternity rights."

I could tell, from Gareth's face, that he wanted to say these issues, at least, weren't ones for Simmons to deal with. She must have seen that, too, for she said, "I know custody is not your problem. But someone has to raise these questions with her parents. Who would do that, except you?"

I was thinking it should be the Department of Children and Families, or a social worker when, with a swiftness resembling Dr. Purcell's, she was gone.

"I feel like I was just flattened by a steamroller," Gareth said. "Two steamrollers."

"You sort of were."

He shook the list he'd made so the paper rattled. "Looks like we've got more homework. As if we didn't have enough—"

"Peggy can do a lot of that," I said. "The records part, I mean. The information about friends and others back home we'll have to get from Mrs. Norris."

"If she gives it to us," he said gloomily. In his business, he had to develop a facility for quickly reading parents. In their limited contacts, there had been a marked lack of willingness to cooperate.

I thought again that I was not looking forward to meeting Mrs. Norris, but tried to banish my negative thoughts and give her the benefit of the doubt. It wasn't her fault that I'd dealt with far too many difficult private school parents. I didn't yet know whether she'd be the "leap to her child's defense" type, or the "none of this is my fault" type. I'd seen both. But Gareth's comments so far inclined me to think we'd be dealing with "not my fault," "my child is such a trial," and "please, I really don't want to be bothered."

Hoping Gareth wouldn't notice, I patted MOC and vowed to be an involved, but not a helicopter parent.

"Where are we?" he asked, and then, without waiting to see if I had an answer, "It's early, I know, but let's get some lunch."

Lunch sounded like a great idea. The bagel was long ago, and these days, I was perpetually hungry.

We finally got lunch after a journey repeatedly interrupted by faculty and students. Gareth was unfailingly patient and shared what he could, but he was looking more frayed by the moment. Over healthy salads and delicious homemade bread, we talked strategy until Gareth's phone interrupted.

The caller's agitated voice was loud enough for me to hear. A woman, identifying herself as Ruthie, said, "There's a man in Heidi's room. A strange man. I've called Security, but you should get over here."

"Someone's in Heidi's room," he told me, already on his feet and moving.

I hurried after him, sadly abandoning the lunch I'd been enjoying. It was a challenge to keep up with his taller stride, made longer by his sense of urgency. I was panting by the time we got to the dorm.

We arrived at the same time as three security officers. "Watch this door and the rear one," he told two of the officers, "if he comes out, grab him." He instructed the third, a Middle Eastern looking man with a thick black beard and fierce eyes, to come with us as he hurried inside, taking the stairs two at a time.

At the top of the stairs we found an agitated woman waiting for us. "The dorm door was locked, Gareth. It absolutely was. You know how careful we are about that. I have no idea how he got in." She paused for a breath. "Sorry. This is no time for explanations. Just this way, Gareth. Joel is blocking the door." She smiled when she said it, a smile I didn't understand until I saw Joel.

The man blocking Heidi's door was the size of refrigerator, and his bulk didn't look like fat. Whoever had invaded Heidi's room without permission wasn't going anywhere. As the man she'd called Joel stepped aside for Gareth, the intruder in the room jumped through the door, knocked Gareth aside, and bounded for the stairs. That little trespasser was fast! And he was heading straight toward me. Maybe thinking if he knocked down the pregnant lady, it would distract the others and he could escape.

Well, sorry, but I wasn't having that. Not with MOC to protect. I stepped back and stuck out my foot. He tripped over my leg and went sprawling. A notebook fell from one pocket, and the phone he dropped as he tried to break his fall landed at my feet. I scooped both of them up as Joel the Refrigerator, and the man from security, both looking like no one a sensible person would tangle with, grabbed his arms and hauled him to his feet.

"Ruthie," Gareth said, ignoring the man's increasingly agitated demands for the return of his property, "can you check Heidi's room and see if you can tell whether anything has been disturbed. And Joel and Amad, will you keep a firm hold on this gentleman while I check and see if he's taken any of Heidi's possessions."

Not only did the man struggle with those holding him, he actually tried to bite Gareth as his pockets were searched. I couldn't tell what he did, but the security guard Gareth had called Amad just seemed to move his hand slightly, and the intruder gasped and stopped trying to bite. He was short, maybe five eight or so, skinny and probably, from the speed with which he'd attempted his escape, a runner. He was also, the credentials in his pocket revealed, a reporter. And yes, also a thief. An inside pocket held photos of Heidi and her family, Heidi and a friend, Heidi with a guitar, along with her iPod and a small turquoise notebook decorated with sequins and paisley swirls.

According to his license and press credentials, the intruder's name was Damien Black and he worked for Boston's most incendiary paper. Black was still struggling to escape and loudly protesting that this was a false arrest and they had no right to detain him as Gareth got out his phone and called the police.

I rubbed my leg, bruised from where he'd slammed into me. Bruises and an interrupted lunch. It was the story of my life. Suzanne says I need to take it easy. She says she never gets bruised or put in danger. But I'm the trouble shooter who gets called when schools want their troubles shot. Trouble shooting is often not a very genteel business. And honestly, what would she have me do? Let the stinker get away with stealing Heidi's property?

I could feel time slipping away as we waited for the police to arrive, the cell phone in my pocket wiggling anxiously with calls I couldn't take. The whole time—it probably wasn't much more than ten minutes—Black never stopped complaining and demanding that we return his phone. That made me concerned about what was on it. Had he taken pictures of her room? Her dresser drawers? Her photos? Her notebook? Let that phone get back in his hands, and those pictures would fly away to his computer. With an inward sigh, I realized most likely they already had.

We shared those concerns with the officers when they arrived, or rather, I did, because Gareth was already on the phone to the school's lawyers, putting measures in place to block the publication of any photos Black might have taken. I gave the officers the items he had taken from Heidi's room, along with his phone and his notebook. "We're very concerned about this student's privacy," I said. "As well as the theft of her property." A uniform who looked young enough to be my son took notes, and after what seemed like an endless give and take, Black was led away.

Gareth was still on the phone when the man from security put a cautious hand on my forearm. "Are you all right?" he asked. "Because you don't look all right. And what that man did was so wrong, running at a pregnant lady because he thought you were vulnerable." There was what might have been a smile behind the beard when he added, "He does not understand. American ladies are tough. Simmons girls are tough."

"I'm okay, thank you," I said, realizing that I sort of wasn't. That I was pretty shaken by the man's behavior. So many ways MOC was changing things.

Gareth finished his call, then took a moment to introduce me to Ruthie Martin, the dorm mother and a reading coach, her husband Joel, who taught biology and coached field hockey and wrestling, and the man who was seeing what I had missed about myself, Amad, from security.

Then we headed back to his office at a frighteningly brisk pace. "Well, we surely didn't need that," Gareth said, on his phone to the security chief about beefing up their system.

Soon enough, it would be time for him to meet with his student body, which sent us through another round of "I don't know what to tell them."

I reminded him of what we'd discussed earlier, and this time, he was calm enough to listen. Still, I was a little worried as we walked toward the auditorium. Speaking of worries, I also needed time to check my phone and see if there was news about my mother's emergency, but there was no time.

I shouldn't have worried about Gareth.

He was shaky for about three sentences. Then he settled back into being a headmaster who respected his student body. Because of who they were—a self-selected group of students who felt deeply invested in their community—and because of who he was, the meeting went well. He explained that Heidi was still in the infirmary, that she was in a troubled state and seemed unsure of what had happened, and that they were bringing in experts to help her. He told them that it appeared that she hadn't been aware of her pregnancy, that the birth had been a surprise.

He was stunningly frank with them, and it looked like the majority of his students appreciated his candor and were willing to keep open minds until they had more information. He assured them that information was being developed and promised to keep them informed as he knew more. He told them that there would be counselors available if any of them felt a need to talk to someone. He urged any of them in whom Heidi might have confided to come and speak with him. Then he invited their questions.

The first question was the one that would occur to anyone—how could she have failed to know she was pregnant? He offered what he knew, and also offered to bring in an expert to explain it further if they wanted. There was concern about Heidi abandoning her baby. How could she do that? Again, he was forthright. He told them pretty much everything we knew. That she hadn't known she was abandoning a baby because she didn't believe she'd had one, and some of the reasons why that might be true.

I was watching their faces. I could see there was puzzlement, and some disbelief, but I could also see that they were considering it. How someone might be traumatized into repressing any memories of an event. They didn't need to be told about date rape, and memory erasing drugs, and young girls who were exploited after drinking. The media was full of such cases. Some of them, at least, had known girls who'd been victimized.

He reminded them of the school's procedure for investigating infractions and urged them not to make judgments until they had more information.

I beamed like a proud mother. Goodness knew they could use some clear thinking, open communication, and honesty. What a radical concept—don't leap to judgment until you've gathered all the information and considered it. Keep an open mind and consider other people's circumstances. I wanted to put him on the nightly news. Send him to Capitol Hill as a role model. The whole meeting was an incredible lesson in civics, in community, in citizenship. These kids made me hopeful about the future.

There were doubters, of course, and cynics. I could see those faces, too. I didn't know if they would rush back to their dorms and spew their opinions on twitter or Facebook or snapchat or whatever current medium they were using. But for the most part, it appeared his students were willing to wait for more information.

The questions went on, and he came right back at them with questions of his own. What did they know about Heidi? Had any of them any reason to doubt what she was saying? Did they have reasons to believe she was a liar? To their knowledge, had she lied about other things? Had she been secretive? Did she appear to have been hiding a pregnancy? Had she confided about the baby to anyone?

He took all the time they needed. More than an hour, with a solid give and take. He slipped in a warning about reporters on campus, and urged them to be vigilant and call security immediately if they saw strangers on campus or in the dorms. He was concluding it with a reiteration of his request that they keep what they knew within the community until more facts were developed, when the door to the assembly room burst open. A tall, elegant woman with thick, perfectly cut, multi-processed mahogany hair strode in. She planted herself in the middle of the room, pointed at the headmaster, and yelled, "Gareth Wilson, I went to the infirmary and they told me I couldn't see my daughter Heidi because she was sleeping. That's totally unacceptable and you know it. I will not be treated this way!"

She had a big voice. It bounced off the walls and hurt my head. I could see that it had the same effect on Gareth. She wasn't dressed or coiffed like someone who yelled in public places, but she did look like someone used to getting her own way.

She was followed by an even taller man who stood sideways in the door, half with her, half not. His brush cut and wide-footed stance gave him a military look. His deeply lined face wore the expression of someone who rarely saw anything that met his standards and expected life to keep dishing up disappointments. The stepfather, I presumed.

In even louder tones, she said, "I insist that you to take me to my daughter this instant."

Sometimes, to understand why a child or an adolescent behaves in a particular way, all you need to do is meet the parents. In those few sentences, and with such a public display of self-centered arrogance, indifference to her daughter's condition, and the inappropriateness of interrupting a school assembly, Heidi Basham's mother had told everyone that she was not a person to whom a troubled or abused child could go for advice or comfort or rescue. All around me, I could see students exchanging glances and nods, and murmuring quietly. Sometimes a picture absolutely is worth a thousand words.

Gareth did not leave the podium. He inclined his head politely. "Mrs. Norris. General Norris. As you see, we are in the middle of a meeting. I will be with you in a few minutes. You're welcome to stay and listen, or wait for me in my office."

Whether they knew it or not, they had been dismissed. The General knew, and in the rigid lines of his body and his lifted chin, I read that he was not accustomed to being dismissed. Mrs. Norris opened her mouth wide, like an opera singer about to hold forth. Then she looked around at the sea of staring faces and seemed to realize where she was.

"Five minutes," she said, and swept from the room. She was wearing a flowing, asymmetrical black silk appliquéd jacket that screamed expensive over slim black pants, but she made it seem like full court dress and train.

There was an audible sigh when the door had closed behind them.

"Of course, Heidi's mother is upset," he said. The English—the Welsh—are so good at understatement.

The meeting finished with a reminder that their advisors and counselors were available, and that while cookies and fruit would be in their dorms and in the lounge, it would be nice to leave some for others even though Mrs. Willoughby, in the kitchen, made the world's best cookies. It was a nice, homey touch that reminded them they were in a community.

Then we both beat feet back to his office. Our original plan had been for me to take a break to catch up on some office work, then he and I were going to meet with Heidi's roommate and some of her friends, then move on to craft the school's public statement. I also wanted a moment to check my messages and see if there was any news about my mother's emergency.

Obviously, that schedule was now changed.

He paused in the hall for a moment, preparing himself. I was already starting a mental to-do list and bracing myself for what might be waiting among the calls stacking up on my phone, when he said, "I hope you'll come in with me, Thea. The presence of an outside expert might have a calming effect on the Norrises."

By hope, he meant he wanted me there. And he was the client.

"Perhaps not so much calming as reminding them of their manners?" I patted his shoulder. "Cast me in whatever light you want." He grinned, and I added, "And I'll try to have your back."

I was tempted to say, "I've got your six," like the cops do, but I exercised restraint. The truth was that I didn't want to have his back just then—there was little more unpleasant than an upset and entitled parent berating a headmaster—but he was right that my presence might remind them of the judgment of the wider world and encourage them to act more civilized. Often, parents waded in without listening, ready to go on the attack before gaining full knowledge of the situation. Often, also, the parents' behavior revealed how little they actually knew about their children. This meeting looked like it was going to involve both of those things, and I really, really needed to find a few moments to check my messages.

"Grateful," he said, and swung into motion again. He had an amazing way of going from utterly still to fully engaged and moving.

I followed after him, my phone relentlessly vibrating. One day soon, I was sure, I would yield to the impulse to throw it on the ground and run over it. Probably not on a day when my mother had an unknown emergency, though.

CHAPTER 5

Lorena Norris was sitting on one of Gareth's couches. Occupying might be a better word, since although it could have seated four, she had planted herself dead center and spread out her draperies in a way that left room for no one else. There was a tray on the coffee table in front of her with a silver coffee urn and a plate of Mrs. Willoughby's cookies. Both coffee and cookies seemed untouched. The General paced behind her, pausing to draw himself up to his full height when we entered. I expected him to speak, but despite his posture of someone about to spring, he let her go first.

"Mr. Wilson, I cannot believe that you were not at the airport to meet us and that, having finally made my way here, I was forbidden access to my daughter," she began. "It took us ages to rent a decent car."

Ah, how quickly the "us" had morphed into "I." If I'd been Gareth, I might have said, "Lady, what's this 'finally made my way bullshit,' I sent a car. Don't you know I'm dealing with a campus crisis?" but Gareth had more tact.

As I wondered how they'd missed the car he sent, he shook his head like one might do with a fractious child and began to explain. "Lorena, we've only had a few minutes of conversation regarding this matter. Let me give you the facts as we currently know them. Then you can ask your questions, and perhaps by then Heidi will be awake and I can take you to see her." He hesitated. "You should know that this has been an extremely traumatic experience for her and on doctor's orders your daughter has been sedated. We will go over there, of course, but she may not be awake."

I must be hopelessly naïve, or hopelessly hopeful, because I could not believe that her first words hadn't been, "Is my daughter okay?" or "How is Heidi?" If not in the assembly, at least in here. But her pressing concerns seemed more to involve her priority and standing and how she should be treated than with the condition of her child. I hoped I was wrong and the show of concern would be forthcoming.

"This is Thea Kozak," he was saying. "General and Mrs. Norris, Heidi's parents. Thea specializes in trouble-shooting for private schools."

The general looked down his nose at us. "You can't handle a little thing like this yourself?"

Little thing? Maybe if you were used to war. But on an ordinary, human level, this was hardly insignificant. There had been an unexplained pregnancy involving a girl too young to consent. A tiny infant who had been abandoned and left to die, still struggling to survive, whose future would have to be decided. A tiny little girl who was this woman's granddaughter. The mother, a child herself, was deeply traumatized and facing potential criminal charges. There was also a potentially serious situation with respect to that young mother's mental status. The police would be investigating. The press, other than the one we'd sent to jail, was camped outside the campus drive, salivating for a juicy story that could deeply damage the school's reputation. The only "little thing" here was the man's mind.

Gareth gestured toward the coffee pot. "Perhaps you'd like some coffee while I walk you through it?"

The General snorted. "A Scotch would be more appropriate."

His wife perked up and gave him a smile. Gareth didn't look at me, but it was pretty easy to read his mind. *You see why Heidi wanted to come here?*

"We can do that if you'd prefer." He crossed to a tall mahogany cabinet. "Single malt or blended? Water or ice?"

"Single. Ice."

When the coffee tray had been shifted to a sideboard and the Norrises had their drinks, Gareth explained the circumstances as he knew them, including Heidi's insistence that she had never had sex and couldn't have been pregnant. He described the visit from Dr. Purcell and her speculations about Heidi's condition, laying heavy emphasis on the words "trauma," "fear," and "repression." "Of course, Dr. Purcell will be available to meet with you tomorrow, and she can explain it far better than I can."

I waited for them to jump in with a thousand questions, all the questions parents would naturally have in this situation. Was Heidi really all right? What about the baby? How was she? Where was the baby? Had Heidi said anything about the baby's father? How were the police approaching this? Was Heidi at risk of being arrested? Was Dr. Purcell concerned about Heidi's mental health? No one jumped. The General was focused on inhaling his drink. She drained her glass more slowly, her face an absolute blank as Gareth continued to explain.

He told them how the police had responded so far, and what they might expect in the days to come. The possible crimes Heidi might be charged with, and some of his strategies for heading those off. "Of course, you'll be our best informants about her. About her prior mental state, her background. About how this might have happened. About who the father might be."

Lorena Norris was about to respond, her mouth twitching and her forehead knotting—signs I knew we both read as the beginning of denying all responsibility—when Gareth popped a zinger. "Your granddaughter is in the NICU at Boston's Children's Hospital. They're concerned about immature lungs, but the doctors say she's a sturdy little girl, just under four pounds, and they're very optimistic. I believe social services has taken temporary custody, but of course, you'll want…"

Her hand flew to her chest, the fingers spreading like a pale white fan with magenta tips, as her breath hissed out. After a moment, she found her voice. "Granddaughter? Grandmother? You've got to be kidding. As if I had anything to do with this. This all happened on your watch, Mr. Wilson, not mine."

"Dr. Wilson," he said, not quite successfully suppressing the ironic smile that tugged at the corners of his mouth. "The doctors say their best guess is that the baby was conceived in August, if not earlier. Heidi didn't arrive at Simmons until mid-September. You of course remember, Mrs. Norris, that we agreed to a late start for her because of her last-minute acceptance and your schedule complications?"

Mrs. Norris looked like she didn't remember any of this. In any case, she didn't acknowledge his comment. She rose from the couch, her hand still flapping against her chest. "I am absolutely not that baby's grandmother. I am too young to be a grandmother."

"And Heidi is far too young to be a mother. But unfortunately, it has happened." He reached for his phone. "Would you like me to check and see if she's awake yet? I know you're anxious to see her."

The woman who had disrupted a meeting and, in front of the entire student body, expressed outrage at being kept from her daughter, and who had demanded to see her daughter immediately, now sank back down on the couch and picked up her glass. "I'd like to finish my drink first. I'm afraid I'm a bit shaken by all of this."

Not that the observing eye could see. But perhaps I was being unkind.

Her husband had helped himself to a second, more generous dose of Scotch and now stood staring out the window, his back to the room.

I didn't have the patience to wait them out. Gareth could do that for both of us. I was about to suggest that I leave them and go return some phone calls when his secretary came in.

"Excuse me for interrupting, but there's an urgent call from her office for Ms. Kozak."

Magda. My breath caught as I imagined what that urgent call might be, but I tried to stay calm as I excused myself and walked to the door, dreading what I might learn. I even took a moment to reassure Gareth that I would be right back. He clearly didn't want to be left alone with them.

I was very grateful to be getting out of this room. It had all the tension, and none of the charm, of drinks at an English house party where some of the guests had guilty secrets. I half expected the cast of Downton Abbey to join us. We could have used some of Maggie Smith's snippy remarks.

The General turned and stared at me with his dark hawk's eyes as Gareth said, "You can take it in the office next door."

I excused myself and left.

"Thea, how are things going there?" Magda asked when I picked up. "What is their problem?"

It was the perfect question in more ways than she could imagine. "Young teen who gave birth in the bathroom, dumped the baby in the trash, and now claims she's never had sex and couldn't have been pregnant."

"Terrible" she said. "Is the baby okay?"

"She's a preemie, but she seems to be doing fine."

"And the girl? The baby who had this baby?" Dour as she was, Magda was also very maternal. She was so over the moon about my prospective baby, I'd probably have to name her Claudine Magda if we had a girl. It sounded good and solid.

"We're still figuring that out." But I couldn't wait any longer. "Magda, why did you call me? Have you learned anything about what my mother's emergency is?"

I held my breath as I waited for her answer.

"It's your father," she said. "All I could get from your mother was that he's had a heart attack, and then she hung up on me." She drew in a breath, uncomfortable with having to give me bad news. "Then I tried your brother, but he wasn't answering, so I started calling hospitals. All I could learn was which hospital he is in. I'm sorry, but you know how they are. They will not give out any information about a patient to someone who is not a family member. And though I've tried, I cannot reach anyone in your family to get more information." She paused. "I am so sorry, Thea."

"Which hospital?"

I had my notepad open, ready for the information. She gave me the name of a Massachusetts South Shore hospital and I wrote it down, wishing my mother had taken him to one of the Boston hospitals. We can all be such medical snobs.

I was going through the motions of being efficient and professional. I wanted to scream and pound on something. I was having some trouble breathing, and thinking none of this was good for little MOC.

"Thanks," I said. "I'll call them right now. How is everything there today?"

"The usual," she said. "We need more help. You and Suzanne are too busy to hire anyone. And your secretary…" She stopped. I already knew her opinion of my new secretary. "If you don't get to it soon, I'll hire some help." Before I could authorize her to do so, though it was more of a threat than a promise, she changed the subject. "Will you be coming back tonight or do you need that hotel information?"

"Hotel," I said. It was clear that I wouldn't be coming home tonight. Home was a word—and a goal—that seemed to get farther away instead of closer. I'd temporarily abandoned my real estate search after a house hunting disaster, but I longed for a place to settle down. I didn't want to bring this baby home to a tired rental apartment. But that was for the future. Right now, I needed to figure out where I'd be sleeping tonight.

Magda gave me a number and an address for The Caleb Strong Inn and I wrote them down. "I told them you might be late," she said. "Reviews say it's the best place around. Also, it's supposed to have a good breakfast. That's one reason I picked it. And I say that because I want you to eat breakfast. You know how you are, and it is not good for our baby."

Our baby. Well, I suppose it would be. At least my baby had people claiming it.

I tried the hospital number, inquired about my dad, and got the information that he'd been admitted. That put my anxiety through the roof. I had to get out of here. I had to go there. I had work to do here before I could leave. I tried the nursing station on his floor, where the phone rang without being picked up. When it was finally answered, I was put on hold and then disconnected. I tried again and got no answer. I guessed they were insanely busy. Hospitals often were. I would try again later. I squeezed my fists in frustration, then forced them to uncurl, reminding myself to breathe. Babies liked it when their mothers breathed.

I took another quick minute to call Andre and let him know that I wouldn't be home, and share the news about my father's heart attack. Then it was time to get back to Gareth and see what was happening.

They were still in his office. Still drinking. There was no sign of all that urgency to visit Heidi. I still hadn't met the girl, but I already felt very sorry for her. There was an expectancy in the air, like Gareth had asked a question and was waiting for an answer that wasn't forthcoming. Maybe he'd asked about Heidi's summer, trying to figure out what had happened. That was something I didn't want to miss, even though I wasn't optimistic that he'd learn very much.

I entered quietly and slipped back into my chair. No one looked at me. The General was back to staring out the window, and Lorena was busily dosing herself with more medicinal alcohol.

"Mrs. Norris," Gareth said, in the patient tones of someone questioning a confused person, "what about a boyfriend?"

"Heidi? A boyfriend? You're joking, Dr. Wilson. Have you seen my daughter?"

I hadn't seen her daughter, but Gareth's description hadn't been unflattering, and anyway, weren't parents supposed to love their children and find them beautiful, regardless? Besides, for a predator, Heidi's youth and innocence might have been all that mattered. Heidi's mother was reminding me way too much of my own. Another self-centered woman who couldn't be pleased. Who couldn't see her daughter for what she was. Maybe Heidi's decision to come to Simmons had partly been recognition that since she could never win with her mother, she needed to find a place where she could make a life of her own. If so, she was wise for one so young. I'd beaten my head against that wall for years.

I reeled in my speculations. I was jumping to conclusions far too quickly when I was supposed to keep an open mind. Perhaps, giving her the benefit of the doubt, this was all the product of shock.

"I have," Gareth said. "She's a lovely girl." He let that go a couple beats, but Heidi's mother seemed oblivious to the message. "Somehow, Mrs. Norris, your daughter got pregnant."

"In the usual way, I presume," she said.

"But you said she didn't have a boyfriend." He hesitated a moment, and asked an inflammatory question. "When you say she didn't have a boyfriend, did you mean Heidi was casual about boys? Engaged in what today's young people call 'hooking up?'"

"Of course not, Headmaster. She didn't date and she didn't hang out with boys. I'm offended you'd suggest such a thing."

Her tone was pure acid, but Gareth didn't back down. "What about a friend who was a boy?"

Lorena Norris shook her head.

"What about any parties where something might have happened? Do you remember Heidi going to any parties last July or August?"

She shook her head. "She's not exactly a social butterfly."

"Nights when she didn't come home?"

Another shake.

"Came home late? What about coming back impaired or confused?"

Mrs. Norris had seen nothing. Based on her knowledge of her daughter, or what she was sharing at any rate, this must have been an immaculate conception.

"Did you notice any withdrawn or troubling behavior? Loss of appetite? Moodiness? Difficulty sleeping?"

"Gad, Headmaster," she said, "you sound like a pediatrician. Heidi was fine. The only problem she was having was that she'd decided she didn't want to go back to her school this year. She didn't feel like she fit in and wanted a change of scene. I think that's how she put it. She said she'd read about Simmons and it sounded perfect. All greeny and crunchy granola."

The ice in her glass clinked. "She was having some trouble adjusting to our marriage. She and The General rub each other the wrong way."

"Is she your only child?"

Mrs. Norris nodded.

"What about her father? Is he in the picture?"

"I should hope not."

I leaned forward, curious about how this would go.

Gareth raised an eyebrow. "Can you elaborate?"

She and her husband exchanged the networking signals of people making sure they're on the same page with their lies. I may be a consultant, not a shrink or a cop, but I've observed and evaluated plenty of people who don't plan to tell the truth. There's a way people arrange themselves when they're going to lie—the amateurs, anyway. There's a lot of lore about looking up to the right or to the left, but it's more of a whole body thing. In my humble opinion, anyway.

"What difference does it make?" she said. "He's not here, is he? And we are. What difference does any of this make? She made a mistake. She's obviously going to pay for it. How it happened doesn't matter now."

Heidi had been only fifteen.

I wanted to shake the woman until her teeth rattled. She seemed so indifferent to the situation her awfully young daughter was in, despite having flown all the way across the country to get here. Despite having made such a show of demanding to see her daughter. I was beginning to wonder what she wanted to see? Just eyeball the girl to establish that she was still alive? Or was it that she and The General planned to recruit Heidi into some campaign of lies because there were things they wanted to hide?

Did she really not understand that somehow her daughter had gotten pregnant at fifteen and that the circumstances were important, or did that not matter to her? Did she have no ideas—or curiosity—how a girl without a boyfriend whose mother thought her too unappealing to attract one had gotten pregnant? Wasn't she concerned about why Heidi claimed never to have had sex or been pregnant?

I was doing it again—the thing my cop husband cautions me about—letting my speculation get ahead of the facts. Of course, we weren't getting any facts, were we? I had to get focused. I shoved back my creeping exhaustion and my anxiety about my dad, nixed my overwhelming desire to crawl into clean sheets and sleep, and shifted my gaze to Gareth.

"I think it will matter very much, Mrs. Norris," he said. "To this community. To the police. And to Heidi herself. You'll understand better when you see her and get a sense of her condition. I was asking about her father, your ex-husband, because unless his parental rights have been terminated, or he's deceased or otherwise unavailable—and we have nothing to our records to show that—we need to contact him about his daughter just as we contacted you. In our last conversation, you assured me you would contact him. Have you done that? Is he aware of Heidi's situation?"

Lorena Norris stretched, like a cat just waking up, an indulgent move that signaled indifference to anything but herself. "He really doesn't matter," she said. She shook her head. "He'll only complicate—"

Gareth, the world's mildest man, looked like he wanted to hit her. "Mrs. Norris, you said you would contact him. Do I correctly infer that you have not?"

She smiled the smile of a woman used to being forgiven every transgression because she was so attractive, and didn't answer.

"Well, if you haven't, you need to confirm that we have his correct contact information so we can be in touch with him at once. When I looked at her records this morning, after we spoke, I found notes that we had contacted you multiple times because the information we have on file for Heidi's father is incorrect, and that you indicated the information regarding her father would be forthcoming. It appears we never received it."

What was perhaps a deliberate omission on her part would still look like Simmons being careless.

He poised his pen over the yellow pad on his desk. "If you could—"

Mrs. Norris's chin lifted. "This really isn't necessary. She doesn't want anything to do with her father."

Gareth's normal calm was beginning to fray "I have no information to suggest that. While it may be the case, legally, he's still her father. Unless his parental rights have been terminated. Have they?"

"No." The word was spat out as though she wished they had. Ironic, since her own level of care and concern was far from parental.

"His name please, and how we can be in touch with him?"

She folded her arms defiantly and swung her body like a sulky child. "Tell him, Bradley. Make him understand."

The General stepped behind the couch and put his hands on her shoulders, like he was her bodyguard. She was an extremely pretty woman, if a hard one, and had what looked like a lush body under her draperies. "We have a restraining order against Ted Basham, Dr. Wilson," he said. "He has made no end of difficulties about our marriage and about my moving into the house. Into 'his' house, as he puts it. Lorena and I decided we'd had enough and got an attorney to assist us. If you call Ted Basham, you'll be inviting a three-ring circus onto this campus. The man is nothing but a trouble maker."

"I believe we have to."

Of course they had to contact him, but to broker a temporary truce, I said, "Perhaps we should talk to Heidi and see what she wants. She might want to contact him herself."

The General was staring daggers at me, which made me think that Heidi *would* want her father contacted, despite her having told Dr. Purcell that her father was too busy for her.

Mrs. Norris emptied her glass and stared sadly at the naked ice.

It was a dumb suggestion. Regardless of Heidi's wishes, her father had to be contacted. Still, Gareth shrugged and picked up the phone. "I'll see if she's awake."

He spoke quietly into the phone and then replaced it, turning to the Norrises with a look of regret. "I'm so sorry. She's still asleep. I can take you over there, Mrs. Norris, and you can sit with her until she wakes up. Or I could go ahead and take you to my house, get you settled, and we can have the infirmary call you when she wakes."

I read that as a question, but they didn't respond until he said, "Which would you prefer?"

"We'll drop our things and freshen up."

"We have a lovely guest suite at the headmaster's house, and my wife is looking forward to helping you get settled."

"Thanks, but we've booked a room at a nice local place," The General said. "The Caleb Strong Inn. Looks like it's just down the street. It got good reviews on Trip Advisor."

So much for Gareth's strategy of keeping them on campus and under his thumb. This couple didn't seem like they'd be easy to keep under anyone's thumb.

Gareth flinched, an almost imperceptible move, and I knew what he was thinking. There was no way to tell what this cold, entitled woman might say if someone shoved a mike in her face and asked about her daughter, but we could both bet that it would be something that wouldn't help Heidi's situation.

"We were so hoping you'd stay with us, where you could be close to her. At a time like this, a young girl really needs her mother."

"She should have thought of that before..." But Lorena Norris never finished the sentence, because her loving spouse dug his fingers into her shoulders, a none-too-subtle message to shut up.

"Before you go," Gareth said, "Mr. Basham's contact information?"

She flounced with irritation, but set down her glass and dug through her purse. In the tones of a sulky teenager, she divulged the necessary information.

"And of course, we will need to finish our conversation at your earliest convenience," Gareth said.

"What conversation?" The sulky teen again.

"About Heidi's condition, and how it may have come about."

She most desperately wanted to repeat her earlier answer—in the usual way—but his look stopped her. She sighed. "Very well, Headmaster. When we've gotten settled."

I wanted to say, "Don't let them go yet," sure that once they were out of this room, our chances of getting any useful answers would diminish, but it was his show.

"I should tell you," he said, "that Heidi has asked that her mother visit alone. In her current condition, she feels uncomfortable seeing General Norris. Dr. Purcell has given the infirmary staff instructions to that effect."

Another conspiratorial glance between The General and his wife, but no other response. I couldn't imagine the man cared, given his apparent indifference to his stepdaughter, but perhaps his peremptory sense of entitlement meant he couldn't be told what to do. Maybe all that unspoken communication was because they had a plan to pressure Heidi about something. All we could do was hope they'd comply with Heidi's wishes.

The Norrises were gathering their things when Gareth's phone rang. He listened, and despite his best efforts to keep emotion off his face, I could see that he was getting more bad news. Seriously bad news. My thoughts were running toward the over-eager DA looking to arrest the sleeping Heidi when he sighed and said, "All right, then. Send him in."

Turning to the Norrises, he said, "Mr. Basham is here. What would you like—"

That was as far as he got before the door banged open and Heidi's father hobbled in. He was on crutches, with one leg in a cast, and a bandage on his forehead. He hopped and thumped across the room until he was within striking distance of The General.

"Fuck you very much, Bradley," he said. "Did you really think I wouldn't find out?"

CHAPTER 6

I had a brief vision of two rutting elks, antlers lowered, pawing the ground, as the two of them faced off. Norris was tall and trim and looked like he could hold his own in a fight. Basham was about the same height, but broader, and even with the handicap of crutches and only one working leg, looked like he'd never backed down from fight and wasn't planning to back away from this one.

From the couch, Heidi's mother watched with the ugly fascination of a woman who loves a good fight, especially if it's over her.

This was one sick bunch of people. Not a soul in the room who seemed to be there for Heidi, and a lot of people who were there for themselves. Except for Gareth. No wonder she'd wanted to get away from all that and into a community that was responsible and caring. Under the guidance of this team, a troubled, neglected, and vulnerable fifteen-year-old could easily have fallen prey to something. Someone. Who that someone was we still weren't getting any handle on, and it didn't look like any of these so-called adults were going to help with that.

I was relieved when Gareth stepped between them before one of the crutches became a weapon.

"Who told you?" General Norris demanded.

"Who didn't?" Basham said. "Lorena's sister. Heidi's roommate. Heidi's friend Ronnie. There may have been others." He turned his back on the Norrises and faced Gareth. "But you didn't call me. Why was that? Did these weasels pay you extra to keep my daughter's life a secret?"

"I didn't have your correct contact information in my files." Gareth remained standing between the two of them. "Apparently, neither you nor Mrs. Norris provided it. I would be happy to update you with everything we currently know. I believe General and Mrs. Norris were just leaving?"

"But I haven't seen my daughter yet," she protested, forgetting she'd just opted for heading to the inn and checking in. Forgetting that she'd just been told that Heidi was still asleep.

"Really, Lorena?" Basham said. "It's nearly five p.m. Your plane landed at two. What were you doing all this time?"

"That is none of your business, Ted. But since you've asked, Dr. Wilson told us that Heidi was sleeping. We've been discussing the situation while we're waiting for her to wake up."

"Sleeping for hours in the middle of the day? That doesn't sound like Heidi."

"She just gave birth," Gareth reminded him. "The circumstances are traumatic. The doctor prescribed a sedative."

"A lot you care, Ted. When is the last time you were in touch with our daughter?" Mrs. Norris was standing now, her hands on her hips, looking ever more like a defiant child.

"Last night, Lorena. She was feeling tired and crampy and thought she might be getting her period. She said it had been irregular lately. What about you? When did *you* last talk to her?"

Lorena Norris joined her husband in studying the encroaching darkness outside the window.

"This isn't helpful," Gareth said. "You are all here about Heidi, so let's focus on that. Whatever personal difficulties there are among you, I hope you'll set those aside to help your daughter through this difficult time."

Lorena Norris tossed her hair and didn't reply.

The General muttered, "She's not my daughter."

Ted Basham said, "Sure."

Someone recently suggested that my next career move ought to be to become headmistress of an independent school. It only took a couple scenes like this to remind me that I'm never going to be temperamentally suited to the job. This was just an extreme version of what Gareth dealt with day in and day out. Lately, I'd been leaning toward law school, when I wasn't contemplating becoming a hermit. Human behavior all too frequently leaves me disappointed about the fate of the human race. I was going to have to do some attitude readjusting before little M, or O, or C arrived.

Basham returned to the bone he'd been chewing. "Last month, Lorena? Last year? Oh, excuse me. I forgot. She was just home for March break. She was just fucking home a month ago with you two and neither of you noticed she was pregnant? How in the hell could THAT happen? Did you ever even look at her? Take her shopping for some spring clothes, just in case spring ever comes to New England? What about wrapping your fuckin' arms around her? I'll bet my bottom dollar—the only one I've got left since you took me to the cleaners—that you never even touched our poor child. You only wanted frigging custody so you would get the support check. You've never given a damn about Heidi and you know it."

"I was busy, Ted. Bradley and I—"

He mimicked 'Bradley and I' with a twisted mouth. "Busy? You hadn't seen her in months, Lorena, and you were too busy to pay attention to your only child? Too busy doing what? What did she do for that two weeks? For the two weeks that you refused to let her spend with me?"

He smacked his crutch down hard. "I would have put my arms around her."

He crutched over to her, getting right into her space. The General moved to protect his wife.

"That is quite enough from all of you," Gareth said quietly. When you want to be heard, they say, whisper.

"Thea, if you would take the General and Mrs. Norris across the hall to the lounge, and finish the conversation about Heidi, I'd be very grateful."

His gesture toward the door was all authority, and they went. I thought they were supposed to be leaving, but maybe Gareth thought their being upset might have loosened their tongues. Upset or lubricated with Scotch. And we did have information we wanted from them.

I followed them into a comfortable and quiet lounge, saw them settled in chairs, and asked if I could get them anything. Unsurprisingly, they both opted for more Scotch. I slipped back into Gareth's office, made them fresh drinks, and went to work.

Now I had new information, or at least a new door that had been opened.

I settled into a chair with my pad and pen. "Since that's when the baby was likely conceived, let's talk about Heidi last summer. Can either of you recall any time last summer when Heidi was missing for a night? Or came home impaired or intoxicated? Any time when she seemed upset or withdrawn?" A question Gareth had already asked, but I wanted to try again.

They hadn't.

"Did Heidi spend much time out of the house?" Babies, after all, could be conceived at any hour of the day.

The General shrugged.

Mrs. Norris said, "She was too young to have a job, so she was doing volunteer work with kids at a day camp down at the elementary school."

"What kind of work?"

"Some ecology thing," she said. "They had these raised bed gardens that they'd made and were growing flowers and vegetables. She was quite excited about it. Heidi loves gardening. It's one reason she came here."

This was the first time her mother had demonstrated any knowledge of her daughter's life.

"Tell me more about that. Who was she working with? Did she have friends there? Counselors or teachers she was close to?"

"She never talked about that. She only spoke about the children. How excited they were when their plants started to grow. When one of their tomatoes turned red, she was over the moon."

"So, no supervisors or other teachers she spent time with outside of work?"

Mrs. Norris shook her head. Her husband was staring into space, appearing indifferent to the conversation, utterly still except for one agitated foot.

"Can you give me a sense of her personality?"

"She's quiet," Mrs. Norris said.

"She's very chatty," The General said.

I smiled. "She's more talkative with you, General, than with her mother?"

"No," Mrs. Norris said.

"Yes," The General said. "Always clattering around the house, listening to music or looking for something to eat."

In short, a teenager. "Generally quiet, occasionally talkative?" I pretended to make a note. "Was Heidi with you all summer? She didn't spend time with her father?"

"She was with him for two weeks, the end of July," she said. "It's part of our divorce agreement."

"About four days in mid-July," he said.

Did two weeks seem like four days to him because he wanted Heidi gone? Was she exaggerating or trying to shift the window of conception to when Heidi was with her father? Did these two even live on the same planet? A former classmate who does domestic relations law told me that often the couples she deals with don't appear to have even met, never mind been married to each other, but these two were newlyweds.

"Where does Mr. Basham live?"

"I don't know," she said. "He moves around a lot. Traveling for work, all of that."

I waited.

"New York."

"Who were Heidi's close friends when she lived at home?"

"Why does any of this matter?" she said. She'd swilled down what I thought was her third drink and I could tell she wanted to ask for another.

Gareth had already answered that, but I gave it another try. "I know it's confusing, so here's why we're asking for all these details about Heidi. Because one thing we're trying to do here is protect your daughter. I don't think any of us want Heidi to go to jail, do we? Verifying her story, and showing that she's not a liar, is essential. Obviously, part of protecting her involves getting as much information as we can about the circumstances of your granddaughter's conception."

The General moved his body in a way that, in a woman, would have been a flounce. I didn't have a word in my vocabulary for a man-flounce.

She opened her mouth to voice an objection when I used the word "granddaughter," even though that was what the little girl undeniably was. I didn't give her a chance. "Yes, we expect the police will ask the same questions, but we're going to be a more sympathetic audience, and can help to shape her story, to explain why a girl who believes she's never had sex has just given birth." I smiled sympathetically. "Those of us who care about Heidi are focused on supporting and protecting her; the police will be focusing on criminal behavior. They may not be kind and we'd like to prepare her for that."

Again, she was going to say something. No doubt a harsh comment about Heidi and sex. Again, I cut her off. I didn't want to hear it. She could go to her hotel and say any bad thing she wanted to say about her daughter to her husband. He was far more likely than Gareth or I to be a sympathetic audience. "Also, of course, the therapist who is seeing her will need background, so going over it ahead of time will save you time and money—"

She gave a vehement shake of her head, and her hair flew back, revealing large diamond studs. "You're not expecting us to pay for that?" she said. "For her therapy?"

The short answer was yes, but I could leave the harsh financial realities for Gareth. "I think, after you've seen your daughter, you'll understand helping her through this isn't a short-term thing."

Now *she* flounced, which was ridiculous behavior in a woman her age, which I assumed to be mid-forties. Almost as ridiculous as The General's flounce. An expert who read body language would be having a field day, but these flounces, sighs, glares, folded arms, and rude silences? They're all wasted on me. "Now, her friends?"

"I don't understand why we're talking to you. Why we've gotten shuttled off to some second-string official while Dr. Wilson talks with Ted."

"You've already had more than an hour of Dr. Wilson's time," I reminded her. "And I'm sure in the days ahead you'll get as much as you need. However, Ted is Heidi's father, and at the moment, he's quite upset."

"I don't see why I have to be here," The General said. "Lorena can answer your questions."

Mrs. Norris gave him a withering look and he went back to staring into empty space.

Then why didn't you just stay home? I barely caught the words before they escaped. I don't see, I don't understand, I don't want. Honestly, could they be any more negative? I wanted to knock their heads together. After the many things I've dealt with, working with private schools, combined with their indifference to Heidi, I wasn't too sympathetic with their narcissism. Not with a child they had not yet seen lying in the infirmary, dealing with the traumatic aftermath of childbirth. Not with my dad in the hospital in I didn't know what condition. I was *doing* my job, trying to help Simmons—and Heidi—deal with this situation. And they weren't helping. Not the school, not their daughter, not themselves. This would not go away just because she wanted it to, no matter how much she and her husband drank. And try as she might, she couldn't, as I suspected she hoped to do, drop it in Gareth's lap and hightail it back to the other coast.

Still, I used my softest tone as I continued, "It would be very helpful to us if you could—"

She gave a long and very put-upon sigh. "I really don't know who her friends were, Ms. Kozak. Heidi didn't like to bring people home. She said our place was sterile and unpleasant and that we were always drinking and it embarrassed her. As though adults aren't allowed to live their own lives in their own homes. She wasn't always like that, of course. She was a very sweet little girl. I understand that teenage girls always behave impossibly toward their mothers, and Heidi was no exception."

That's right, I thought, *lay the blame on your difficult child.* She didn't seem to grasp that the operative word here was "child."

Heidi hadn't been old enough to drive. Most of her comings and goings would either have involved being driven by her mother or a friend's mother, or walking or taking a bus or a taxi. Or Uber. Lyft. I always forget about these new ride services. They don't operate around rural Maine.

The simple fact was that Lorena Norris would have had to work at not knowing what her daughter was up to. And if she was telling the truth, we weren't looking at an angry, estranged teen who spent the majority of her time away from her family because she was acting out. We were looking at a sad child who had been replaced in her mother's affections and forcibly separated from a father she loved.

I would circle back to the question about friends. For now, I moved on. "What about teams or clubs at school, or organizations she belonged to? There would have been people there who knew her."

"She wasn't much of a joiner. There was a radio station, and she worked there for a time, and of course there was her guitar teacher. I don't remember his name, but I can look it up when I get home. Charlie something. I think he was the only thing she was sad about leaving when she came to Simmons, even though they assured her she could continue her lessons here."

The General cleared his throat and said, "Not Charlie. William," and she shot him a look.

I made a note. A male music teacher she was very attached to was a possibility. Someone she was alone with for long periods of time, and could be certain that her mother wasn't paying attention. A mother who likely wrote the man regular checks and couldn't even remember his name.

"Did you ever get the sense she might be getting too attached to him?"

"He was in his fifties, Ms. Kozak."

As though that answered everything. As though a man in his fifties was too old to hold a young teen's interest or to be a seducer. "What about colleagues at the radio station? Or an advisor?"

Lorena Norris shrugged. "I really don't know."

"Best girlfriend?"

"Stephanie Smirnoff, across the street. They've been pals since kindergarten. But Stephanie's gone off to boarding school, too, and I have no idea how to get in touch with her."

"You could contact her parents and ask, couldn't you?" I said.

I made a real note this time. Two young girls, close friends, who both decide to go to boarding school at the same time. Did it mean anything?

She cast a quick glance at her husband. "Stephanie's mother and The General…they didn't…don't really get along. I'd prefer not to stir things up."

I couldn't see how trying to locate a friend of Heidi's would stir things up between the neighbor and her husband,

and where Heidi was concerned, things were already stirred up. Maybe she'd feel differently after she'd seen her daughter. Maybe all of this was just an attempt to protect herself, or to give herself time to process what had happened. It would be a huge shock to any parent, and she had just had to throw some things into a suitcase and fly here from the West Coast. Tomorrow morning, when she was rested, she might be more forthcoming. Or she might have had more time to formulate her lies.

Was I becoming too cynical, or just less naïve about human behavior? Recently, someone had accused me of "acting like a cop." I didn't think it was true, but there were days when I wished I had some authority behind me that could persuade people to answer my questions honestly.

"Don't talk about me like I'm not right here, Lorena," he said. "Nina Smirnoff is a nosy, interfering bitch who had the audacity to lecture me about my relationship with my own stepdaughter. But look, if you think it will help Heidi, go ahead. Call her. Get a phone number for Stephanie. Or give Ms. Kozak Nina's number and she can track down Stephanie. I'm sure we can leave that in Ms. Kozak's capable hands."

He turned his back on us and drifted over to the window. Whatever earlier impulse he'd had to comfort her was gone.

"I'll find you Nina's number," Lorena Norris said, looking eager to off-load the task of contacting her to me. So eager she opened her bag, got out her phone, and scribbled something onto a small piece of paper. She handed the paper to me, and I checked the handwriting before putting in my briefcase.

What a day. There was my mother thinking I was being difficult, and I was thinking Mrs. Norris was being difficult, and she was thinking Gareth was being difficult. Everyone needed a decent meal and some rest. But everyone also needed some answers and the quest for those prevented any of us from seeking rest.

"Maybe this will be easier in the morning, when you've had a chance to rest," I suggested. "Let's find out if your daughter is awake. But please be thinking about how this might have happened. About the names of anyone who might help us determine the facts about Heidi's situation. As her mother, you're the best source."

I wanted to say, "pregnancy," but it seemed to draw such negative reactions from her I used the euphemism.

Heidi was awake, Gareth confirmed, but since Ted Basham had been with him when he got the call, Basham had gone to the infirmary to see her. Gareth suggested that the Norrises get settled at their hotel and he would call them when Heidi was ready for another visitor. He reiterated Heidi's request that Mrs. Norris visit by herself, and I saw them share another of those conspiratorial looks. I made a mental note to have Gareth remind the nurse in charge that Heidi didn't want a visit from her stepfather.

What a miserable mess.

They left spitting and snapping, Mrs. Norris's nose way out of joint because, though she seemed not to care much about her daughter, she cared a lot about not being bested by her ex.

I didn't care about any of them. Well, I cared about Gareth, and I thought I'd come to care about Heidi. I'm a big defender of the underdog, and the vulnerable, and she was definitely both of those.

I gave them time to get good and gone, then stuck my head into Gareth's office, explained that they had left, and told him I'd be in to discuss the situation as soon as I'd made some phone calls.

Once I had a room to myself, I checked my voicemail. There were some work calls that needed to be returned, but nothing from my family. I handled the work calls because they could be done quickly and the clients would be pacified. Then I checked texts. Again, nothing. I started going through my family roster again, desperate by now for some information about my father's condition. By some miracle, despite getting no response from my mother or my brother, I was able to reach my Uncle Henry.

"Thea, dear," he said, "is everything okay with you? We've been trying to reach you all day."

I wasn't sure what version of trying to reach me involved not taking my calls, returning my calls, initiating any calls, or leaving me any messages, but the snarky reply that came to mind—How, by mental telepathy?—would get me nowhere. Besides, I might not get along with my mother, but I had no beef with my favorite uncle. "I've been calling," I said, wondering if for some reason they'd been calling me at home, where no one would ever expect to find me on a work day. "I'm here in Massachusetts working on a boarding school crisis."

He made a quiet "Hmm" sound. "I'm afraid we've got a bit of a crisis of our own."

My stomach knotted. "Tell me everything. Tell me what's happened with Dad. Mom left a message that there was an emergency, but she didn't say what it was. Thanks to my staff, I know he's in the hospital, but I haven't been able to get any information about his condition."

He hesitated so long I thought I'd lost the connection. And then, because my life is so full of negative stuff, I decided he didn't want to tell me the worse news. At last he said, "I'm sorry, Thea. It's definitely a heart attack," he said. "He's in the cardiac care unit."

"And no one called me? No one called me? What's his condition? What if he…" I checked myself. Yelling wouldn't help. And it wasn't his job to keep me in the loop.

"He's stable for now, but you should be here, dear, just in case." He didn't need to finish the sentence.

I couldn't help myself. I said, "I should be there? It's that serious? But no one has tried to reach me, Uncle Henry. No one. Not even you or Rita."

I thought his silence acknowledged the truth of my statement.

My office brain immediately started making lists of what I had to do before I could leave. It was the story of my life that I often had to be in two places at once. I'd become adept at handling things by phone as I rushed from one place to another. But there was no way I could handle my dad's heart attack by phone. And I was far from done here at Simmons. Sometimes I could call in someone else from our office, but there was no one with the bandwidth to handle this. I'd just have to stick some bandages on the current situation, head to the hospital, and see how things were.

"Are you at the hospital now?" I asked.

"Of course."

"I'll be there as soon as I can. In the meantime, please ask Mom or Michael to call me."

"I'll try Michael," he said. "Your mother's…well, she's in kind of a state right now."

I wasn't surprised. Mom is tough as nails and a brilliant organizer and a professional volunteer who scares everyone in her orbit into cooperating. Her soft spot is my dad. They might bicker and disagree, and he was far kinder, but basically, like many well-married, and long-together couples, they were joined at the hip. He was her first priority and she was his. I'd learned that the hard way— expecting him to take my side when she was being cruel and unreasonable—and having him back her instead. Ah. Family. My own, and, as I was seeing here, poor Heidi Basham's.

Dammit. I needed to be here. I had so much work to do.

I couldn't stay.

"Is Michael there?"

Another long silence. I knew what this was about. Michael had been there, probably with Sonia. But Sonia didn't like unpleasantness—hovering by a sickbed was not her thing—and she didn't much like anything that wasn't about her. No doubt she'd dragged Michael off for a meal, one that would last several hours. But if that was the case, why the heck wasn't he answering his phone? I knew the answer to that, too. Because he'd turned it off, not wanting to be disturbed in case there was bad news. Sometimes it was hard to believe we'd been conceived by the same parents and raised in the same house.

"I'll be there as soon as I can," I repeated. "Please. Call me if…"

"I will," he said. "And please, Thea, drive carefully."

As if that time I'd driven off the road and been in an accident had been from careless driving instead of being rammed by a bad guy. I suppressed a sigh. Families are complicated. "See you soon."

My mind racing, I braced myself to give Gareth the bad news, and headed back to his office.

CHAPTER 7

I planned to fill Gareth in on the little I'd learned, get caught up on his information, and head for the hospital. He'd be unhappy with my departure. He had a traumatized student, irate and incompatible parents, an anxious student body, and a faculty hoping for answers. By morning, that group would no doubt include the police again. I expected to find him pacing the room. Instead, Ted Basham had returned after a remarkably short visit with his daughter, and he and Gareth were sitting in comfortable armchairs, each holding a drink. Gareth was looking weary, but composed, Basham like a man seriously in need of the drink he was holding.

Gareth nodded toward his glass. "Can I get you anything?"

Sure, I thought, *a split personality? A superpower that included being able to be in two places at once.* I felt like I was being drawn and quartered by the powerful pull of my dual obligations. "No thanks. I'm fine." A drink at this point would render me useless on both fronts even if mothers-to-be could drink.

I took what was supposed to be a calming breath and pulled out my pen and a pad of paper. I still like taking notes by hand, the act of writing helps to register the information in my brain, though now I often use my phone's recording ability as backup. I looked at Gareth. "I've just had some bad news." He flinched as I rushed on. "My father's had a heart attack. He's in intensive care. I need to go..." I tried to think what to say that wouldn't alarm him. "We can catch up on the last hour or so, then I have to leave. Assuming things are stable, I'll be back in a few hours."

When he didn't say anything, I started in. "Let's catch each other up. How's Heidi?"

It was Basham who answered. "She doesn't know what hit her. Sorry. That's a poor choice of words. She...uh...she really doesn't believe that she was pregnant. Or didn't know that she was. She's sure she hasn't had a baby, despite the evidence of her own body. I guess I'm going to need to talk to that shrink tomorrow. Get a clearer idea about what's going on. I sure hope she has some insights."

"Dr. Purcell says that getting a handle on Heidi's situation may take a while," I said. "It will take time to build a relationship that will enable Heidi to confide in her."

Basham nodded. "Makes sense to me. But I'd appreciate Dr. Purcell's insights."

He was an attractive man in an artsy way. Tall and broad-shouldered, with longish hair, black jeans and a black shirt. A couple of interesting, handcrafted rings and some bracelets. Copper, and some of those fund-raising things that look like big rubber bands. He'd said he had spoken with Heidi often on the phone, so maybe he would have more information for us.

"We will do our best for your daughter," Gareth said, "but you'll need to get Heidi her own lawyer. The school's attorneys have been advising us, but she's not their client."

"I get it," Basham said. "Can you, or they, suggest someone?"

Gareth located a paper on his desk and offered it to Basham. "Here are some names and numbers."

Basham nodded, like everyone needing their own lawyer was something he understood, made some notes in his phone, and tucked the paper in a pocket. "Okay," he said, "what do you need from me? How can I help?"

"Information," I said. "Insight into Heidi. Into how this could have happened. The how, the when, and the who. Your ex-wife said Heidi didn't have a boyfriend."

"What Lorena probably said," he interrupted, "is that Heidi wasn't attractive enough to get herself a boyfriend, when Heidi is lovely. Sweet and fresh and so natural looking and unspoiled. She's sick, that woman is. I can't believe I didn't see it years ago. Can you imagine being competitive with your own daughter?"

Suddenly, he dropped his head into his hands and his shoulders slumped. "I should have fought harder for custody. I should never have left Heidi to deal with that pair. I travel a lot, which is not a stable situation for a child, and she said she'd be okay. I shouldn't have believed her. She's a sweet girl. Trusting. I thought she'd be all right, which was wishful thinking on my part. She just doesn't have the skills to protect herself against that."

"Against what, Mr. Basham?"

"Narcissism. Indifference. Abandonment. On Bradley's part, I think genuine dislike. When he went after Lorena, who looks hot even if she's colder than the North Pole, he didn't bargain on getting a kid, too. I don't know what he thought was going to happen. Lorena doesn't give two damns about Heidi, but the minute she thought I wanted custody, it became another one of those battles she just had to win."

He squeezed his head between his hands like he was trying to keep it from flying apart. "I suppose they have no idea who the father of this baby is? Who the bastard is who…"

"Do you?" I asked.

He stared at me like it was an idea he'd never entertained before.

"You said the two of you talk on the phone. I get the impression that's a fairly regular thing?"

He nodded. "It depends on my schedule, which isn't always my own. But we try to stay in touch."

"Regular even before she came to Simmons? While she was still living in California with her mother and stepfather?"

He nodded again. "We try to talk every week or two. It doesn't always work out, but we try."

"Did she ever say anything that might have suggested the father's identity?"

"No." He considered. "Heidi's kind of a late bloomer. She really hasn't been interested in boys."

"What about boys who might have been interested in her?"

"She's never mentioned any. There are some boys here she's talked about, Ronnie and Jaden, but the impression I got was that they're friends, not boyfriends. And there wasn't anyone back home that I ever heard about."

"What about times when she might have been blank about what happened? Sometime when she might have gotten drunk or gone to a party…"

"Heidi doesn't drink," he said. "Or party."

This wasn't helping. He might know something, perhaps even something he didn't know he knew, but he was refusing to dig in and be analytical. Playing the wronged and abused father of his "sweet little girl" was useless to us, and to Heidi. He needed to understand that his obligation to step up for his daughter involved more than criticizing his ex or being charming. I stared at the man lounging comfortably in his chair, enjoying Gareth's good Scotch, and contrasted it with my image of a frightened girl alone in the night, delivering a baby.

Ignoring my partner, Suzanne's, frequent admonition to treat people with kid gloves, I put some steel in my voice. "Something happened to her, Mr. Basham. From everything we've heard she was not a girl who partied or drank, and you've just agreed that's true. But somehow, whether she consented to it or was even aware of it, a sex act took place and she got pregnant. It only takes once. Someone is responsible, and knowing the circumstances may help us—us and the police—to understand why she's in denial. Whether it happened under traumatic circumstances or she was seduced by someone she trusted. Whether she might have been in a situation where she was drugged and taken advantage of. There are date rape drugs where the victim has no memory of the events."

His head was in his hands again. Despite the circumstances, he didn't want to think about this. "Why do *you* need to know? Why not the police?"

I had to get out of here before my depressing vision of a child being raised in a household with this man and Mrs. Norris overwhelmed me.

Luckily, Gareth took that one. "The police do need to know and they *will* ask these questions. Of you and your ex-wife. And Heidi, of course. The difference is that they'll be looking for a crime. Crimes plural—a crime on the part of whoever got her pregnant at fifteen, and a crime on her part for abandoning her baby. If someone hadn't found that baby so quickly, she might have died. We're asking these questions in part because we're trying to get ahead of them—to shape the story in the light that's best for Heidi. Figuring out how we can support her and protect her from prosecution, if possible. Dr. Purcell will be an important resource for Heidi there."

There was the sound of sloshing ice as Gareth drank. I was envious. Sometimes a fortifying drink really helps. A relaxing, mellowing drink. A "take the edge off your fear" drink.

I could have used some mellowing. My father was in the hospital, and I was delaying rushing to his side to explain things that any truly sensible and caring parent would already have known. Trying to extract cooperation when cooperation should have been eagerly offered.

"That's a part of it," Gareth said, continuing to explain why we were asking our questions. "The other reason for these questions is the nature of this school. Since you've been in regular contact with Heidi, I'm sure she's told you about Simmons. We endeavor to build a real community here, Mr. Basham. Being a part of this community means that everyone takes responsibility for his or her behavior. For actions that are harmful to others. Heidi chose to come here because of who we are. By doing that, she accepted our values and agreed to live by them. Now she has done things that the community finds abhorrent—abandoning a helpless newborn and claiming that the child wasn't hers. Then claiming that she has never had sex or been pregnant, when the clear evidence is to the contrary. That's a lot of ways she's violated the community's values."

He hesitated again, then said, "Part of my job is to help the community understand. Initially, they are going to think it's not possible that Heidi didn't know she was pregnant, and to see what she did as a betrayal of our shared values. I need to help them see how Heidi's position could be true for her. Help them understand how this isn't black and white, it's complicated. Psychologically and physically complicated."

Looking wretched, Basham held out his empty glass like a supplicant. "At the risk of acting like Lorena…could I have another?"

Like the rest of the world would, I flashed on Oliver Twist.

"Of course."

Gareth refreshed the drink and went on with his explanation. "One of the reasons Heidi needs her own attorney—someone to protect her interests—is that I have mixed loyalties here. My loyalty to Heidi, as one of my students, and my loyalty to this school, and the community we've created. We have a unique philosophy here—one that isn't for everyone, one that's important to the students who choose to come here. I need to retain my current students and continue to attract like-minded students for future classes. To do that, I have to take whatever steps are necessary to protect the school's reputation."

He nodded at me. "That's one reason Thea is here. To help us shape the message and protect our community. And crass as it may sound, Mr. Basham, we've sent our acceptance letters to next year's applicants. I need to do my best to ensure we enroll a strong class for next year. Obviously, a scandal like this—"

He held up a hand to ward off Basham's protest. "The press will call it a scandal, Mr. Basham, even if we don't. But this event calls our whole approach, our philosophy of an open and responsible community, into question. It also reflects on our ability to take adequate care of our students, which is very important to any boarding school's parents. We have to meet these issues head-on and deal with them honestly and openly. Under the circumstances, Heidi's interests may differ from ours."

Basham stared at the floor, his knotted hands resting on his knees. "Are you saying you might ask Heidi to leave?"

Gareth nodded.

"Heidi is happy here," Basham said, shaking his head as though shaking off a burden. "It's a good place for her. It would break her heart if she had to leave. And I can't...she really can't come live with me." He sighed. "I travel too much. She'd be alone too much. And I don't see how I can send her back to...to them."

He stared down at his hands, which were decorated with intricate, heavy silver rings. "You can't send her away, Gareth. It would be too cruel."

Gareth stared out a window where there was nothing to see. He was such an admirably decent man. It was rare that people told each other the truth.

I was noticing that despite their very limited acquaintance, Basham had used Gareth's first name in a most familiar way. Were those pauses genuine searches for thoughts or consideration of the next manipulation? I had the uneasy feeling Basham was hiding something.

And we were no closer to understanding what had happened to Heidi.

"She has no idea how this pregnancy happened?" I said.

He raised his arms in a helpless gesture. "She's never had sex. She couldn't possibly have gotten pregnant. If that's what she says, that's what she believes. Heidi is no liar. This isn't something she's faking or asserting to cover up bad behavior or some secret relationship." He shrugged like this was all beyond him. "That's not the kind of person Heidi is."

"Her mother says she spent a couple weeks with you last summer—"

"Five days," he said bluntly, cutting off my question. "Just five days. That's all that miserable bitch I used to be married to would allow. The agreement says two weeks, and she futzed around and changed the plans so many times I only ended up with five days. Not because Lorena was too attached to Heidi to be apart from her, but simply because it was another opportunity to jerk me around. Like I said, she doesn't really care about Heidi."

I bit my lip, because my smarty mouth wanted to say, "And yet, knowing that, you left her with her mother." He talked a good game, but I wondered if he'd really put up much of a fight, given the demands of his own life. I wanted him to prove me wrong.

"And in case you have some crazy idea that this might have happened on my watch," Basham continued, "I can assure you that that's impossible. We went on a four-day sailing cruise up the coast of Maine that Heidi chose. Small boat. Lots of people. Tight quarters and no time when she could have gotten together with anyone, even if there had been someone to get together with. Which there was not."

He dusted his hands together, a startlingly loud noise in the quiet room. "We all...anyone who's thinking clearly and doesn't want to evade responsibility, that is, understand this pregnancy couldn't have happened here at Simmons. It happened before she got here, so it must have happened on Lorena's watch. Not that Lorena was paying any attention. Self-centered doesn't begin to—"

We were not going down this road again. "So you have no idea who..." I interrupted.

"No idea about who, Ms. Kozak, and no idea about how. When. How could I? I wasn't there."

He raised his head and his eyes were blazing. Eyes can be the mirror of the soul and they really can blaze. "Lorena should. She *was* there. She was supposed to be taking care of Heidi. I support her so that she can take care of Heidi. But I don't suppose she—"

"She says she has no idea."

"She has an idea, all right. She's just not deigning to share it with us."

I was inclined to agree with him. Lorena Norris had claimed to know nothing, but her indignation had been as much at the necessity for obfuscation and self-protection as it had been genuine indignation. I'd met Lorena Norris's type before. The independent school world was full of them. Women—and men—glad to offload their children and the responsibility for raising them onto the shoulders of institutions. Often children they'd abdicated responsibility for years before they sent those children to boarding school. Children who'd been struggling to raise themselves. It was rarer that such parents would choose a place like Simmons. They'd go for prestige, name recognition, schools that might get their kids into good colleges. But then, they hadn't chosen Simmons. Heidi had.

Time was passing. My anxiety was increasing with every minute that I wasn't on the road, and we were getting nowhere. Better to wait 'til the morning. I had one more question, though, a random one I didn't expect him to answer. "Is there anyone you can think of who might have been in and out of the Norris's house on a regular basis, someone Heidi might have trusted? Or someone who might have taken advantage of her?"

Basham looked startled by the question. Then his fists clenched. "In and out of the house? Someone she would have trusted? Maybe not trusted, because they aren't trustworthy, but I can think of at least three people who were in and out quite frequently. Two of the general's junior officers and Lorena's slimy cousin Dennis. And there's that guy, Will, who taught Heidi to play the guitar. Only I think he doesn't come to the house anymore because all that noise bothers The General."

Just when you think you can fold up your tent and slip away. I wasn't surprised. People often came out with the important stuff when I thought I was done. Usually I left time for it in my interviews. Not tonight. Tonight my concentration was already leaving this room and driving way. And dammit, this needed to be followed up.

Basham was surprised, though. As if, despite what we'd been talking about, and despite the dramatic events that had brought him here, he'd never seriously considered the possibility that someone had taken advantage of his daughter in a way that violated all the rules of decency, and he couldn't conceive of such a betrayal of trust and seduction of innocence. It was almost as though, despite having been told about the baby and being made aware of Heidi's condition, he, too, believed that his daughter was still an innocent virgin and an unexplained pregnancy and delivery hadn't really happened.

He needed to get himself over to the hospital and see that baby for himself. If Lorena was a grandma, he was a grandpa. There was an innocent newborn in this situation that no one was thinking about. I wasn't supposed to be, either. I was supposed to be thinking about my client, the Simmons School.

Eager as I was to be gone, I dropped back into my chair. "Tell us about them," I said.

"Which one?"

"All four of them."

Though he tried to hide it, I could tell Gareth wished I hadn't asked the question. He was tired, too, having been up much of the night, and had other things to deal with besides Ted Basham. And a family that probably wanted some of his attention. Morning would come just as fast whether we were prepared for it or not.

"If you'd prefer, Mr. Basham, we could pick this up again in the morning," he said. "I'm sure you've had a tiring day."

I shot him a look. Didn't he understand how important this was? It needed to be followed up now, before Basham had time for second thoughts, but he and Gareth were on a different page. With relieved sighs and the downing of the last of their Scotch, they shook hands, and Basham crutched out to his car to head for Gareth's house.

When the door had closed behind him, Gareth gave me an embarrassed look. "I know," he said. "We risk losing momentum. But it would have taken time. There are other things I have to deal with. And you've got your father."

I thought he'd made a bad call. This might have been our only chance to get those spontaneous revelations. Often, people talked more freely under stress and disclosed things they otherwise wouldn't. It sure looked like that was the case with Basham. But Gareth was the client so he got to decide.

So many other things—crafting a press release and a message to be delivered by phone to the parents—would take a long time. But he was toast and I had a family emergency. We would meet again early in the morning. As though just remembering it, Gareth scooped a file off his desk and held it out. "Copies of Heidi's records," he said. "Not much there, but I thought you should see them."

I stuffed the file and my notes in my briefcase and headed out to my car. Before I started driving, I quickly checked my phone. No updates from anyone. Did their silence mean news too bad to tell me over the phone? My anxiety filled the car like a cloud. I could almost smell the ozone from my snapping nerves.

As I hit the road, I told Siri to call my brother Michael. I went directly to voicemail. My mother didn't answer. Uncle Henry didn't answer. The night was spookily dark as I drove far too fast toward a hospital south of Boston, imagining the worst.

CHAPTER 8

I couldn't help calling one more time as I raced through the night. I needed to know what was happening. It was only when I looked at the speedometer and saw I was going 95 that I forced myself back under control. I didn't want to get stopped for speeding. I slowed down, even though 80 felt slow as molasses, and called someone I hoped *would* answer—Andre. He picked up on the first ring, his usual calm and control replaced by a flurry of questions. "What's going on with your father? Have you seen him yet? How's your mother doing? How are you doing?"

I tried to answer them calmly, but I'm not so good at calm when the issue involves me. I guess I save my calm and control for my clients. I got as far as, "I don't know anything yet, except that it's a heart attack and he's in the cardiac care unit. I'm on my way to the hospital now. And no one is answering their phones," before I dissolved into tears.

"Do you want me to come down there?" he asked.

Of course I wanted him. But I hated to drag him out into the night for a long drive if everything was fine. "Let me see what the situation is when I get to the hospital," I said.

"Call me when you know. I'll come if you need me."

"I will."

We didn't disconnect, though we didn't talk. Sometimes I think we do our best communicating when we're just silently together, listening to each other breathe. After a while I said, "I'm scared."

"I'm sure you are." And then, because he knew me so well, he said, "But don't drive like a maniac, okay. Little MOC wants to stay safe. And I want both of you to stay safe."

MOC. Mason, Oliver, or Claudine. A child in grave danger of going through life being called Mock no matter what name we chose or what sex it was. Unlike most couples, we hadn't wanted to know the sex of our child. We wanted the surprise. Never mind that it meant our friends didn't know whether to buy pink or blue. We didn't have a baby's room to paint, so that wasn't an issue. And we would meet whoever it was when the time was right. All we knew so far was that we were definitely going to be the parents of a nocturnal acrobat, quite possibly a kickboxer, and someone plagued by hiccups. That sure was going to be fun. Which made me think about Heidi again. How was it possible to have missed her baby's kicks and hiccups? Were there babies that were quiet and still?

"Thea? Are you still there?"

"Still here. Thinking about the situation at Simmons and wondering how that child could not have known she was pregnant."

"It happens."

"I know. It happened. So how are things there? All quiet? No one has been murdered today?"

"If they have, no one's told me. So, tell me about your student. Wait. Check your speed and then tell me about your student."

"I'm only going eighty," I said.

"Only?" he said, and laughed. The man was so scarily competent he could drive eighty miles an hour in reverse.

"My student? The poor girl insists she's never had sex and that the baby isn't hers. Her mother and stepfather are clueless. Or indifferent. Her mother says the girl is too unattractive to have a boyfriend. I think the two of them are hiding something, though I have no idea what it is."

"What the mom said about her daughter? Bet that got your back up," he said.

"It did. Then it turns out that the mom failed to notify the dad, even though she said she would. He got word anyway and showed up on crutches, absolutely furious. Now mom is stonewalling, while the stepfather says 'not my problem,' and the dad is angry and flailing. He may have something for us, though. The dad. We were close to getting it, but then Gareth ended the meeting, and who knows whether he'll still be forthcoming in the morning."

"And you were angry about that."

"You bet. Frustrated, anyway. When someone is willing to talk, you don't shut them down. Guess who I learned that from?"

He made an affirmative noise and asked, "When will you be coming home?"

"I don't know. I'm hoping for tomorrow night. It depends on what happens here. On the parents and the press and how the situation develops. And of course, what's going on with my dad."

He made a comforting sound.

"Boy, do I wish you were here," I said. "You would understand how to get to the bottom of things. This girl didn't have a boyfriend. Mom says there's no time where she can't remember what happened to her. Or came home from a party intoxicated or didn't come home at all. Or where she later seemed upset or distant or depressed or showed any signs of trauma or changed behavior. You'd be able to get more out of her. The mom, I mean. She really needs to be leaned on by a tough guy like you."

"While you have to be polite." He sympathized, then moved on to the essential question. "Any thoughts about what she's hiding? Or why?"

He had a lot more faith in me as an observer than I had in myself, but I considered his question. Had I noticed anything? Things I might have dismissed because of her overall demeanor? There was something. When I asked about people in and out of the house, Mrs. Norris was going to say something, but the stepfather shut her down. I told him about that. "And the stupid ass of a stepfather just keeps saying 'She's not my daughter,' like none of it is his concern."

I paused while I skimmed around someone in the fast lane going fifty-five, and realized what his questions had just led me to. "He, or they, are definitely hiding something. I'm pretty sure they have an idea what happened."

"Wish I could help," he said.

"At least I've been trained in Detective Lemieux's school of interrogation."

"Interviewing," he corrected, then said, "Give 'em hell." It was there in his voice, the sound of a detective who's intrigued by a case. "Get the mother alone and try again. And the stepfather. Sometimes those military tough guy types can be disarmed by a pretty woman."

"If I ever get the chance."

"Getting back to the girl. She could be lying," he said.

"No one who knows her thinks she's lying. It sounds more complicated than that."

But I hadn't met her. She could be lying. Lying to protect someone she cared about? I wasn't sure how we'd find that out. Dr. Purcell? Heidi herself? Her friends?

I slowed down to weave my way through a clot of cars poking along in all three lanes, wishing for the zillionth time that I had a carpoon—my fantasy device for punishing annoying drivers—mounted on my hood. Then I could have some fun out here. Recently, I'd resolved to have more fun, live a more normal life. So far, it wasn't working. Crisis and dysfunction continued to be my normal.

"Dr. Purcell, the psychiatrist, says trauma can do this, can make a person repress something so deeply they genuinely believe it never happened. She's thinking this is a psychological reaction to trauma or extreme fear. My money would be on a date rape drug, or extreme intoxication, some situation where she could have been unconscious and raped and have no idea that it had happened to her. Or on someone who terrified her into repressing an assault. Either way, without more information to explain it, Heidi's version of the story sounds dishonest and improbable, which is a big deal in this community."

I realized that he didn't know anything about the Simmons School. "Her having a baby and abandoning it. Her denying that she had a baby at all. It's a bigger deal here, I mean, because this school is all about personal responsibility and being an honest member of the community. If they think she's lying and has betrayed their values, she's going to be asked to leave. And if she leaves, she has to go back to her awful mother. The dad travels and is never around—"

"Thea, calm down," he said. "You work for the school, remember, not the student. And check your speed."

I'm pretty independent and not so good at taking advice, but over time, I've learned to listen to Andre, so I slowed down a little and made myself stop gripping the wheel like it was someone's throat. Sometimes I don't realize how wrapped up in things I can get. But Andre knows. He also knows how attached I can get to some of these kids.

"Good," he said, as though he was watching me via a hidden camera. "Wish I could put my arms around you."

"Me, too." Despite our crazy lives, and the dangerous things that have happened to us, being with Andre was the safest place I knew.

Rain began splatting against the windshield. April showers. Except these April showers looked more like sleet. I flipped on the wipers and slowed a little more.

"What about the stepdad?" Andre said. "Could that indifference be a pose? You think he could have done it? He'd certainly have access, and he wouldn't be the first man to marry a woman so he could get at her child."

I considered Andre's question. "He seems so supercilious. He's a general, and he acts like one. Like a man who wants to boss us all around and shape us up, and then march away and leave us to handle things. He doesn't strike me as someone who'd be attracted to a fifteen-year-old."

But that could all have been a smokescreen. Plenty of women had been fooled by such men. And anyway, that kind of targeting behavior was not about normal attraction and men who targeted children were damned good at hiding it.

"Some fifteen-year-olds can be pretty hot," he reminded me. "And mature for their age. Or innocent and childlike, not yet into puberty. Both of those can attract the wrong type of men."

"I haven't met her yet, but I don't think that's Heidi. She's more like a plaid flannel hippie. Definitely not the flaunt-her-body type. After all, she was nearly eight months pregnant and nobody noticed. Not even her own mother and she was just home for two weeks in March."

"That's sad," he said, and I thought about Ted Basham's comment to his wife. If Lorena had hugged her daughter, how could she have missed the pregnancy? It was sad to think of a child flying all the way across the country to visit a parent who never touched her.

A yawn came over the air. "I'm going to bed. Someone who will remain unnamed got a call at an ungodly hour this morning and now I'm short on sleep."

"Sorry," I said. We both loved a good night's sleep and this pregnancy was making me regard sleep with a far deeper appreciation. Not that he hadn't interrupted my sleep plenty of times. When a homicide detective gets a call, he answers.

"Call me when you know something," he murmured.

I imagined him arranging his pillows and pulling up the covers. "You bet."

He was gone. I was alone again in the dark. The metronomic slap of the wipers and the hiss of the tires created a sense of being in a bubble as I raced through the night. It lasted until the GPS announced that my exit was coming up. I moved into the exit lane and followed the blue hospital signs. My anxiety, which I'd kept at bay while talking to Andre, was back—a huge hand squeezing my stomach and interfering with my breathing.

I pulled into the parking garage and wound my way through the echoing darkness into a parking space near the exit stairs. I am easily spooked by parking garages at night. My life has been eventful enough that I am entitled to be wary about what lurks in the dark. Tonight, at least, I had no reason to expect that I was being followed by bad guys. This bad lay in real world circumstances that had nothing to do with my work. Still, I checked my surroundings carefully and paused a few times to listen for footsteps. The lighting was terrible, faint and a sickening yellow.

My feet clattered down the slippery steps of a stairwell that smelled of urine, coffee, cigarettes, and fear. I was sure I'd added my own fear scent by the time I reached the bottom and pushed through a heavy door into the hospital itself.

CHAPTER 9

A kindly woman at the information desk directed me to the cardiac unit, a place of bright, sterile lights, the *sotto voce* hum of machinery, permeated by the anxious beeping of machines that kept track of the inhabitants' vital functions. When I gave my father's name to the stern, harried male nurse, he shook his head. "Only two visitors at a time," he said. "Are you family?"

I suppressed the smart-assed urge to say, "No. I just like to visit strangers who've had heart attacks." Smart-ass tends to be my visceral reaction when I'm terrified. Instead, I simply said, "I'm his daughter."

The sternness softened. "Come with me," he said. I followed him down a hallway crowded with equipment and into my father's room. From his comment about two visitors, I expected to find my mother and Michael. Instead, I found Uncle Henry and Aunt Rita and was immediately smothered in familiar embraces, comforted by the well-known scents of Rita's perfume and Henry's aftershave. Released, I moved toward the bed, where my father—my larger-than-life, big-voiced father—was sleeping, still and pale against the pillows, connected to an array of wires and tubes.

I kissed him and squeezed his hand. Told him to snap out of it. Then I drew Henry and Rita into a corner. "What do we know?"

Their words poured out in an overlapping jumble, the gist of which was that he'd had a mild heart attack and they were keeping him overnight for observation. The mild part was good, but no one reacts well to the idea of "observation," particularly with respect to a beloved family member. It always smacks of obfuscation. What did "mild" really mean? What were they observing? And why? These days, hospitals send people home before they've even stopped bleeding. It sounded fishy, but they didn't know. Rita and my dad, brother and sister only eleven months apart, had always been like twins. Right now, she looked almost as bad as the man in the bed.

"How long has he been like this?" I asked, and then, not waiting for a reply, "How long has he been here?"

I got another chorus of overlapping responses. Hours. He had been restless and cranky, earlier, wanting to go home. Then he'd fallen asleep, and had been like this for hours. Backtracking, Rita explained that he'd been feeling a little light-headed in the morning, and my mother had wanted to take him to the emergency room. He'd refused. He was finishing some project in the office, so he wanted to wait until he felt better and go in to work. By the time she persuaded him to go to the ER, he was having chest pains. They'd done one of those cardiac catheterizations and things looked fine. They would watch him tonight and send him home in the morning.

The man in the bed looked anything but fine to me.

"We convinced your mother to go down to the cafeteria and get something to eat. She hasn't eaten all day. You know how she is," Rita said. "She should have gone with Michael. I mean, he should have insisted she go with him, but you know how Michael can be. He and Sonia did that, 'We're just stepping out for a moment,' thing and disappeared. They didn't even ask if she, or we, wanted to join them."

She checked her watch and frowned. "That was nearly five hours ago. That Sonia…" None of us liked Sonia, who was utterly self-involved and brought out the worst in Michael. But she stopped herself from saying the obvious—that my dad had had a heart attack and was in a precarious situation and I hadn't been here at all. I'd been dealing with other people's problems.

I would have felt guiltier if I thought my mother had been waiting for me all this time. But since she'd failed to let me know what was going on or where she was, that could not have been the case. Logically, since I was without information and she and I have zero psychic connection, I couldn't have rushed to my father's bedside. She wouldn't see it that way.

Where I did feel guilty was thinking that my father might have needed me.

"Mom didn't call me," I said. "Or leave any messages about what was happening. I tried a dozen times to reach her or Michael and got no response."

Rita patted my arm and looked away. "We know," Uncle Henry said. But he hadn't called me, either. Perhaps assuming Mom had called me and I simply hadn't responded. Family. Maybe how Heidi's mother was behaving wasn't so strange after all. Perhaps all families are dysfunctional?

Still, I felt rotten that the situation had seemed critical and my mother hadn't bothered to include me. A single phone call without a useful message did not count as inclusion. All the complaining she'd undoubtedly done since didn't change that. This wasn't about our relationship and however good or bad it was. This was about our family.

My brain was whirling. What could be worse than wanting to scream at my mother for not including me in events that would make me want to scream? I couldn't help wondering why she hadn't called. Why Michael hadn't called. What was wrong with them, to think I didn't want to be involved? Even when obligatory family events were nothing short of torture, I always showed up.

My mother believed I was too wrapped up in my job. Had she used this as an opportunity to make a point? Truth check, Kozak. If one of them *had* called, would I have stopped what I was doing and rushed here? Bad as the situation at Simmons was, the answer was of course. Except that I'd been so immersed in Simmons's problems, I had stayed to clear a few things up, hadn't I?

Stop it. This is not about you, Kozak, I reminded myself. Whatever had happened before, I was here now. Here and wanting Andre with me—my own personal piece of family. Someone on my side. But he would only be one more person anxiously pacing, probably excluded from the room, given the two-person rule.

Why was I even thinking about sides?

How did one do any of this right?

I'd call Andre and update him, now that it looked like my father was stable. He'd sleep better knowing he wasn't about to be summoned here to deal with a crisis. My father would be going home in the morning. If only he didn't look so awfully sick.

"Have the two of you eaten?" I asked. I was sure my mother had forgotten her normal care-taking habits in the face of this.

Reluctantly, Rita shook her head. "We haven't. We didn't want to leave him. If you wouldn't mind…"

"Go," I said, making shooing motions.

It was only then that she studied me, and her drawn face lifted in a sudden smile. "Oh, Thea, how wonderful!" She swept into another hug. "Your mother didn't mention…" A hesitation, then, "Oh dear. Does she know?" A meaningful glance at the bed, and then, "Does your father?"

I shook my head. "I was going to tell her tonight. We were going to have dinner to plan that shower for Sonia." Rita and I both burst into tears. True, my father knew that he was going to be a grandfather. Michael and Sonia had announced their pregnancy practically on the day of conception. He'd be a great grandpa. It was a role he'd been preparing for all his life. But, despite our differences, I was his favorite. He would be thrilled that Andre and I were finally having a baby.

What if things got much worse and MOC never got to know this wonderful man? I stifled the thought.

"Go get something to eat," I said. "I'll be here. I've got your cell numbers. I'll call if anything happens."

They left. Against those hospital admonitions not to use cell phones, I made a quick call to Andre. Then I sat. My father lay unmoving, his stillness utterly terrifying. From time to time, something would beep, or someone would come in and perform some procedure. The leaden minutes passed like hours. I felt like I had been in the room for half of my life. I hate hospitals.

Despite my efforts to be present here, in the cold stillness my mind drifted to Simmons, and Heidi, and a small baby everyone was ignoring. It was horrible to imagine that tiny human being born with no one around who cared about her. No loving, worried face peering down at her. No warm hands comforting her. No reassuring voice crooning her name. The poor infant had no name. With an effort, I pushed those images away.

Concern about my dad merged with my other worries until I was a cauldron of anxiety. I had the sense that bad things were happening at Simmons, but restrained myself from checking my phone for messages. In my haste to get here, I'd left my briefcase in the car. I wasn't leaving my father alone to go and get it, so I couldn't fill the time with work.

I was glad I was alone when my father woke up. It gave us some special time together. He seemed weary, but very much himself. "Everyone's making too big a deal about this," he said. "All this darned hovering professional medicine to establish that something happened, it wasn't serious, it's over, and maybe I should get some rest. How are things with you and Andre? Crazy as ever?"

"We have some news," I said, and guided his hand to where our little acrobat was performing tonight's act.

"Wow!" he said. "A baby! You are in for it now, you know. This is just how you were. Your poor mother never got a decent night's sleep. She thought she was going to give birth to a monkey." He was grinning like I had never seen him grin.

"You're going to be one busy grandpa," I said.

The grin stayed on his face. "I can't wait. One of them better like fishing." He dropped his hand back onto the covers, and I took it and held on. "Somehow, I don't see Michael and Sonia's child as a fisherman." He laughed.

"Maybe she will turn out to have a mind of her own." I could say 'she' because we knew they were having a girl.

"So what are you having?" he asked. "Did you do that testing?"

"A baby. That's all we know. We wanted to be surprised."

"Oh. You'll be surprised all right. Just you wait. You got names?"

"Mason, Oliver, or Claudine. We're calling it MOC."

"That's going to stick, you know. Kid will be ready to graduate high school and you and Andre will still be calling it MOC."

"I know."

He grinned. "Your mother know?"

"I was going to tell her today. At dinner."

"Oh. Right. Sonia's shower." A grimace. "She's going to be mad at you."

"Because I told you first?"

"You bet."

"Rita and Henry know, too."

"Brace yourself, then," he said. "She's going to be double mad."

"I never could do anything right."

"I know. It's not you. It's just...she worked too hard to have you. All those miscarriages. It changed things. It's never been about who you are...and then when Carrie..."

Carrie. My adopted sister. My little sister who was murdered. Getting involved in that investigation was how I met Andre.

My dad lost his train of thought, sighed, and closed his eyes. "All this medical business has made me very tired."

I've spent enough time in hospitals to know they are not restful places. "Try to get some sleep, if they'll let you," I said. "Morning will be here soon and you'll be going home."

"Happy news. I hate this…" he murmured and drifted off.

The hum of machinery did its thing, and I nodded off, too, until someone dropped something in the hallway with a huge clang. Hospitals are so restful.

Eventually, my mother returned. I wasn't foolish enough to expect joy or an embrace. Well. I was that foolish, but I've learned to suck it up. She was on the attack even before she was fully in the room. How dare I tell Henry and Rita about my pregnancy before telling her? She went on for a good twenty minutes. Another time I might have argued or, my new strategy, simply walked away, since this was all about self-importance and her not being the first to know, but the circumstances called for patience and compassion. I dredged some up and let her have her say. From time to time, so entrenched were her habits, that she turned to the silent figure in the bed for confirmation. Each time it stopped her cold. But not for long.

When she ran out of steam, I said, "I wish you could be happy for me."

Henry and Rita returned to say they were going home to get some sleep. Asked that we call if anything happened.

The doctors came by to examine and consult, and urged us both to go home and get some sleep. They said he seemed fine. They didn't expect any changes. They would call if anything happened, but expected a quiet night and planned to discharge him in the morning.

I needed a few hours of rest, so I said I would get some sleep and check back in the morning.

My mother, of course, refused to leave.

Michael and Sonia never returned.

CHAPTER 10

———◆———

Back in the car, I checked my phone. The evening at Simmons, it seemed, had been blissfully quiet. I wasn't sure I believed that. No doubt it would start up again by morning.

The roads were empty, but with ridiculous unseasonable snow splatting down, it took a while to get back to the little town where Simmons was located. Not eighty-mile-an-hour conditions. Times like this, when we get snow and slush instead of welcoming flowers, I wonder why any of us live in New England.

I parked, grabbed the overnight bag that lives in my car, and headed inside, feeling like a vandal as I crept into the inn. I hoped they'd simply left an envelope and key. Instead, despite the late hour, a tall, bent, weary man in a Mr. Rogers cardigan was waiting. He greeted me, led me to my room, explained how things worked and said there was still cake and other desserts in the breakfast room. Then he padded quietly away.

I wanted cake. I needed sleep.

I did a slapdash toilette that consisted of brushing my teeth and braiding my hair, set my phone alarm for six, changed into my nightgown, and crawled into bed. I didn't know if my phone would ring during the night with news about my father, but just in case, I set it right beside my pillow. I also didn't know whether when I woke I might be making my excuses to Gareth and heading back to the hospital, or going back to pasting Band-Aids on his problem.

It was probably a nice room and a nice bed, but I was too distracted, and far too tired, to notice. I woke only a few hours later from a horrible dream in which I was the person who had to operate on my father to save his life. I'd just picked up the scalpel when the sounds of doors opening and closing, and loud footsteps on the stairs, pulled me from sleep. It seemed like a lot of commotion for such an early hour.

Maybe the proprietor was already up and making breakfast? But no. A quick glance at the clock said it was only four a.m. and the man who checked me in said breakfast was at seven. I went to my window and looked down into the parking lot. The outside lights were on, and despite the rain and the fog, I could see Mrs. Norris getting into a shiny black car while The General put their luggage in the trunk.

Leaving? It didn't make sense. They'd barely seen Heidi. Barely spoken with Gareth and not at all with Dr. Purcell. The police hadn't had a chance to speak with them. Nothing had been decided about Heidi's future or about the baby. What on earth was going on?

Maybe they were moving to a different place to stay, but it was an odd time to be doing that. My finely-honed instincts for bad behavior said they were heading out of town. Just beyond them, hovering patiently, was a man with an umbrella. When he lowered it, I recognized the tall man with thinning hair who had greeted me last night. As the car drove off, I grabbed my robe and hurried downstairs to see what I could learn.

If he was surprised to see me, it didn't show. "Was that General and Mrs. Norris?" I asked.

He nodded. "Going to the airport," he said. "They're heading back to California. She said something had come up at home and they were taking an early flight. She said the school would pick up the tab for their room."

He shrugged. "Since I didn't have authorization from the school, I required them to pay and suggested they seek reimbursement. She was mad as a wet hen about that. But this is a business, and I've been stiffed before."

"That was smart," I agreed. "There's no reason for the school to be paying. But why on earth would they leave suddenly like this?"

He shrugged again, as though despite being in the business of housing and feeding transient strangers, human behavior puzzled him. "Some people. You'd think she'd stick around, what with that poor child of hers having that baby and all. There must be a lot of things to be sorted that no way could be sorted that fast. Legal stuff and decisions about the baby. Folks sure can be strange, even about their own children."

He had that right, I thought, even as I wondered how he knew so much about the situation. I had no idea how much had been on the news, but it wasn't likely that the Norrises had been identified and certainly not Heidi, who was a minor. Was it possible that Lorena Norris had confided in him? That would be bizarre even in an already bizarre situation.

My mind was running at high speed, trying to analyze what the Norris's stealthy departure did to Simmons and the whole situation. Wondering how I was going to tell Gareth about this, and whether I should call him right now. Arguing the pros and cons with myself as I stood in the hallway in my bathrobe while a patient man holding a dripping umbrella waited to see if I needed something.

If I did call Gareth, he might be able to head them off at the airport. But even if he went to the airport, was there any way he could stop them? Probably not. If she wanted to abandon her child, there wasn't much Gareth could do to stop her. I supposed that even if I called the police, they couldn't stop her. They'd sure like to question her, though. I'd put money on that.

My loyalty was to Gareth. However useless it might be, I felt that I had to tell him what was happening. I said, "Excuse me. I'd better tell the headmaster," and made the call. Instead of Gareth's sleepy voice, I went straight to voicemail. I left my message and shoved the phone in my pocket.

I was operating on only a few hours sleep. I wanted to go back to bed. But the kindly proprietor was still hovering, so I figured I'd ask. "Pardon me for prying, but you seem to know rather a lot about the Norrises' situation. Was the story about Mrs. Norris's daughter on the news?"

He shook his head. "Just that there was an abandoned baby at the Simmons School, and that the police are investigating. No names, of course, the mother being a minor and all."

He must have read my skeptical look, because, after a hesitation, he said, "When people are upset, they talk. Actually…" He lowered his voice and gestured for me to follow him into the kitchen. "Actually, I overheard most of it last night, when the Norrises were arguing. Before they went out again. When I had to go upstairs to ask them to please be quiet because they were disturbing our other guests."

He looked at me as if inviting me to share his bafflement at human behavior. Obligingly, I said, "People sure can amaze you."

"I knocked," he said, "and no one answered. She was saying that they had to do something and he was saying that the girl had gotten herself, and them, into this mess and she could get herself out of it. Then she said, 'Heidi's only sixteen,' and he said, 'Old enough to get herself knocked up.' And she said 'I don't see how' and he said 'In the usual way, I suppose' and she said 'But who's the boy, Bradley, she's never even had a boyfriend,' and then she said 'What about that music teacher?' and he said, 'What about your creepy cousin?'"

My host, whose name was Austin Palmer, a name I vaguely remembered as having something to do with cursive writing, popped a single-serving cup into the coffee maker and looked at me. "Figure at this point I might as well stay up. You want one?"

A sensible person with a demanding day on the horizon would have gone back to bed, but there was more to be learned here, so I said, "That would be great. What else did they say?"

He shouldn't have been telling me any of this, but I wasn't about to complain. When he hesitated, I added, "I don't see how they can come all this way and then abandon the poor child like this. Her child or that poor little baby."

Nodding, he turned to the rack of coffee pods and said, "Regular or decaf?"

"Regular, thanks."

I have no use for decaf. If I'm going to drink coffee, I want to get some bang for my buck, even if I am hoping to go back to sleep. Then I thought about MOC, and how the baby needed sleep and I was supposed to go easy on the coffee, and said I'd pass. He offered cocoa instead. MOC likes cocoa.

He removed his coffee, added cream and sugar, popped in my cocoa pod, and moved seamlessly back into his story. "She said 'You leave my family out of this,' and he said 'Well, she's your kid so this is your mess. It was probably the kid who cleans the pool' and she said, 'Don't be silly, it's far more likely to be Crosby and Ramirez. I've seen how they watch her.' That's when he got very loud and told her to shut her damned mouth, he didn't want to hear another word about that. I knocked again because they were getting louder and it sounded like name-calling was about to start."

He looked like a man who'd stumbled on a couple in flagrante. Perhaps, by his standards, arguing loudly enough to be overheard, particularly about a subject as personal as a child's unexplained pregnancy, was as bad as any other improper public display.

But his story wasn't finished. "I waited outside their room to be sure they were done and would quiet down. It was quiet for a moment. Then she said, 'Well, it could have been one of them. They're always in and out and looking at her like she's not just a kid.' He made some kind of sputtering noise. She said, 'Well, it isn't impossible.' He said, 'Shut up.' She said, 'Heidi complained about you. And them.' Then she raised her voice and said, 'Oh, God. Bradley, you didn't...they didn't?' He said 'shut up' and some other words I won't repeat and something about getting the girl back to California so they could deal with this. So I knocked again."

He stopped, like he'd realized maybe he shouldn't be telling me this, then said, "She finally jerked the door open and said 'What?' like she had no idea why I might be knocking. I explained about the noise and she just made an aggrieved sound and said they'd had a hard day. Behind her, he was on the phone, and it sounded like he was trying to book flights to California. I left them to it and went back downstairs. An hour later, there was another commotion and they both went out."

He considered. "That was around eleven. I didn't hear them come back. I'd gone to bed. Then, a few minutes ago, she knocked on my door, told me they were leaving, and that I shouldn't charge their card, the school would take care of the room."

It might be reasonable for me to expect the school to pick up the tab for my room, but not the Norrises. But many of the comments and actions I'd observed screamed cheapskate. Good thing the proprietor had insisted on payment.

He gestured toward a plate of cookies. "I know it's an odd hour, but they're very good. Or I could get you a muffin?"

I'd missed dinner, sitting with my dad, and I was hungry. "That's very kind of you. I'd love a muffin."

He ducked his head like someone unused to compliments. "It's a small thing, Ms. Kozak. I'll be right back."

He disappeared through a swinging door and was back quickly with two muffins on a plate. "You know," he said, "I'm sure the papers will make her out to be a monster, but I'm already feeling quite sorry for that poor girl. Heidi. I shouldn't say it, of course, but the Norrises are not pleasant people. One can only hope perhaps her father is a better parent."

"I feel sorry for her, too."

I noted he'd called Heidi by name. The news hadn't reported her name, so this, also, had to have come from the Norrises.

With parents like them, who needed enemies? A little after four in the morning, pitch black outside, and the two of us were sitting at the table gossiping like friends. I figured I might as well ask another question or two. "So, they were actually arguing about who might be the father of that baby?"

"They sure were. She got really defensive when he mentioned her cousin. Then, when she mentioned some people he'd brought to the house and wondering whether it might be one of them, and mentioned that Heidi had been concerned about them, he got ugly and shut her down real fast."

The plot, already as thick as long-cooked porridge, had just gotten thicker.

I figured I'd pushed it as far as I could, so I took my muffins and cocoa and headed for the door. "Thanks for these. I'll see you at breakfast."

"Any time after seven. Tomorrow…uh, today, I mean…we're making whole grain granola pancakes with bananas and pecans, whipped butter, and real maple syrup."

I didn't care what came up or if the world was ending. I was going to have some of those pancakes. MOC loves pancakes.

"Well, I'd better let you get back to sleep." He disappeared through the swinging door while I hurried upstairs.

I gave up on Gareth calling me back, and was settling down into what I now knew was a deliciously comfy bed, when my phone rang.

As every cop's significant other knows—when the phone rings in the middle of the night, your heart stops. This goes double for when your father is in the hospital, even if they say they're just watching. My hand traced a rapid, unsteady course, and picked it up. Did my "Hello?" sound as shaky to the person on the other end as it did to me?

Let it not be about my father, I thought. Maybe Heidi's father had beat feet for the airport, too. Maybe their whole story was bogus, Heidi was none of the things we'd been told, and her parents were fleeing before the truth came out. But I doubted that was what was going on. Why had her mother come here in the first place, if she didn't intend to deal with her daughter's issues?

As soon as I heard Gareth's own shaky, "Thea?" I felt a wave of relief followed by guilt and an immediate wave of renewed anxiety.

"You got my message?" I said.

"Your message? No. I've been on the phone for the last half hour. I haven't gotten any messages."

My stomach lurched. If he didn't know about the Norrises, it had to be something on campus. Something wrong with Heidi? Something had happened with the baby? Unless the cops had jumped the gun and arrested her, and while I'd met cops who were irredeemably bad, he'd seemed to think he was dealing with reasonable ones.

"What?" I said it too sharply. "What is it, Gareth? What's happened?"

"It's Heidi," he said. "The infirmary called. She's disappeared."

CHAPTER 11

"I'll meet you there," I said. "But there's something else you need to know. It's in my message. The General and Mrs. Norris just decamped for the airport. According to the proprietor here, they're on their way back to California. Maybe they've taken Heidi with them?"

"Damn that woman! Cover your ears," he said, and muttered a string of obscenities. "I'll see you at the infirmary. You know how to find it?" He rattled off some directions. It sounded pretty simple.

I put the phone down and jumped in the shower. That horror dream had left me sweaty. It was a two minute soap and rinse. No time to wash my hair. I have the world's most impossible hair, long, curly, and willful. To wash and dry it so it looked smooth and professional, would have taken an hour I didn't have. I just bundled it into a thick braid. I jumped into my clothes, hoping they were right side out, shoved my laptop into my briefcase, grabbed my raincoat, and hurried down the stairs.

I'd been looking forward to those wonderful pancakes for breakfast, and now I was probably going to miss them. An especial pity because breakfast was my favorite meal and I knew what I would be missing. I also knew it could be a good long while before I got another chance at food.

Even though I'd paused for a shower, Gareth was just getting out of his car when I arrived. When he walked around and helped Ted Basham out of the passenger seat, I understood. Basham had had to be woken, too, and get himself dressed, not the easiest of tasks when you're on crutches.

The nurse who met us was probably in her sixties. Ash blonde hair, a pleasant face, and an aspect that would normally have been motherly and comforting if she wasn't so distraught about having lost a patient.

"It was only fifteen minutes," she said. "I'd checked on my two other patients and gone down to the kitchen to make one cocoa. When they don't feel well, that's when they're likely to get homesick, and I've found that cocoa and some of Mrs. Willoughby's cookies usually helps, especially in the middle of the night. Heidi had been restless and weepy and I'd given her another dose of the sedative that Dr. Purcell prescribed."

Her hands were twisting in a nervous knot as her eyes jumped from Gareth to Ted Basham. "She was asleep. I swear she was asleep. She was such a sweet, obedient girl. I never thought—"

She reached in the pocket of her scrub top and pulled out a folded tissue, unwrapping it to reveal a pill. "I found this under her pillow."

She shook her head and focused on Gareth. "The door was locked. We keep it locked, you know, so no one can get in or out, because sometimes their friends like to sneak in, and sometimes they do want to take off, if they've been bad, see, and think they might be in trouble or if they're worried about school work and getting behind. It's safe, keeping the door locked like that. If the fire alarm goes off, the door will unlock, see. It's just a precaution, because they're kids, and while the kids here are good kids, they don't always have the best judgment. And so we…"

She stuttered to a stop, recognizing that she was giving too much general information and too little of the specifics. "I don't see how she could have gotten out."

"But that's not the only door," Gareth said.

"That other one's always got an alarm on it," she said. "It would have gone—"

She turned and hurried toward the back of the building. "Oh dear. I suppose I should have looked, only I would have heard…" floated back to us.

The back door was ajar, the floor wet with rain. And no alarm had sounded.

Sometimes these kids didn't have the best judgment, but they could be pretty ingenious and many of them were technically savvy. If it *was* kids who had helped Heidi disappear. Plenty of adults were ingenious and tech savvy as well—and plenty of them used those skills for bad purposes. I wondered again if the Norrises had swooped past and carried Heidi away. But someone from campus security should have noticed them coming and going. We'd have to check.

I wondered who else it might have been. I was getting an awful feeling in my stomach.

Gareth sighed, turned away, and got on the phone to security. From what I could hear, it sounded like they hadn't seen a student out on her own, and no unfamiliar cars had arrived or left. He put things in motion to start them searching the campus. Then he called Joel and Ruthie, in Heidi's dorm, and the dorm parents in the dorms that housed Heidi's closest friends. Setting all the usual things in motion.

He shifted his focus back to the nurse. "Are her clothes gone?" He thought a moment, and then revised his question. "Did she have clothes here?"

The woman—her name was Helen Brooks—nodded. "A friend brought her some clothes."'

"Do you know her friend's name?"

"It was that sweet little Bella. Heidi's roommate."

He turned to us and raised his arms in a helpless gesture. "I really don't know what to say. This is another unexpected event in a day—and night—of unexpected events. We'll find her, of course. The campus isn't that big, security has monitored who goes in and out, and the students don't have cars."

I was supposed to be helping him. At this point, though, I didn't know what to do. I'd developed a dark turn of mind lately, and yesterday's events hadn't helped. I was imagining very bad things.

"Your other patients," I said, "they didn't see or hear anything?"

"I'm sorry," she said. "I've been in such a rush since I found her gone, I haven't gotten around to asking. I mean, they should be sleeping, but under the circumstances, it should be okay to wake them. I'll go do that right now."

"I'll come with you," Gareth said.

"Wait," I said. "Do we know if this has been on the national news? The story about the baby?"

My dark mind turning. What if it wasn't a friend who'd helped Heidi escape? What if someone had taken her? Someone other than the Norrises. Someone who'd heard the story on the news, and hurried here to silence her? They wouldn't have used Heidi's name on the news, but a bad actor who knew about Heidi and where she went to school could have put two and two together.

He gave a grim nod.

"Mr. Basham, did you tell anyone about this? About your coming here, and why?"

"People told me, remember?" he said, and repeated the list he'd recited earlier, when his ex-wife had asked him how he knew. Lorena's sister. Heidi's roommate. Heidi's friend Ronnie. The roommate and Heidi's friend I could understand, but how did Lorena's sister know. Know in time to notify him and get him here? And then I realized that I had no idea where he'd come here *from.* And I noticed that he hadn't answered my question.

"Where did you come here from?" I asked.

"New York."

"Do you live in New York?"

He nodded. "Sorta."

"And did you tell anyone you were coming here?"

"Why does that matter?"

He sounded like his ex-wife. Why, why, why. It was like dealing with children. "Because if Heidi didn't leave on her own, or with the help of her friends, or with her mother, we'll have to widen the circle. A circle that might include whoever is responsible for Heidi's pregnancy. Someone who, quite possibly, didn't know the trouble he was in until yesterday."

Basham's face wore lines of chronic tension, like he was used to expecting, and getting, troubling news that had to be dealt with. Now those lines got deeper and he was looking around like he was searching for an avenue of escape. But what he said was, "I'm sure that she's okay." Which made no sense at all under these circumstances, unless he knew something about Heidi's disappearance.

I should have kept my mouth shut until we knew more. The most likely scenario was that we'd find Heidi back in her dorm room, or with one of her friends.

Gareth was already heading upstairs with Helen Brooks, the anxiety on his face a mirror of that on Basham's. While the two of us waited downstairs, I figured I'd use the time.

As I led Basham into a small sitting room, I had to fight a powerful desire to tell Gareth I quit, then go back to The Caleb Strong Inn and climb into my comfy bed. I'd pull the ruffled chintz extravaganza that served as a bedspread over my head, whimper like an abandoned puppy, sleep a few hours, and enjoy those pancakes.

What ever made me think I liked my job?

CHAPTER 12

My instinct last night in Gareth's office—that if we didn't get information from Basham right then we might never get it—had been right on the money. This morning, and to give him the benefit of the doubt, it was pretty darned early for anyone to be functioning, he seemed to have forgotten about the four people he'd mentioned last night who might have had access to Heidi.

Access to Heidi. It was such an ugly phrase. When people ask what I do and I tell them I'm a consultant, their eyes glaze over. They don't imagine students lured out onto frozen ponds, or a cult of male students preying on naïve freshmen. They don't think of massive egos and the corrupting power of money, the terror of stalking, or the drama of students involved with faculty members. They picture Abercrombie and J. Crew. Bean boots and Uggs and plaid pajama pants, bikes and scooters and ultimate Frisbee, not the fierce anger of a 6' tall black female basketball player or a penny-pinching school in New York City where the headmistress's mission is to save young African American girls.

After his third head shake and reflexive "I can't remember," I asked if he'd like coffee and went to the kitchen to make some. The coffee didn't help. I was contemplating torture as a reasonable form of information gathering—I was a civilian contractor, after all, and not the government—when Gareth reappeared and said we were moving back to his office.

Back in his office, securely behind the authority of his impressive desk, Gareth told Ted Basham about the Norrises.

Basham took the news of General and Mrs. Norris's suspicious—and precipitous—departure with admirable calm, as though it was no more than he'd expected. "She's never been the hang around and wring her hands type, and Norris doesn't care a fig for Heidi. But it's highly unlikely that she took Heidi with her. Too big a cramp in her style. They were both delighted when Heidi wanted to come here. Aside from the money, of course."

He shook his head. "You'd better call her, though. Update her about Heidi's disappearance and see if you can get her back here. It's unlikely to change her mind, but you never know when something's going to prick that bitch's conscience." He shrugged, like it wasn't his problem, and added, "Someone has to make some decisions about Heidi and that baby's future. She's the custodial parent. It's her job."

He was displaying the same disdainful and cynical attitude toward his ex that we'd seen yesterday, but today it felt like his heart wasn't in it. Yesterday's caring dad who spoke to his daughter often on the phone was missing. He didn't seem overly concerned about Heidi's situation. He fidgeted like someone eager to dump any responsibility for this mess and be gone, and looked like someone who hadn't gotten any sleep.

"Is there someplace I can get breakfast?" Basham asked.

"I can call the dining hall and have some food sent over," Gareth said.

"That would be great," Basham said. "And please, can you excuse me for a little while. I have to make some calls. People are expecting me in New York today."

Gareth directed him to the room I'd used with the Norrises yesterday.

"Did you call the Mrs. Norris?" I asked, when he was gone.

"You said they left."

"I said the owner of the inn told me they were heading for the airport. They don't know I saw them leave, and *you* have no reason to think they've left. You should call them. Right now. Tell them Heidi is missing and you need them in your office as soon as possible, and see how they react."

"If they're not already on a plane."

"They've been gone not much more than an hour, hour and a half, so that's unlikely. But if they don't answer, leave them a voicemail. It's due diligence."

He looked at me blankly, so I explained. "This isn't just about Heidi, though she's our immediate concern. It's about the school. How you handle emergencies. How you communicate and how that's consistent with the place you want this to be. If the Norrises want to blow off her kid, that's their bad act. You still need to be making a record of being responsible and responsive. You want to have acted properly, not from who they are but from who you are. From what the Simmons School is. To be a positive example for your other parents of how Simmons cares for its students."

He stared at me like he didn't understand what I was saying, and I realized that he didn't. He was about the day-to-day running of the school and about a creating and sustaining a community with a particular set of values, while I was about damage control and making a record of responsible caretaking. He was about living it, and I was about proving to the world that he'd done a good job. He didn't see the value in calling the Norrises, if they had indeed decamped, because of what it said about their commitment to Heidi. I needed to make sure that down the road he could show that he'd done everything possible for his troubled student, including being responsible with respect to her parents. Keeping them informed. Trying to involve them. After that the choice was up to them. Experience has shown me that parents were likely to be outraged at any sign of inattention or carelessness on a school's part, even if they were indifferent to their own responsibilities.

I could explain in detail later. Right now, we wanted to be sure they'd been called before they got on a plane. "Make the call," I said. "Now."

Wearily, he picked up his phone. He needed to pace himself or today would be a complete disaster, and I kept making his to-do list longer. Okay. Truth. If we didn't find Heidi, today was already going to be a disaster. But he could roll with it better if he wasn't exhausted. If both of us had the energy to deal with what lay ahead. And disaster was supposed to be my specialty.

I watched him dial the number, and then he said, "Mrs. Norris, Dr. Wilson here. I'm afraid there's been a new development."

He listened, then said, "Heidi has left the infirmary without telling anyone. I'm calling to see if she is with you."

I could hear her squawk of indignation from across the room.

He said, "No. Of course we're searching the campus. We're doing that now. But in the event that we don't find her—" he said.

Another squawk and a flurry of words that I couldn't make out.

Gareth stayed admirably calm. "No," he said, "we just discovered this ourselves within the past hour. What this means is that we have to explore every possible avenue. Identify who she might have left with. People she knows from back home as well as ones she knows here. You are the one who knows her best, so we certainly will need your help with that. Right away. This morning. I'm sorry to wake you so early, but I need you here in my office as soon as possible."

He listened again, and said, "You're what? You're at the airport? With your daughter in the midst of a crisis? When nothing has been decided about her future or your granddaughter's future?"

He was playing it well, dropping onto his sofa as he settled in for an argument. "No, Mrs. Norris, impossible. No phone chat could possibly be adequate. Nor you being out of touch for the six hours or more it will take to fly to California. I cannot emphasize too strongly how critical this situation is. Your daughter is missing. Vanished in the night. At this point, we have no idea whether she left of her own volition or whether someone else was involved."

He gave that a moment to sink in, then continued. "I think you will want to be here. No. Let me be clear. Your presence isn't optional. You *need* to be here, no matter what happens next. Here, not on another coast trying to handle this by phone. You are the custodial parent. Whether we find her or not, there is inevitably going to be police involvement. And the press. And when she's located, Heidi will need your support—"

He waited through another interruption, a sardonic smile on his face, then said, "Whatever General Norris's pressing business is, I'm sure he can handle it on his own. He'll understand that you have your own pressing business here. *Your* responsibility is to be available to your daughter."

He took a deep breath, and I watched him set his hook right into the center of her denial. "She will need you here, Mrs. Norris, on this coast and available, whether it's in the event that her decision to flee triggers a police decision to arrest her, or if it turns out that she has been abducted. And of course, as things fall in, if it becomes necessary for the Simmons School to determine that she is no longer a good fit for our community, you will need to be here to take her back to California. I hope that that will not happen, but in the event, it is essential that you are available."

The squawking got louder. I didn't really need to hear her words. The tone was sufficient.

"And there is the matter of the child. The infant. Someone must assist Heidi in making decisions about her parental rights. And that someone is *not* the headmaster of her boarding school."

This time they must have heard her squawk all over the airport.

He waited until the noise subsided, and said, "You've been here twelve hours, Mrs. Norris, during which time no decisions have been made regarding your daughter. I have to say I find your decision to leave so precipitously, and with so many matters unresolved, incomprehensible. I would remind you that it is you, and not Mr. Basham, who has signed the contract with this school, and who is financially responsible for Heidi, whatever that may entail over the next few days."

When all else fails, use the contract, and the money.

Minutes ago, he'd seemed fuzzy and exhausted, now he was doing just fine. "I'm very pleased to hear that, Mrs. Norris. I look forward to seeing you in my office as soon as possible."

He disconnected and said, "She's coming back."

A little after five in the morning. The day had barely begun. Gareth already looked exhausted and I felt like I'd been flattened by a steamroller.

"We're going to have to tell the police about this," Gareth said. "And once we do, any chance we have of protecting Heidi or our student body from questions and intrusion is gone. They're not going to cut us any more slack."

"You haven't told them?" I said.

His shoulders lifted and fell. "I'm still hoping we'll find her somewhere here on the campus and it won't be necessary. I've had the house parents and dorm residents checking, and security is going through the other campus buildings. We're not done looking, but so far, there's no sign of her. One thing that really troubles me is that she doesn't have a coat. She went from her dorm to the hospital in an ambulance, and then security picked her up and brought her back here to the infirmary. She didn't take her coat with her. Helen Brooks thinks the friend who brought her clothes didn't bring a coat. There isn't one missing from the infirmary, as far as Helen can tell. So unless someone else visited her and brought her one, she's out there in this rotten weather without one."

Heidi lost to us without a coat. It was just a symbol, I knew, of a much bigger problem. The whole business was just such a disaster. For Heidi. For her classmates. For the school. My specialty was damage control and right now, I couldn't begin to think of how to contain the damage. Heidi's disappearance, along with the evidence of deliberation in her not taking her pill, made the situation so much worse. It's harder to spin 'abandoned the baby and then ran away herself', whatever her mental state. Running always looks guilty.

Last night's rain and sleet had abated, but the dawning light disclosed a foggy, misty gray world with soggy, dark ground and wet black tree trunks and mushy patches of snow, the remnants of last night's late-season event. It looked like the landscape of a horror movie, not a pleasant school campus in spring.

My phone vibrated. Given my father's situation, I wasn't ignoring any calls. It was a number I didn't recognize, so I ignored it. But staring at my phone triggered another thought. "Does Heidi have a cell phone with her?"

Gareth didn't know.

"Call Helen over at the infirmary and ask whether, at any point, she saw Heidi using a phone. A cell or a landline. Have her ask the other patients, too."

I wasn't sure why it mattered, or how much. Only that it might help us to know if Heidi had called someone. Normally, I was good in situations like this, thinking of possibilities and getting ready to handle the trouble that came. Today my brain was sleepy and slow. That didn't stop me from being bossy. Or, to put a more positive spin on it, directive. This morning I was all about being directive.

With Mrs. Norris back under control, it was time for me and Gareth to get back to other pressing matters. He to get on the phone to security and his staff and get updates on the search for Heidi. Me to focus on Heidi's father and what he might know that would help us help her. Things he really wasn't likely to have forgotten in just a few hours. I mentally rolled up my sleeves and headed into the small lounge I'd used with his ex-wife last night. He was pacing and gesturing as he spoke into his phone. I smiled, waiting while he finished a call and put his phone in his pocket. Then I gestured toward a chair and waded in.

"Those four men you mentioned last night," I began, the instant his butt touched the chair cushion.

"I really don't remember—"

Don't be combative or confrontational, I reminded myself. Channel Suzanne.

"Of course you do. It's just been a hard night. Let me refresh..." I made a show of flipping through my notes. "Let's see. Yesterday, when I asked about people...about men, of course, who were in and out of the house and could have had access to Heidi, you said there were four."

I hated using the phrase "access to Heidi" but that was the reality.

I checked my notes again as he wiggled on his chair, restless as a toddler, even looking toward the door as though wondering if he could escape. "You said there were two younger officers who worked for General Norris who were in and out of the house regularly. Let's start with their names."

"You're not a cop," he said, in exactly the same tone my little sister Carrie used to say, "you're not the boss of me."

And last night, I'd thought I liked him. If I had a child and she'd just delivered an unexpected baby and then disappeared, I would be in a terrible state. I would be moving heaven and earth to find her and understand what had happened. I'd be calling the police and the headmaster and everyone else I could think of, trying to locate her and know if she was safe. I'd be insisting that whoever had sex with my daughter and fathered that child be both locked up and castrated. I wasn't seeing any of that here.

Well sorry, but I wasn't having this. I might not be the boss of him, but somebody had to look after Heidi's interests, and there weren't a lot of candidates lining up for the job. "No. I'm not a cop." I manufactured a wry smile. "And for that, you should be grateful. Last night you were very eager to discuss these men, Mr. Basham. We're all trying to help Heidi here, so tell me, has something happened in the intervening hours? Has someone gotten to you? Have you been persuaded by someone that it is not in Heidi's interest to try and identify the man who fathered her child?"

He studied his shoes like there would be an exam later. Wet, muddy shoes, which seemed odd since he'd only come from Gareth's house and the infirmary. But it was raining out, and he moved slowly. He was so deliberately avoiding my gaze that I wondered if I'd hit on something. Something was making him reluctant to cooperate. I searched for a way to move him.

"Mr. Basham, do you love your daughter?"

"What? Yes. Yes, of course I love my daughter. What kind of a question is that?"

"A pointed one," I said. "Someone had sex with your daughter when she was only fifteen and got her pregnant. From what both you and your ex-wife have said, it doesn't sound like this was a couple of kids experimenting or a pair of too-young lovers who lost their self-control. It sounds like exploitation. The critical question is: who was in a position to do that?"

I could imagine Suzanne conducting this in a totally different way. All blonde sweetness and smiles and patting his hand in sympathy as she nudged him to do the right thing. Maybe she would have had better luck. Maybe I was better against brutal thugs and armed militia members and not recalcitrant parents. But Suzanne had been too busy to come, so like it, lump it, the Simmons School, and Ted Basham, got me.

I tried to summon some sweetness. "I know this is a hard business to get your head around. She's your child and you feel protective. You want to protect her privacy. But in this situation, trying to protect her by being silent about the potential fathers of her child—and of your granddaughter—doesn't protect her. It protects them. It allows their exploitation of her to go unpunished. I can't imagine that's what you want."

The trouble was, I was running solely on assumptions here. I hadn't spoken to Heidi or her friends. I didn't know that there wasn't a secret boyfriend. But if her denial was genuine, as Dr. Purcell felt it was, then this was not a love child.

He went on studying his shoes.

"You mentioned Heidi's guitar teacher?"

"Will," he said. "William McKenzie. But he's almost my age."

I put Basham's age at about fifty. "Tell me about him."

"But…" He began gearing up for another argument about how it didn't matter and I wasn't the police. I read minds, and I could see it coming.

Sometimes it helped to ask questions to get the conversation rolling. "How long did she take lessons from him?"

"Two years."

"Did she like him?"

"She loved him. He was talented and funny and he made her feel creative. Sometimes I'd walk by when he was teaching and they'd be jamming together and laughing."

He stopped. "You know. That was about the only time I ever heard her laugh. I don't expect Lorena and I were any picnic to live with, even before General Asshole entered the picture. Lorena was so jealous when I showed Heidi any attention that I guess, to avoid conflict—"

He buried his head in his hands, twisting it sideways like he was trying to get the top off a jar. "I stopped giving her attention. It's ironic, really, Ms. Kozak, that I've spoken with Heidi more in the months she's been here than in the couple years before that."

He raised his head and gave me a boyish smile. The kind of "aw, shucks" smile that had probably been getting his failures excused all his life. He and his ex, in their own ways, both believed charm and looks excused bad behavior. "But you wanted to know about Will."

I nodded. "Where did her lessons take place? Was it always at your house? Former house?"

"It was, but—"

Another pause. I guessed he was one of those people who didn't think things through, but rather discovered his own thoughts and feelings from what he found himself saying. "After Norris was in the picture, he found the sessions irritating and Heidi started going to Will's place. So I guess…" He looked surprised. "…a year and a half now, she's been going to his place."

"So Will had access, and a lot of time alone with your daughter?"

"But he's my age. And he cares about Heidi. I was jealous of that. Their closeness. She would confide in him instead of me."

And we all knew how easily that could spill over into inappropriate behavior. But was it the kind of relationship that could result in trauma and denial? Was he the type of man who might use drugs instead of seduction? Or was the relationship such that Heidi might lie to protect him?

"She never acted secretive about him, about Will? Or, conversely, like she might have a crush on him?"

"Not that I ever saw. You should ask Lorena."

Right. I should ask Lorena, the woman he'd said was indifferent to their daughter and didn't give a damn about her. A truly great suggestion. Of course, I *would* ask Lorena. I just didn't have high hopes. And why did I get the sense that he was holding something back? Something about Will.

"Lorena's cousin?"

"Dennis," he said, pouncing on the name. "Now there's a better suspect! He's a male Lorena. Interested in nothing and no one other than himself and what pleases him."

"Do you have any reason to think that seducing Heidi would have pleased him?"

He shrugged, unwilling to consider my question, then gave me a "Do we really have to do this?" smile.

I continued, not charmed. "Would he have had opportunities to be alone with Heidi?"

He went through the head holding ritual again, like squeezing and shaking might bring up useful answers. This conversation was making me sick. Either the conversation or the smell of bacon and sausage that was creeping into the room. That must be the breakfast that had been sent over. I love breakfast, but right now, I was so overtired even the smell of food made me sick. Basham was also making me sick. I wanted to see protectiveness. Outrage. A father ready to kill whoever had done this to his daughter. Instead, I was seeing curious surprise at his own reactions, like a kid discovering something colorful at the bottom of a tide pool or studying a zit in the mirror.

A stronger wave of sausage came at me and my stomach flipped.

"Excuse me," I said, and went to find a bathroom.

CHAPTER 13

I hovered in the powder room, feeling miserable, wondering whether I just didn't know enough about Heidi to be sure of what I was seeing. What if she wasn't the shy innocent who had been described to me, but instead a great actress and manipulator? What if her denial wasn't the result of trauma or some terrifying event or an assault she was unaware of but simply that she'd had an affair with her music teacher and now was faking amnesia or repression to cover her actions? Could she have fooled someone as experienced as Dr. Purcell?

Even if it were true, we'd still want to protect her. She was very young and young teens made mistakes and did stupid things all the time. The responsibility still rested with the adult. But her choices made a difference. Not to any lawyer brought in to protect her interests, but to the Simmons community and to how we made our decisions.

Should I have talked with her friends before making any judgments or trying to interview her parents? It was pretty early in the day to haul her friends over here and start asking them questions. When I was done with the familial see no evil and hear no evil—Basham and his ex were clearly willing to *speak* all kinds of evil—I'd get Gareth to arrange for me to meet with those who were closest to

Heidi. Meanwhile, I'd started down this road. I might as well finish with Ted Basham before Mrs. Norris arrived. It looked like an unpleasant day all around, but no one ever promised me a rose garden. The occasional bloom would be nice, though.

When I got back to the little lounge, Basham wasn't there. Before I jumped to the conclusion that he'd scarpered like his ex, I stuck my head in Gareth's open door. He and Basham were bent over a tray laden with a breakfast feast. Bacon, scrambled eggs, sausage, toast, muffins, croissants, and good strong coffee. I wanted those pancakes back at the inn, but would settle for eggs, croissants, and coffee. Maybe a muffin, despite my middle of the night snack. Today my wonky morning stomach said skip bacon and sausage.

"Join us, Thea," Gareth said. When I hesitated, he looked at me like I'd gone slightly loony. He knew I liked to eat. I decided my stomach had settled down, and joined them.

Basham ate like a man in a hurry, which was how I usually ate as well. I've heard it's not good for our digestion. I hadn't even gotten food when he set down his empty plate and stood. "Where's the loo?" he asked.

Gareth, grinning, gave him directions and Basham hurried away.

When he was gone, I said to Gareth, "When I'm finished with Mr. Basham, I'd like to talk with her dorm mother and some of Heidi's friends."

He nodded.

"Gareth?"

He turned toward me, his expression quizzical. I guess my tone was laden with portent. In matters like this, I sometimes feel like the queen of doom and gloom, unless it's like someone's nagging mother.

"Did you call the police? Have you told them Heidi is missing?"

He didn't reply.

"Would you normally call the police if you had a missing student?"

His sheepish nod was answer enough. "But what do I say?"

"You ask for their help. You do exactly what you'd do with another student. You describe the situation—her delicate condition and troubled state of mind, the fact that the doctor has prescribed sedatives, your uncertainty that she's capable of making sensible decisions right now. The mystery of the open door and the alarm that didn't go off, which suggests someone else was involved. You say that last night's weather was dreadful, and you're concerned about her welfare."

I let him process for a minute, then said, "You can't let this slide. Especially if you want good on-going relations with them. Which you do. Not just in this situation but in the future. You don't want to damage your credibility."

He knew all this. He'd just let this crisis push him into tunnel vision. That's why I was here.

"But Heidi?" he said.

"If she's out there hiding somewhere, or if someone has aided her escape, or, worst case, someone has taken her, how do you help her by not trying to have her found?"

I gave it a beat. "And how does inaction reflect on the school? Simmons isn't about hiding things or keeping secrets. It's about open and honest communication. Open with your students. Open with their parents. Open with the police. If you believe Heidi is telling the truth—her truth— you've got nothing to hide, right?"

"But you're already talking about shaping the story," he countered.

"And isn't 'we believe her' part of the shaping that story? Isn't looking after a vulnerable child part of the story? Isn't the fact that these *are* children, still in the process of becoming adults, still vulnerable to adult manipulation, part of the story? What about innocent until proven guilty? You want to concede the field before we've even started?"

It struck me then that I was tired of helping people tell the story. Weary of trying to get even well-intentioned people to listen and take my advice. Tired of crises and bad events and death and danger and people who didn't think it mattered. I wanted to leave poor baffled, temporarily indecisive Gareth standing there and go call my husband and ask him how he did it, day in, day out, year after year, without growing cynical and sour. I felt like I was curdling. My resilience was ebbing. I was getting too old to run on little food and less sleep and a steady diet of personal and professional crisis. By the time MOC arrived, I would be what the medical profession called an "elderly primigravida." It sounded like a dinosaur.

This was not about me, I reminded myself sternly. I was here to do a job, not to indulge in a bout of poor me. "Eggs and toast," I said, reaching for a delicious-looking blueberry muffin the size of Rhode Island. "Then I'll finish with Basham and we'll talk about our strategy for the day."

Gareth patted my shoulder. "This isn't easy," he said.

I filled a plate and went back to the little lounge, and a moment later, though I was expecting Basham, Gareth appeared. "Is it always like this?" he said.

"Like what?"

"Like impossible to get a handle on people?"

"You're good with people, Gareth," I reminded him. "But this is worst case scenario. Crisis does not bring out the best in many people. Their impulses to lie and defend themselves at the expense of those around them click in. Plus, in our world, there are so many families who've sent their children to boarding school not for the student's benefit, but to get rid of them. They've sent their kids away because they don't want to deal, or don't know how to deal, and now they're being forced to deal. They don't want to face their own failures. They want to keep handing their problems back to you. And sometimes, they've been complicit in creating the problem, and they don't want to accept that responsibility, either."

"I can see that with the Norrises. But yesterday, Ted was so attentive."

"That was yesterday. Yesterday he *was* thinking of Heidi. He was also trying to show us, and his ex, that he was the better parent. Excuse my language, but that was part of their ongoing pissing contest. Today, he's back to thinking about himself. What he might need to protect and how he's going to go about that. About responsibility. About the awful possibility that he might have to find a way to be a full-time dad and not just a loveable telephone dad."

"Ugly," he said. "Disappointing."

"We've both seen it before, Gareth. We have to keep our focus on what's best for the school. And on Heidi. Sometimes *in loco parentis* really means moving beyond the loco parents and trying to do it better."

Gareth's grin came and went. "What does he need to protect, anyway? If he's telling the truth, this didn't happen on his watch."

"Big if. Besides, people lie for a lot of reasons."

"And I thought I was cynical."

"I prefer to think of myself as a realist."

I looked down at my rapidly cooling plate. "I'm going to eat now, Gareth. Then we can talk."

"Right," he said. "Forgetting my manners."

"We'll get through this."

"I know."

He backed away, like someone leaving the presence of the Queen, and moments later, Ted Basham arrived.

Breakfast had not put Basham in a more cooperative frame of mind. He plunked himself back down on the couch and folded his arms like a defiant kid. He and Lorena must have been quite the pair when they were together. It was not attractive behavior and brought out the side of me that wanted to whack him upside the head. I squashed the impulse and pulled out an encouraging smile.

"Lorena's cousin Dennis," I prompted.

He shrugged.

I looked around. Was there a weapon that might nudge him into cooperation without doing serious harm? The umbrella stand offered a few possibilities, both sturdy umbrellas and a thick walking stick. "He came immediately to mind when I asked you who might have had access to Heidi. Why was that?"

"Because Dennis lives to nail anything female that he can. Because he has an ugly, vulgar mouth and it's always running on about this hot chick or that one and how cleverly he seduced them."

"He's known Heidi all her life."

A shrug. "Yeah. But I don't think that would matter."

"How does Heidi feel about him?"

"She thinks he's funny. He used to bring her little presents. Do magic tricks for her."

"Sounds like he is fond of her. But you still think—"

"He was fond of money," Basham interrupted, "and he thought that being nice to Heidi would make Lorena more amenable when he wanted to borrow some."

"Did it?"

Another shrug. "He's had some generous helpings of my money over the years."

"He pay it back?"

Basham gave me a look.

"What about General Norris's money?"

"Far as I know, Bradley Norris doesn't have a lot of money."

"I guess you don't like Cousin Dennis much. Any particular reason to think he might have seduced your daughter? Have you observed unusual behaviors? Things Heidi might have said? Things Lorena might have said?"

"I try not to talk to Lorena."

I waited.

"Other than just who he is? Not really. But he was around. And he tried to hit me up for money a while back. After Lorena and I were divorced. I turned him down flat, and Ms. Kozak, he's just the type to take a sick kind of revenge like that. He would think it was amusing. You should ask Lorena. She's always been protective of her cousin, but faced with something like this, you might be able to move her off the mark."

I kept Cousin Dennis in the active suspects column, got some basic locating information, and moved along. "The two younger officers who were frequently in the house. Tell me about them."

"Tweedledee and Tweedledum?" he said. "Lt. Alexander Crosby, thus Sandy or Dee, and Lt. Aaron Ramirez, who despite being a lieutenant is genuinely dumb. Crosby is a big guy, bristle-cut, shifty and sharp-faced. Despite the glasses, he looks like he's always ready to pick a fight and would just as soon stab you in the back. Ramirez is smaller, dark, with a too-ready smile, a real Latin lothario. They look as different as night and day but they act like salt and pepper shakers. Always together. Always scrambling to please. Norris likes having sycophantic young men around him. Maybe that's what generals do. I'm afraid that's not the world I travel in."

I wondered, if he'd been absent for some time, how he knew so much about the comings and goings at his ex-wife's house and decided not to ask. I also wondered why I got the feeling he was impatient to be done with this and gone. Was he planning to bail, like his ex-wife? Take off as soon as I let him off the hot seat?

"Why did they come to mind, Mr. Basham?"

"Ted," he said. "Please."

"Ted."

"You asked who was in and out frequently. Who might have had access."

"Tell me more about them."

"I don't *know* more about them. Because I didn't have access. I'm just going on what Heidi said. That they were always around. That when The General and my ex weren't sitting around drinking and laughing it up, he always had people in and out of the house like it was his office. And the two people Heidi mentioned most often were Dee and Dum."

"Did she dislike them?"

"I don't know. I think she just wanted…" He considered. "Some peace and quiet. Some semblance of family. Family dinner. Family breakfast. Some time with her mother when it wasn't a three-ring circus. Of course, Lorena likes a circus, especially if it revolves around her. Attentive young men to refresh her drink, compliment her cooking, her looks, pull out her chair. Never mind that it meant she had even less time for Heidi. If her daughter wasn't going to be the cute little girl, a useful accessory to the beautiful mom, she had no time for Heidi. That didn't stop Heidi from wanting her mother to care. I think her decision to come to Simmons was a sign she was finally giving up."

Lorena ought to meet my mother. They could have a field day talking about their difficult daughters. And boy could I relate to the challenge of pleasing an unpleasable mother. But I could ponder on that another day. I wanted to be done with Basham as much as he wanted to be done with me. I needed to call the hospital and check on my dad.

Besides, despite Cousin Dennis, I thought this was all pretty useless. I decided to give it a few more questions and then cut Basham loose. "Was there ever anything Heidi said that suggested she had concerns about either of these young men?"

He shook his head.

"What about a crush?"

"On Dee or Dum? You have to be kidding."

"No, I'm not kidding. A lonely, impressionable young girl, and a couple of attractive young men primed to be attentive to the family to please their boss?"

"Heidi's not the crush type. If anything, she's too serious. And she wasn't interested in boys."

"Mr. Basham. These were not boys."

I didn't think he got it, but I made one last effort. "Mr. Basham. Ted. Dr. Purcell, the psychologist you will meet later today, is suggesting that what Heidi may be suffering from is what you might call 'emotional amnesia,' the result of some traumatic or terrifying experience which has caused her to repress all memory of the event. I know my questions may seem vague or random, but what I'm looking for is anyone who might have caused such trauma in your daughter's life."

He looked at me curiously and said, "Emotional amnesia?"

"As opposed to the kind produced by a blow, an injury, or an accident."

"Emotional amnesia. I like that."

I looked longingly at the umbrella stand. That sturdy walking stick would make an excellent weapon. Sometimes I worry that my exposure to so much violence is making me a more violent person. Curbing the impulse, I stood. "I'll take you back to Dr. Wilson now, and we can see if there's any news about Heidi."

His relief was all over his face. He ruffled the shaggy hair in what was clearly a practiced move. A boyish 'forgive me, I'm just a lad who is very new at this' gesture. "You're disappointed in me," he said.

That was an understatement.

CHAPTER 14

Gareth had two men with him, detectives, I assumed, and a scared-looking boy. Probably one of Heidi's friends who worked with her in the greenhouse.

As we entered, the two cops turned to stare, first at Basham, then at me, maybe wondering if I was Heidi's mother.

The boy, his eyes fixed firmly on his clenched hands, was saying, "I don't know where she'd go, honest, Dr. Wilson. She's not from around here. She doesn't know anyone except us other students. I just hope she's okay."

Clearly they hadn't found her hiding under a bed or in a closet while I was off attempting to interview Ted Basham.

Gareth introduced us to the two cops, Sgt. Miller and Detective Flynn, and to the boy, Jaden Santoro, and explained to them who we were. We shook a round of hands and I took a chair.

Basham remained standing. "Thought I'd head back to your place, Gareth," he said. "Take some weight off this leg for a while. You can call me if you need me. You know your own number, of course, and..." A flourish as he produced business cards and handed them around. "...here's my cell."

Basham was manager for a pretty famous band. That explained the artsy look and the travel. Perhaps the bi-coastal addresses. And maybe the touch of narcissism, a minor infection from hanging around people who were always in the spotlight and professionally self-involved?

Miller told Basham to keep himself available, they'd want to speak with him later. Basham, flashing his charming smile, agreed. They made an appointment to speak in the early afternoon, then Basham crutched noisily away.

I wondered that they let him go so easily, but that was their business. I slid Basham into a file called 'later' and focused on the people in the room. I didn't know what ground they'd already covered, so I figured I'd better sit on my hands and let them direct the conversation. Not my usual style, even with cops running the show.

"Thea," Gareth said, "to catch you up. As you know, security has searched the campus. Now we've got local police out retracing their steps. So far, they've found no sign of Heidi, so we're talking to people who know her. We've just started talking to Jaden. He's a friend of Heidi's who works with her in the greenhouse."

"Jaden," Sgt. Miller said, "can you think of anyone we should speak to who might have some idea where Heidi might go?"

The boy shook his head. He was a slight boy, with dark eyes and thick, mussed hair, and he looked scared to death. I sat on my hands for about twenty seconds, then, because I thought Miller was leaving important ground uncovered, I intervened with a question before the detective could dismiss the boy and move on to other friends.

"Have you spoken with Heidi since yesterday morning?" I asked.

The knotted hands tightened. The boy stared at me and I could see how badly he didn't want to answer. "I know you're worried about being disloyal to a friend, but under the circumstances, Heidi may not be making the best decisions right now. We need to find her so we can take care of her. So—did you talk with her?"

He nodded.

"When?"

"Last night."

This was going to be like pulling teeth. I was surprised that neither of the cops had intervened yet, but it seemed they were willing to let me ask some questions. "What time last night, Jaden?"

"Nine."

"Did she call you?"

A shrug, a clench of his hands, and then, "Yes."

"On a cell phone?"

He shrugged, a nebulous gesture that I took for a "Yes."

"What did you talk about?"

The boy looked at Gareth. "It was a private conversation, Dr. Wilson. Do I have to talk about it?"

"I hope you will, Jaden," he said. "I suppose Heidi asked you not to tell anyone?"

The boy nodded.

"We're not trying to get her in trouble. We're trying to keep her out of trouble, and make sure she's safe. You can help us with that."

Jaden folded his arms. "This isn't going to help. I don't have any idea where she is," he said.

He was the only one who believed he was telling the truth.

"But you did know that she was planning to leave the infirmary?" Gareth said.

Again, the boy didn't answer, but we all knew that that was an affirmative.

"Do you know why she left?" I asked.

"She was afraid." He gave the answer up reluctantly, like even that much information was a betrayal of Heidi's trust.

Now Miller jumped in. "Who was she afraid of?"

"Not a who. At least, she didn't mention any who. A what. What people would think of her. Do think of her. She...you've got to understand..." The boy was strangling the sleeve of a gray hoodie tied around his waist. "Heidi loves it here. She says that she hasn't been happy in years. Her parents used to fight all the time when her dad was home, and then her dad would be gone and she'd be stuck there with her mother, who doesn't like her. Then they got divorced and her mother married this awful man that Heidi hates. Coming to Simmons has really changed her life, and now they—"

He looked at Gareth. "I mean you. The school. You're going to throw her out for being pregnant when she didn't even know she was."

He abused the gray sleeve a little more and studied his shoes. None of this was easy for him. It was true that students at Simmons were more used to speaking their minds and expressing opinions openly than at many schools, but Gareth was the headmaster, a major authority figure, and there were two intimidating cops in the room. Plus, at Jaden's age, peers were most important. Peers and friends. He'd promised a friend he wouldn't talk. Now we were pressuring him to break that promise.

"I know what some people are saying. That it's not possible that she didn't know," Jaden said. "But I believe her." He looked around at us and shook his head. "Heidi isn't a liar. That's not who she is. She loves that we're honest with each other here. She says it's the first time in her life when the people around her are honest. She says that there was no one in California that she could trust, except her best friend Stephanie, who also went to boarding school, and her music teacher, and she only saw him an hour a week. Everyone lied to her and tried to use her for their own purposes. Her mom especially. But also her dad, even though he tries to get it right. She calls her dad Peter Pan. And her stepdad is just a creep."

He hunched his shoulders, like he knew he wasn't supposed to call a grown-up a creep, especially to other grown-ups. "That's what she calls him. General Creep. She says he—"

Just as suddenly as his words had started pouring out, they stopped. He'd come to a confidence he wasn't comfortable betraying.

"Look. I don't know where she is. Honest. She wouldn't tell me because she figured that you might want to talk to me, and she knew I wouldn't lie."

We could circle back to what he did know, and learn more about Heidi's relationship with her stepfather. For now, there was other information to be gathered.

I was thinking like a cop again.

"She called you because she needed your help with the door, didn't she?" I said, putting a guess into words. "Because she could trust you and you knew how to deal with that alarm."

He nodded. "There are lots of things I'm not good at, like sports and stuff, but electronics?" He couldn't resist a small grin. "Plants and electronics are my thing. That door was a cinch." God. He was so young. It was just unfair for these kids to be caught up in something like this.

Miller was giving me a strange look. These should have been his questions. But he had the grace—or the good sense—not to interrupt. In my experience, that could be a rare quality in a cop.

"No one saw you visit Heidi."

"Because I didn't. I visited Paul. He's a friend, too, and he needed some of his books so he wouldn't get behind."

Damn. The question we hadn't asked and now needed to follow up on—who had been to visit the other students in the infirmary. "But you don't know where Heidi went? Where she is?"

He twisted the sleeve and shook his head vigorously.

"Did she say anything that might have been a clue? You know that we…" I swept a hand to indicate Gareth and the cops, "are really worried about her safety. She doesn't have a coat, and you know what it's like out there. She's just had a baby, and she should be watched over. And resting. There could be complications. You just said that she doesn't know anyone around here. So where could she go?"

"I don't know. Really. I don't know. She said she'd be safe, but I don't know what she meant."

He looked ready to cry, so I moved on, checking with Miller before I asked my next question. "Who might know, Jaden? Who should we talk to?"

He gave three names. Her roommate Bella, Ronnie, another boy who worked in the greenhouse, and a girl named Tiverton.

Then I sprang my zinger. "Heidi was afraid of her stepfather, wasn't she?"

He nodded.

"Did she tell you why?"

There was a long silence that neither Miller nor Flynn interrupted.

Finally, he said, "I'm not supposed to tell you this. It took her six months to tell me about it and we're really good friends. We tell each other everything. I guess we're kind of like family to each other. She doesn't have any brothers or sisters, and neither do I. And you know, working together in the greenhouse, it's really peaceful. Comfortable. Comforting, I guess. A safe place where we're both happy. Away from our crazy families. Where it's easy for us to talk."

The sleeve died a death by strangulation, the ripping sound audible in the quiet room. "The General. He's always accidentally walking in on her." The boy's hands made quote marks in the air. "In the bathroom. In her bedroom. When she's dressing. When she's in the shower. And her mother doesn't believe that it happens, which makes Heidi feel helpless. But what if...you know...what if he did something to her? Something she can't bring herself to talk about even to me?"

There were tears in his eyes.

I was still struggling to form a picture of Heidi, but this added something interesting—that she'd been able to create a pretty deep friendship and inspire loyalty in this boy. And added The General back on my suspect list. Heidi had been very specific that she didn't want him here. Emphatic she didn't want him to visit. Did he pose a threat to Heidi's safety? And had he really gone back to California? That was something the cops could check.

He took a breath, ducked his head, and said, quickly, "I don't know how this might help you, but when she heard he was coming here with her mother, she said she had to get away."

CHAPTER 15

Gareth walked Jaden out, leaving me alone with Miller and Flynn. As soon as they were out the door, Miller pounced. "So, who are you really? A P.I., right?"

This was not good. Cops are generally suspicious of P.I.s. "Consultant," I said. "Really. I'm here to help the school deal with this. My specialty is campus crises. Sorry if I was too pushy. It's just that I've spent a lot of time with students at other schools in situations where their information is critical. In cases where something bad happens and the school has to deal with all the implications of that."

I gave it a beat, then said, "I guess you guys have, too."

"Right," Miller said. He had a slightly rumpled look and a comfortable face. He seemed like someone you could talk to. Like the best interviewers, his manner invited confidences. Bad guys often gave those confidences, to their sorrow. But I was not a bad guy. Or bad gal. And I hoped they, and I, could work together on this.

Flynn stayed in the background, which surprised me. But maybe they were a team. Miller the front man and Flynn the observer. Or maybe Flynn brought different skills to the table. Muscle, for example. He was built like a weight-lifter, with a jacket that must have come from the kind of specialty tailor that fitted a chest and arms of that size. There wasn't anything off the rack that would work unless he bought a 48 and had it tailored down to fit his waist. He looked kinda like my guy, only on steroids.

Then Miller surprised me again. "So what do you think? The girl was assaulted by her stepfather and couldn't bring herself to tell anyone?"

Or tried to tell her mother and was totally shut down. It was definitely a possibility. I was already thinking DNA— whether there might be something at the inn that still had Norris's DNA on it. It was worth checking out. A quick answer to our question, and an idea I'd share with these officers.

But I wasn't ready for quick answers yet. "Her father had a list of potential suspects as well. Not including Norris. He was pretty quick to name names, but more reluctant about details." I gave them the names. "You should ask him about them."

Flynn wrote them down.

I thought that while all of this was important, what was of greater importance was finding Heidi. If Jaden was right, and she didn't know anyone except people here on campus, where had she gone? Had she called someone for help? Could we get access to her phone records? Might there be a friend here whose family might take her in? There were day students as well as boarders here, so one of them might have offered shelter. Was it possible her friend Stephanie was in or near Boston and Heidi had gone to her?

When Gareth returned, he had a young uniformed officer with him. The man conferred briefly with Miller and Flynn and left again.

I felt the passage of time, and concern for Heidi's absence, like a physical weight. Despite the time that had passed, there was still no sign of Mrs. Norris. Maybe she had gotten on a plane with her husband after all. It would be the ultimate statement about her lack of concern for her daughter. Or, perhaps, an acknowledgment of choosing her husband over her daughter regardless of what he might have done. Or because she knew what he had done.

I was angry on Heidi's behalf, and stepped on that anger because it was unproductive.

Miller consulted his notes and asked if Gareth could arrange for them to see Heidi's roommate, Bella, and then Heidi's other friend from the greenhouses, Ronnie, and the girl named Tiverton. While Gareth was phoning to set that up, I asked Miller if he minded if I stayed for the interview.

"You've got to stay," he said. "You're our secret weapon."

Responding to my quizzical look, he said, "What's more threatening? A pretty young woman or a worn-out old cop? Or Brian here, looking like if they don't give it up, he'll beat it out of 'em?"

Flynn smiled at that, and suddenly looked far less threatening.

"I guess we all have our strengths," I said.

While we waited for Heidi's roommate to arrive, I excused myself and stepped out to check my messages. Unsurprisingly, no one from my family had called, so I called the hospital and asked for the nursing desk on his floor. Someone answered and assured me he was on track to be released later in the morning. Relieved, I called Andre.

"You're up early," he said.

"I've barely been to sleep."

"What's happening?"

"It's a great big mess. Our girl slipped away in the night and now there's no sign of her anywhere. The mother and stepfather headed off the airport very early this morning, planning to fly back to California. We've tried to catch mom and get her back to help us deal with her missing daughter. She said she was coming but hasn't appeared."

I sighed and he made a comforting sound. "We're just starting to talk to people who might be able to help us find Heidi. And of course the police are involved. Right here. Right now."

I heard him take a breath as he started to process what I'd said and run possible scenarios. "Sure she didn't go with her mother?"

"Not sure of anything, but she doesn't get along with her mother and, according to a friend she confided in, is genuinely scared of her stepfather. But the mom's still AWOL, so we don't know."

"Does the girl have access to a car?"

"Good question," I said. "She's too young to drive. The students don't have cars, but maybe a friend does? Or an older brother or sister? The big question is why she ran. Whether it was really because she was upset by how the community would regard her, or fear of going back home, or was it something more sinister, like she was running away from a specific someone."

"Stepfather sounds like a good possibility."

I agreed. "Look," I said, "I've got to go. We're talking to some of her friends, and the detectives are waiting."

Back in the room, Miller gave me a look and shook his head. "Just a consultant, huh?"

I nodded.

"And the guy you were just talking to on the phone, he's what? Your boss?" He hesitated, then added, "Your partner?"

Cops. They hear through walls. Listen at doors. Are suspicious of everyone. "My husband."

"Right," he said.

I didn't want to play games. We had more important things at stake here than my privacy, and his suspicions could cloud our ability to work together. "He's a detective. Maine state police. Works homicide."

He nodded, somewhat mollified by my explanation. Often, with cops, learning that I'm married to one moves me, in their "us vs. them" world, into "us."

"So how are we going to find this girl?" he asked.

"You're the detective."

"And you're the expert."

I'm good at what I do, but I've never in my life felt like an expert at anything, though I still hold the somewhat naïve belief that there are experts in the world. I really didn't know how to find Heidi without more information, but I did know something about the independent school world, so I had a strategy.

"Keep talking to her friends, for starters. Even if they don't know where she's gone, they may have ideas. May know who else she might have turned to for help. We've already learned a whole lot from Jaden, though I believe he still knows more than he's saying. It may take another interview to get the rest. It's not easy to convince a kid that age that they're actually helping a friend when they reveal a confidence. And it's likely we'll learn more from her roommate, her other friend, Ronnie, and this girl, Tiverton."

I thought Tiverton was a town in Rhode Island. But parents will give their children distinctive names. Probably, the zeitgeist being what it was, every child born this year would be named Mason, Oliver, or Claudine. I did not share this thought with Sgt. Miller.

I wasn't sure he knew this yet, so I said, "Her father said that her roommate and Ronnie both called him when all this happened, which means they were close enough to Heidi to know, or have access to, her father's cell phone number. Her mother wasn't going to tell him."

"Ugly divorce?" he said.

"Sounds like it."

Gareth had barely gotten back when his assistant, the one who worried about him not eating properly, stuck her head in. "Excuse me," she said, "but Bella Hastings is here."

He nodded his thanks. "Send her in."

"Uh…Gareth." She let it hang in the air a moment, then said, "She's very upset."

"Excuse me," he said to Miller and Flynn, and stepped out of the office.

We could all hear the quiet murmur of his voice, and then he came back in, followed by a tiny Asian girl with pixie-cut hair and scared brown eyes. She moved with the bowed head and reluctant gait of someone going to her execution.

"Bella," he said, "this is Thea Kozak, who is working with us on Heidi's situation, and these are Detective Flynn and Sgt. Miller. Bella is Heidi's roommate."

Like a child raised by very proper parents, Bella took a deep breath and then offered me her hand. Hers was cold and trembling. I said I was pleased to meet her. What I wanted to do was put an arm around her and reassure her that Miller and Flynn didn't bite. But that was Gareth's department, not mine. I was still walking a fine line with Miller and Flynn. So far, they'd been fine, but cops tended to be territorial.

I watched her approach Flynn, with his bulky body and his square, hard face like she really did expect to be bitten. And watched Flynn unbend, and smile, and take her tiny hand between both of his. "Brian Flynn, Bella, and relax. I may look scary but I'm really a nice guy."

When she hesitated, he said, "I understand people around here are big on telling the truth, so make that really, really nice," and that made her smile.

I realized I'd been holding my breath, and that Miller had been watching me instead of watching Bella. So maybe he still didn't believe my call with Andre had just been a wife talking to her husband. We would have to see how that played out.

When Bella was settled, Miller took her through the same questions he'd asked Jaden. His questions and my questions. Despite Flynn's reassurance, it took a while before she started giving more than the briefest of answers. She was embarrassed now that she hadn't realized Heidi was pregnant, but Heidi was a big girl. Compared to Bella, almost anyone would seem big, but from her description, it sounded like Heidi was tall like both her parents and big boned like her father. Basham was a lean man but not slight.

"Big," she said, "like wide shoulders and tall. Not fat."

She confirmed that Heidi had had a good relationship with her father and a bad one with her mother, adding that Heidi knew her father was kind of self-centered and unreliable but at least he knew she existed, which her mother didn't. "That's why I called him," she said, "because Heidi needed someone and I knew her mother wasn't it."

She paused a moment, then said, "You know, Heidi and I, I never thought we'd be close. I'm mean, except that we're both from California, we're pretty different. But she's just about the nicest girl I've ever known. Girls, in my experience, often aren't nice. I mean, at my last school, they were really mean and competitive and so were their parents. That's one reason I chose Simmons. I thought they wouldn't be like that here."

She looked at Flynn and then at Miller. "I know people are saying she did an awful thing and so she must be an awful person, but she's not. I don't think Heidi has any meanness in her. I mean like her mother treats her so badly and tries to make her feel awful about herself because she isn't interested in being glamorous or in clothes or make-up and stuff, and she just keeps on being patient and forgiving her mother like she's the adult and her mother is the child."

Heidi was sounding too good to be true, but that was my cynical side speaking. It shouldn't be a bad thing for someone to be nice. I could have used a friend like Heidi when I was a miserable, too tall, adolescent with a chest boys couldn't stop staring at.

"She never said anything to you that suggested she knew she was pregnant?"

Bella gave a vigorous shake of her head. "No way. The night before…you know…the baby? She thought she was getting her period. It had been irregular, so she was glad. Well. Um."

She looked at the three men and blushed. "I mean, yeah, it's a pain, but when she didn't get it, she was worried that maybe there was something wrong with her. She even went and talked to the nurse about it, but the nurse told her that sometimes happened at her age and not to worry."

I made a quick note about that. Another thing we needed to track down. Find out what the whole story was. When that visit took place and whether there were notes about it. Part of my job is to be alert to places where a school might not have adequate procedures or could let something potentially serious slip through the cracks.

"Do you know if the nurse asked if she might be pregnant?"

"I think she did," Bella said, "and Heidi thought that was funny."

Without waiting, Bella addressed the question they hadn't yet asked. "Heidi doesn't lie. That's something that's important to her. I absolutely believe that she didn't know she was pregnant," she said. "She was as surprised at this as the rest of us. I know..." She waved a hand to ward off interruption. "I know people are saying it's impossible. That she couldn't have not known. But I live with her. Yes, she was modest about dressing and undressing, but that wasn't because she was trying to hide something. That was because of the situation in her mother's house. She'd just gotten in the habit because she didn't have much privacy."

"Tell us more about that," Flynn said. "What did she tell you about the situation at home?"

"There were people in and out all the time. Her stepfather—General Norris—and some of the men who worked for him. Her room was just down the hall from the living room, and she said people kept walking in on her."

We could all see that she was holding something back, and Flynn tried to dig it out. "Did she say which people?"

Bella was silent, the silence of someone trying to work out how to share important information without betraying a confidence. Finally, she gave a helpless shrug and looked at Flynn. "I promised I wouldn't tell anyone about this."

I thought I knew what 'this' was, but life is full of surprises, so I held my tongue and waited as Gareth stepped in.

"Bella, right now, we're concerned for Heidi's safety. She's physically and emotionally vulnerable and she's disappeared. Right now we don't know if she's run away or if she's been taken. Either way, we need to find her, and part of conducting a good search for her is having good information. About her state of mind, about what might have happened at home that made her decide to come to Simmons. And about how her pregnancy happened. I know you believe you're protecting Heidi by keeping her secrets, but you might be putting her at risk."

He gave that a moment, and then said, "Sometimes we have to betray a friend's confidence because we care about her. Especially when her safety is involved."

Nobody tried to rush her, which really impressed me. Cops can get impatient and start pushing. But everyone waited until Bella had sorted things out for herself.

"It wasn't just one person," she said. "Heidi's like…well you know, really pretty, and she's got…well, you know, before she gained some weight…I mean, before it looked like she'd gained weight…um…with the baby, I mean, she was—" She stopped, looked around at us as she searched for the right words. "Hot," she said, finally. "She had the kind of figure a lot of girls would die for and yeah, she's not a skinny mini like me. I mean, she says her mother told her she's plain and too heavy, but her mother is a real bitch. Her mother's wrong, too. Heidi believed her, but it wasn't true."

She looked down at her tiny hands, clasped together so tightly as she fought her fear. "What she told me is that her stepfather, and some of the other guys who were in and out of the house, they just kept walking in on her. Like walking into her bedroom without knocking and stuff. Her mother wouldn't let her put a lock on her door 'cuz she didn't believe what Heidi was telling her."

She raised her head, amazement on her face, like she needed us to understand how baffling this was. "So Heidi always dressed and undressed in the bathroom, because that door had a lock. Which is why she was always so secretive about getting dressed. Because I guess, even though she was safe here, she didn't really trust that it wouldn't keep happening."

"Did she say who those 'other guys' were?" Flynn asked.

Flynn, I noticed, not Miller. I wondered how they worked out the roles. Whether Miller was better with boys and Flynn with girls? Despite his initially fearsome appearance, Flynn seemed to have a knack for interviewing Bella.

Bella gave us all a "can you believe this?" look. "There was a man she referred to as her 'funny uncle,' which I thought meant he wasn't an uncle at all, or funny, but just a man who acted in an inappropriate way. And there were two men who worked for The General, and at least one of them did it, too. Kept walking in on her. She didn't use any names. She was very uncomfortable talking about it. It was just, you know, that she needed to tell somebody, I think. When we were talking about why we came to Simmons."

"Did she ever mention her guitar teacher?" I asked.

"Will?" she said.

I nodded.

"He calls her sometimes to check up on her. If she's doing okay. See if she's still playing. He sends her music. Heidi doesn't laugh much, but when she's on the phone with him, it's like she's talking to her best friend."

She didn't seem to find that odd, and I didn't want her to, so I let it drop. I saw Miller make a note, but figured he was on my wavelength about this one and would ask me later.

Even without Will, we had at least three candidates for baby daddy without leaving the house. Poor Heidi. She'd come here because she needed refuge. Now that was coming apart.

Miller moved on to questions about Heidi's disappearance. Running my questions. Had Heidi called her? Bella wrung her hands, lowered her head, and tried not to answer. But she'd been reminded that Simmons was a truth-telling place, so after an uncomfortable silence, she said, "She called me last night and asked if I could help her. If I could think of someplace she could go. But like her,

I'm from California. Sure, we go into Boston sometimes, but that wouldn't be a good place for her. Not right now, even if she could find a safe place to stay."

There weren't many safe places for a young girl like Heidi to stay. So many predators of all ages and sexes. And there was the risk of complications from her delivery. Or someone she'd turned to for help who was a false friend. Even her parents were unreliable. My dark mind was running scenarios involving her mother and stepfather. How far might they go to keep a secret? And whose secret was it?

Where was her father in all of this? Had she confided in him? Might he have been willing to help her disappear? And if so, why? He'd made it clear Heidi couldn't live with him, so what good would helping her to hide do, when it seemed the best result for Heidi would be to get things resolved in a way that let her remain at Simmons? Was he aware of a greater threat, one beyond escaping the humiliating judgment of her peers? When he came for his interview this afternoon, we could ask.

Bella fell silent and we all waited, hoping what was coming might be important. "She asked me to find her purse and get her some money from the stash she kept in her desk. I took her coat, too, because she'd left it behind when she went to the hospital. I didn't even get to speak with her. She was asleep. I'd put her things in a backpack, and I just left it on a chair."

She looked guiltily at Gareth. "I didn't know her plans, but I didn't see how I could not do that much for her. Maybe Jaden knows more."

Not that Jaden was telling us, but we'd all felt like he was holding something back. It wasn't much comfort to know she had money and her coat. Could she have called a taxi? An Uber? Gotten it to meet her somewhere off campus? Could she have left without going through the gate? Her calls would be in her cell phone records, but I had no idea how long it might take to get those. Miller and Flynn could get the number from Bella.

"Just to confirm," I said, "Heidi had her phone with her? That's how she called you?"

Bella nodded. "Can I go now, please?"

I looked at Gareth and saw that he was running the same questions in his mind. Instead of answering, though, he stood. "Thank you, Bella. If you think of anything else that might help us find her, please call me or tell your dorm mother. It's important."

She nodded and headed for the door, looking no more easy about going than she had about coming. Halfway to the door she turned. "Dr. Wilson, do you think Heidi is okay?"

"I hope she's okay," he said. "Two last things. What color is her jacket?"

"Blue," she said. "Ice blue. We went shopping for jackets together last fall. It was so much fun. Because we never needed heavy jackets in California."

"Thank you. And how much money does she have?"

"I didn't count it, I just grabbed the envelope and put it in her purse. But I think it was at least a couple hundred dollars. And she has a credit card."

With a student ID and a credit card, Heidi might be able to get pretty far away. A taxi, a train, a plane? Who knew where she might go? Checking on credit records and whether she'd bought a ticket was outside my realm. That was up to Miller and Flynn.

Before she left, Flynn asked for Heidi's phone number.

We all watched Bella leave. I didn't know what the others might be thinking, but my dark mind was churning out visions of ice blue fabric surfacing in the river that flowed past the campus. Or a vulnerable young girl in a physically depleted state wandering around Boston during last night's awful weather, looking for a place to hide.

Clearly, it was time to consider a new line of work.

CHAPTER 16

I'd interviewed many students at other schools as part of my efforts to be sure schools were taking proper care of their student population, but this felt different. There was something oddly uncomfortable about sitting in Gareth's office and having a succession of students come in, tell what they knew, and depart. Like we were a review board or something. Or cops, like Miller and Flynn. My increasingly cop-like nature made it hard to back away, yet this task felt removed from my job of protecting Simmons. Sitting and asking questions, though I knew it was important, seemed like we were delaying the moment when we'd have to get back out there and resume the search for Heidi. I knew campus and local police were searching even as we sat here. But hours had passed since she disappeared and so far, we had no good clues about where to look for her.

Hours had also passed since Gareth had spoken with Heidi's mother, yet there was no sign of Mrs. Norris. He'd called again, after our interview with Bella, and gone straight to voice mail. Worst case scenario, which I knew we were both imagining, was that she'd blown off their conversation and gotten on that plane to California. If what we'd learned from Jaden and Bella was true, she had good reasons to duck hard questions, especially questions from Miller and Flynn. Like many a mother before her, it sounded like she'd failed to protect a young daughter from predators in her own home. Predators she'd been complicit in bringing there herself.

If what we were hearing was the truth. It was frustrating to have such an information void on Heidi's side. We couldn't know whether she was telling the truth about being unaware of her pregnancy and about her stepfather and other men in the house, but it didn't sound like something she would have made up, especially if she valued the Simmons culture as her friends said she did. The uncomfortable tale of her stepfather's practice of deliberately walking in on her didn't seem like something she'd tell to a boy, even one who was a friend, except in deepest confidence. And if she'd shared something so intimate, wouldn't she also have shared her pregnancy, if she knew?

I wondered what Miller and Flynn were thinking, and where they'd want to go from here?

At the risk of sounding like the detective I wasn't, I used the interval to suggest to Miller that they might find some items with The General's DNA at the inn if everything hadn't already been cleared away. He didn't argue or even look at me funny, just nodded and left the room briefly to make a call.

There was another discreet tap on the door and Gareth's assistant, Peggy, ushered in our third witness. If Bella had entered like a timid mouse, Ronnie Entwhistle came in like a German shepherd trained for crowd control. While his name suggested something from Hogwarts, he was more Refrigerator Perry. Angry, frustrated, concerned, and impatient. He was a shade of brown so dark he truly was almost black, and so handsome one instantly understood that black *was* beautiful. He shook our hands with one that swallowed all of ours except Flynn's, a shake and squeeze that had a 'let's get on with this' brevity. Then he perched on the edge of the chair Gareth had indicated.

He didn't wait for anyone's questions. "Heidi's mother brought the damned stepfather, didn't she?" he said. "Heidi told her not to. Heidi said she'd like her mother to come, but if The General came, too, she'd run away. But Heidi says her mother isn't going to listen to anything Heidi tells her. It's no wonder Heidi wanted to come here, is it?"

Flynn let Miller take this one.

"What has Heidi told you about her stepfather?" Miller asked.

"Probably what Jaden and Bella have already told you. That he won't give her any privacy and it makes her very uncomfortable. He says she's just a little girl and he's looking out for her, but she'd have to be pretty feeble to believe that, and Heidi's not feeble. Her narcissistic mother won't do anything to protect her. Her stupid, self-centered bitch of a mother, I mean."

Miller nodded. "Has Heidi said anything to suggest her stepfather has taken liberties with her? Been sexually aggressive?"

The boy squeezed his big hands together in a gesture I thought was an effort at control. "She hasn't come out and said it, but it sounded like something had happened."

"Can you give us a sense of that conversation?"

Ronnie fixed his fierce gaze on Miller. "It was confidential, sir."

"I understand that, and we appreciate the importance of keeping your friend's confidences, but we've got a serious situation here, Ronnie, one where Heidi may be in danger. She's disappeared. No one knows where she's gone. We have no way of being sure she's safe or whether someone who doesn't have her best interests at heart may be involved. Our best chance of finding her is if we're working with good information. What you know is a valuable part of that."

Ronnie shifted his eyes to Gareth.

"Sergeant Miller is right, Ronnie," Gareth said. "We respect your desire to keep Heidi's confidences between the two of you, but in a situation like this, protecting your friend may mean protecting whoever caused this pregnancy, while putting Heidi at risk. And, as you can understand, she's very vulnerable right now, having just given birth. This is not a good time for her to be trying to manage on her own."

"You just want to get her back here so you can turn her over to them." He jerked his chin toward the two detectives. "Then, even if she doesn't go to jail—" He glared at the two cops, "Which would be ridiculous since she's just as much a victim here as that baby is—" A chin jerk toward Gareth, "And even if they don't charge her, you're going to send her packing back to California where she'll have to live with the bitch and the creep and that would destroy her. I'm not going to help you with that."

He sat silently for a moment, then added, "It's no wonder she ran."

"So you know where she is?"

Ronnie Entwhistle didn't answer.

"What about her father?" Miller said. "You called her father when this happened."

"What about him?"

"He cares about Heidi, and he's worried about her. Evidently you thought he should be involved, since you called him."

"Not really. If her mama is a narcissist, her daddy is Peter Pan. I only called him 'cuz Heidi asked me to."

The boy folded his arms across his chest and glared at all of us. "She didn't want him here because she believed he would be much help. She was scared and wanted someone here who cared about her, somebody who maybe could negotiate with you...uh...the school, I mean, on her behalf, and he was the best she could do. But if you've met him, you must know that when it comes to looking after her, her dad's pretty useless. Otherwise, why would he have left her with them?"

We were learning things, lots of things that illuminated the situation and gave us possible avenues to identifying the baby's father, but in the finding Heidi department, we were making no headway.

Miller tried a different tack. "You think the stepfather is the father of her baby?"

Ronnie stayed silent, but he shook his head.

"She tell you who it is?"

"She didn't know she was even pregnant, so how could she tell me?"

"You really believe that?"

Ronnie was big and tough. He was also just a kid, though clearly a kid with more street smarts than Jaden or Bella. He looked at Gareth again. "Dr. Wilson, what am I supposed to do here? I don't know what I should say and what I shouldn't and I don't know what's going to help Heidi and what might hurt her."

"Let's take it one step at a time, Ronnie," Gareth said. "Can you answer that question honestly?"

"I can. Yes. I do believe that Heidi didn't know she was pregnant. But I think, now that she knows...now that she's had the baby, she may have some idea who the father is. But that's just me guessing. Honest, it is. She never said anything before all this that suggested she knew, and when I spoke with her last night, she just said something really vague."

"What did she say?" Miller asked.

"She said she had no idea that anything had happened but it must have been him."

"Who is 'him'?"

"She didn't say."

"There was nothing in the context of the conversation that made it clear?"

"Clear as mud. It was more like she was talking to herself."

Miller waited for a better answer.

"See, Heidi tells us the truth. Her friends. Teachers. People here at Simmons. That's why she came here, so life would finally let her be honest. But before, in California, she said she'd learned to lie about everything. It was the only way to have any privacy. The only way to keep herself safe."

"Safe from who?"

"Just about everyone but Will. She can trust him, which is why…" Ronnie broke off, glared at us, and shrugged his great big shoulders. "Safe from who? Whom? You know what I know. Someone who was around the house is what I figured."

"Did Heidi have a boyfriend back home?"

About this Ronnie was clear. "Nope. She wasn't interested. Between her parents and the creep, it's no surprise. She hasn't exactly had models for the possibility of a positive relationship."

"That doesn't usually stop people from forming relationships."

Another big shrug. "I can only tell you what she told me. Plus, she said boys didn't find her interesting. Which is dumb, because she's really pretty. She's not all girly and flirty and stuff or all into clothes and makeup. She's just straightforward. It's what makes her a good friend. She's not playing games. She's not trying to get me and Jaden interested in her. She's just, you know, real."

He looked at Gareth. "I don't think they understand about Heidi."

"It's hard," Gareth said, "when they haven't met her."

Ronnie nodded, then told us something we should have known from the start. Something that helped explain why her judgmental mother thought she couldn't have a boyfriend. Why she might have been extra self-conscious about her body and dressing in private. "Not that it slows her down or anything, she's really okay with it, but maybe the reason Heidi didn't have boyfriends, and the reason her mother says she's unattractive, is that she has a partial prosthetic foot. She was born missing three of her toes. A lot of guys aren't going to be cool with that."

CHAPTER 17

It was not politically correct, or Simmons correct, to say, "Why has no one ever mentioned this before?" So I didn't. But I did give Gareth a look. So did Miller and Flynn. Not that it changed anything, and yet it did. Without any information about the ways in which this issue with her foot might impair her, knowing about it made me worry more about Heidi managing on her own, and about her vulnerabilities to seduction and predation. It made me angry with Gareth for not giving me all the facts when he knew I needed them. When knowing as much as possible about a situation was critical to managing it well. Maybe it had been in the file Gareth gave me as I was heading out last night. A file I'd not had a chance to open.

And I'd bet that it gave Miller and Flynn reasons to think Heidi might have been lying about a sexual adventure because it was something no one—meaning the hateful mother and stepfather, and possibly her peers at her former school—believed she could have.

There was a long silence after Ronnie's declaration, so long that he got uncomfortable. He wore the look of someone who thinks they've gotten something very wrong.

"What," he finally said. "You didn't know about her foot? Sheesh, I thought everyone knew. It's not like she tries to hide it or anything. Not that you'd know, seeing her and all. She's just regular like the rest of us. But there are things she can't do so easily, like run fast and do sports. I mean, she can, but she doesn't like to because she's not so good at it, and Heidi already feels like she's not good at so many things. She thinks, because of her mother the bitch, that she's ugly and plain and dumb and useless. As well as a cripple."

His look invited us to share his amazement. "When she's really great."

"Where are you from?" Miller asked.

"Dorchester. Boston. Why?"

"Did you arrange for a friend with a car to come and get Heidi and take her somewhere?"

"Did I what?"

"You heard the question."

Ronnie looked at Gareth. "Is he accusing me of something?"

"He's just asking, Ronnie. Did you help Heidi leave the campus last night?"

"No." He didn't look evasive or anxious or like he wondered how we'd take it. He didn't look like he was hiding something. He just looked really pissed off that Miller had asked such an offensive question.

There was a long silence, then the boy said, "Can I go now?"

Their pact to tell the truth could be difficult sometimes. Miller had jumped the gun. Asked the ultimate question without building up to it first. And now Gareth had to tell the truth—that Ronnie could leave any time he wanted.

Miller tried to backtrack. "We're just trying to make sure she's safe," he said.

"Wish I believed that. But, excuse me if I sound rude, I don't believe you. I think you want to use Heidi as an example to other girls. I saw your boss, the DA, on the TV last night, and he didn't sound the least bit concerned about Heidi. He sounded like someone who wanted to put her in the stocks, like they used to do around here, and let people parade past and insult her. Going on and on about her abandoning an innocent newborn. Well, Heidi's been abandoned, too. And she's innocent. And she didn't know anything about that baby."

He stood, and again I was struck by his size. Still a kid, and yet possessing a massive man's body. "Sorry," he said. "I'd like to help but I can't be a part of that. Unless you can convince me that the DA, and you all, don't have it in for Heidi, then I've said all I'm going to say."

Unlike the others, who'd tried to hide the fact that they were lying, Ronnie was completely upfront. He wasn't going to lie to us, unless his answer to the question about the car had been a lie, but he wasn't going to say anything more. I was sorry for Miller and Flynn. They had a hard job to do. It was also their job to do it well. To do the best job of getting important information. Witnesses were often difficult, reluctant, or wary, and the challenge was to find a way past that to the truth. Part of the truth, in this case, being whether he had any knowledge of Heidi's plans for last night.

When the door closed behind him, no one said anything for a while. Finally, Miller broke the silence. "Well, that went well, didn't it?"

He was looking at me but I refused to be baited.

"Heidi's dorm mother?" I asked, looking at Gareth.

He shook his head. "Sgt. Miller and Detective Flynn are going over there. They want to have a look around Heidi's room."

The lawyer's daughter in me was already wondering whether they could do that when Gareth said, "It's part of the contract here. We have the right." Like he was reading my mind. I hope he couldn't read all my thoughts. And he seemed to have forgotten that I'd asked to speak with Heidi's dorm parents yesterday.

"You do know that a reporter got into her room yesterday, right? And your department has the things he took from her room?" I asked.

Miller nodded. "Got any ideas about where we look for the girl?" he asked, an edge in his voice like he thought I'd had a hand in her disappearance.

"I think you're on the right track," I said. "Look for someone with a car, or connections to a car. Ask the local taxi companies or the Uber drivers if anyone picked up someone matching Heidi's description near the school last night. Give her friends a little time and see if they come up with anything else. Ask the other girls on her floor if they have any ideas. Bella's her roommate, but that doesn't mean she's closest to Heidi. Or ask Bella who else Heidi was friends with. Check her phone records and see who she called. Check her credit card use. One of her parents must know the number. And ask her parents some hard questions about their visits to Heidi last night, and any other conversations they might have had with her. Ask them straight out if they were involved in Heidi's disappearance."

I stopped, because what I was telling them was so obvious. "And we've still got this girl with the name of a Rhode Island town. Tiverton."

I looked at Gareth, "We are going to see her, right?"

"She's in a two-hour lab this morning. We'll see her later."

Flynn gave me another of his suspicious looks and made some notes.

"As for the rest—" Yeah. I know. He hadn't asked. "It wouldn't be a bad idea to put a little pressure on Heidi's mother, see if you can find out what was really going on in that house. Find out if General Bradley Norris did get on a flight to California this morning."

I switched back to Gareth. "No word from Mrs. Norris?"

He shook his head.

I added something to Flynn's list. "And whether Lorena Norris was on that flight."

There were so many loose ends I felt like a spider whose web had exploded as I watched Miller and Flynn depart.

I was glad they were heading over to Heidi's dorm. I needed some time with Gareth without the constabulary looking over our shoulders. He looked like he was ready to have them gone, too. They'd been well behaved, but we had things to strategize about, and didn't want to have those conversations before an audience.

As Miller and Flynn were heading out, Gareth's bustling assistant came in with a handful of pink message slips. She gave the majority of them to him, but there were a few for me as well. I shuffled quickly through them. Work, work, and work. Nothing about my father—a case of no news is good news. I hoped. Still, I excused myself for a moment, stepped into the small lounge I'd been using, and called the hospital. They confirmed that he'd gone home.

Then, because finding Heidi was paramount, Heidi's friends were our best source, and we were now far enough into the day to make it a respectable hour to call California, I got out the number for Nina Smirnoff that Mrs. Norris had given me, and called.

Making a cold call like this, you never know what to expect. What I got was an attempt at a brush-off. "I'm sorry," Nina Smirnoff said when I explained I was calling about from Heidi Basham's school and wanted to reach her daughter Stephanie, "Stephanie isn't here. She has gone to boarding school herself. She wants to put the whole business with Heidi behind her, as do I. I'm afraid I can't help you."

Can't meaning won't. *What whole business with Heidi*, I wondered? I made a few more attempts to persuade her to give me Stephanie's contact information without revealing too much about Heidi's situation, but Nina Smirnoff—so disliked by General Norris for her criticism of their parenting style—was a brick wall. I figured my only option was to shock her. "I'm so sorry to be bothering you with this," I said, "when evidently something unpleasant happened between Stephanie and Heidi. I wouldn't be making this call except that Heidi just gave birth to a premature baby when she believes she's never had sex, and now she's disappeared. She's just sixteen, and scared. We don't know if she's run away, or been taken. We're desperate to find her. Her parents are no help at all, while the police are looking to arrest her for abandoning her baby. I was hoping Stephanie might know something that could help us find her. Or protect her from arrest."

There was a long silence on the other end, while I nursed my guilt at having revealed Heidi's private information. Finally she said, "I don't know. I just don't know. Stephanie wants to be done with that mess at the Norris's. But if Heidi is in trouble? I'm going to leave it up to her. She can call you if she wants. Give me your number."

I gave her my number and then shared one more suggestion. "If she really wants to help Heidi, she'll share what she knows with the police." I gave her Miller's number as well. She sighed, then disconnected without saying goodbye.

What mess at the Norrises'? My dread about Heidi's safety was growing exponentially.

I stuck my head into Gareth's office to see if he was ready for me. He was sitting behind his desk, staring balefully at the telephone, looking like he'd been the recipient of more bad news.

"What's up?" I said.

He glared down at the phone, which was still in his hand. "I think your dark side is contagious," he said. "Not that this situation isn't awfully dark already. I've just called my wife to see that Ted Basham was resting comfortably."

He shook the phone like he was trying to shake something out of it. "Thea, she says he's not there."

"Not there? Did she say where he went?"

He shook his head. "She has no idea. Seems despite his statement that he 'needed to rest,' he never went back there after he left us this morning."

"Is his car gone?"

"Jennie says it's not at the house."

He walked to the window and stared out into the parking lot, looking for Basham's stand-out red BMW. "And it's not out there in the lot."

Had my instinctive lie detector been so far off the mark? Did that pseudo-boyish charm hide not a man trying to duck the buck but a wily manipulator? If so, who was he manipulating? And for what purpose? Did he, like his ex-wife, have secrets he wanted to hide, secrets that Heidi might divulge? Or—and this was an ugly thought—was there some way he thought he could use Heidi as a pawn in his on-going battle with his ex-wife? What if Heidi was in his trunk or he had helped her to hide somewhere? Was he making a stupid, and likely futile effort, to protect his daughter, some kind of "I'm a good dad" bravado? What might he hope to accomplish by that? He couldn't keep her hidden forever. He'd already said his lifestyle couldn't accommodate a child.

We hadn't asked whether Basham had been back to visit Heidi last night. Why would we? He was with us when we went to the infirmary. If he had anything to add, presumably he would have mentioned it. Helen Brooks hadn't mentioned it. And Gareth hadn't noticed his house guest missing during the evening. Nor had we asked Jaden or Bella or Ronnie whether they'd spoken to Basham since they'd called him about the baby. We'd dropped a lot of balls in that interview—like what had happened after Jaden dismantled the door alarm, and whether he'd done anything else to help Heidi get away. Those were absolutely questions that Miller or Flynn should have asked. As I keep telling people—often defensively—I am *not* a cop.

Increasingly, this business was making me feel like I was hanging off a ledge by a few shaky fingers. Gareth's expression suggested he felt the same way.

"Call Security and see if he's left the campus," I said.

He made the call and set the phone down with a crash. Ted Basham, it seemed, had driven away from the campus immediately after leaving Gareth's office.

"Call his cell phone and see if you can find out what's going on."

He found Basham's business card and started dialing. I could tell by his face, and the brevity of his message, that he'd gone straight to voicemail.

Not only Heidi, but both her parents, it seemed, had disappeared.

CHAPTER 18

Gareth looked like a man with a bad headache. This situation would give anyone a headache. Leading a community that believed in honesty and righteous behavior, and negotiating between that community and the rest of the world, was challenging at the best of times. At a time like this, when he'd represented that Heidi was telling the truth, it was going to be hard to go back to his students and put her disappearance in any kind of a positive light.

Mrs. Norris's disappearance, followed by Basham's, didn't help his relations with the police, either, though neither was his fault. Maybe Ted Basham had just gone to run an errand or buy a clean shirt. What we hoped, but not what we believed. Why would he need to lie about that?

I quickly filled Gareth in on my phone call to Nina Smirnoff. "Whatever she knows, she's not sharing it. This is beginning to feel like the blind men and the elephant." I settled into a chair and got out a pad of paper. "I get no consistent picture of Heidi, and her parents are off the chart strange. But something happened in that house. I'm sure of it."

"What am I supposed to say to our parents, never mind the school community?" he said. "First there's the baby and now we've lost the mother."

"You didn't lose her."

"As good as lost her," he said. "We let her slip through the cracks. I know you're good at spinning, Thea, but how do you plan to spin this?"

I stared down at my pad as though there might be some wisdom in the blank white paper or the clean blue lines. "The baby is doing well."

Gareth stared at his own blank page.

I pushed away my uncertainty, pulled out my tiny recorder so I could capture my thoughts as I went, and pushed record.

"The student body at Simmons has self-selected to attend this school because of its reputation for honest discussion, informed debate, shared community values, and a belief in the importance of civic involvement," I said. "The recent events involving a very young mother, a premature birth, and what appears to be a case of traumatic amnesia regarding the circumstances of the pregnancy present a challenge to all of us. Dealing with this complex and difficult situation through rigorous investigation, followed by open discussion and debate, will be a test of our community and its values. However, we're confident that by keeping open minds until the facts are known, and conducting respectful discussion, Simmons will emerge stronger despite this troubling event."

I looked at Gareth. "With a bit of tweaking, you can use that for both your students and your parents."

He moved restlessly behind his desk, reminding me that despite the fact that he wore a suit today because of official meetings, he liked to spend his time outside on the campus, interacting with his students. "It helps," he said, "but it's not enough. We need to find her. We need to find her parents. What kind of people are these, to abandon their child like this? They should both be here in my office, wringing their hands, and asking what they can do to help."

I couldn't disagree. Before I could get him focused on the message and what steps we should take, his phone rang. He listened to what was obviously more bad news before setting it carefully back in the cradle and grabbing his coat. "That was Security," he said grimly. "They've found a blue jacket in that copse of trees down by the river. The spot we call the picnic grove."

My heart jumped. It could be unrelated, but Bella had told us Heidi's jacket was blue. His grim expression echoed the thought that leapt into my mind—had Heidi had been so upset she'd thrown herself in the river? The possibility was too horrible to contemplate.

"You'd better call Miller and Flynn," I said.

His set face said, "I don't wanna," even before his words brushed me off. "I've got to go," he said. He was out the door before I could stop him. Evidently, he planned to handle this without me, despite the fact that I was supposed to be his trouble-shooter. Trouble-shooters have the unfortunate effect of reminding people of their troubles.

No way, I thought. I grabbed my own coat and followed.

He moved fast and with purpose, whipping past his assistant when she tried to stop him to ask a question. He was out the door and into a waiting four-wheel drive security vehicle with lightning speed. Ignoring me when I called, "Hold on, Gareth," he slammed the door and the driver took off, leaving me standing there.

I understood his alarm, but his behavior? Not so much. Maybe Basham-Norris disease was contagious.

Luckily, my Jeep was nearby. I jumped in and took off after him, instructing my phone to dial Miller's number as I wheeled around the green and followed Gareth down a narrow dirt track that disappeared into some trees. The main road was almost clear and dry, but the dirt track was soft and mushy with mud after the recent rain and freak late-season snow.

Miller didn't answer. I didn't want to try and describe the situation in a message, so I said we'd found a coat that might be Heidi's and asked him to call me. Then I concentrated on not putting myself in a ditch or running into the vehicle I was following if it came to an abrupt stop.

I was dressed to look professional in a meeting room, not for traipsing through the woods. Luckily, my boots were low-heeled and water-proof, with thick soles and a sturdy, gripping tread. I live in New England, after all. We carry snow shovels and scrapers and those odd foil emergency blankets in our cars. We carry kitty litter and water and energy bars, extra sweaters and spare wool socks, jumper cables and all manner of stuff "just in case." Just in case included unseasonable weather and snow when we'd already moved on to spring and were thinking of capris and spring dresses. Also, I was married to Detective Extra Careful, the king of serve and protect, so I had the best shovel, best scraper, and a giant bag of kitty litter in case I got stuck, even though my Jeep was supposed to be an off-road vehicle.

The road curved abruptly, and I slammed on the brakes, slewing sideways to avoid running into the car ahead of me. Gareth and the driver were already out of the car, and heading down a wooded slope toward the river. The track we'd been following dead-ended at what looked like a picnic area, with an outdoor area for lectures with rows of stumps arranged like stools. In more inviting weather, it would have been pleasant.

I stood a moment, catching my breath, then jammed my hat on, grabbed my gloves, and followed.

A man in a security uniform, Gareth, his driver, and I stood and stared down at a forlorn-looking blue coat. It wasn't folded, but looked like someone had flung it in haste.

All our eyes focused on tracks in the thin patches of unmelted snow, heading away into the woods and not toward the river. "Did you check those out yet?" Gareth asked.

"We're waiting for Chief Greenberg," the man who'd found the coat said. "I called him just before I called you. He said to wait until he got here and not to do anything to muck up the scene."

He ducked his head, like he was embarrassed. "Except he did not say muck."

Gareth shifted his shoulders impatiently. "Well, where the heck is he? It's not like the campus is that big."

"Um…" This was the man who'd helped Joel the refrigerator hold the reporter who'd been in Heidi's room. The one who'd showed surprising concern for me. His name tag said he was Dalmar Amad. "One of the students found something in a greenhouse that she thought might be a clue to…uh…Heidi Basham's disappearance, Gareth. He went to check it out."

He was a large man with a slight accent, broad-shouldered and competent-looking. Under Gareth's glare, he seemed to wilt.

We heard the roar of an engine and the depressing thunk of metal on metal as the SUV I assumed held Chief Greenberg slewed around the curve much too fast and arrived with a literal bang—the sound of his vehicle slamming into mine. I am very fond of my Jeep, but suppressed my urge to storm over there and yell at him about his carelessness. My bumper still appeared to be attached. We were all distracted. And right now, our focus had to be on that jacket and the tracks leading away from it.

Chief Greenberg's first words did not endear him to me. "Who the fuck parks their car right around a blind curve?" he demanded. "Whose car is it, anyway?"

He shot an interrogatory look at Gareth and a dismissive glare at me. Ex-cop for sure, and unlikely to have been a nice guy when he was a cop. He seemed like a poor choice for a place like this, given the independence and quirkiness of the students, but maybe he was the best they could get. Or gave a good interview that didn't reveal his true character? More likely, Gareth had inherited him.

"Mine," I said, meeting his dismissive glare with one of my own.

"And who the hell are you?"

Before I could explain who the hell I was—a question that Gareth should answer anyway—my phone rang. Miller. I answered.

"What's this about a coat?" he said. "Where the heck are you? Where's the headmaster?"

"Hold on." I held out the phone the Gareth. "Sergeant Miller."

If looks could kill, the one Greenberg gave me would have blown me up and scattered my pieces. I tried not to roll my eyes. Cop vs. cop pissing contests were not my department. I wanted them to all get over their egos and starting thinking about what those tracks meant, where they led, and who was going to follow them. Greenberg? Greenberg and his crew? Gareth and Greenberg and his crew. Did I get to trail in their wake? And now we'd have to wait for Miller, which was my fault. But as I'd told Gareth earlier, my job was to protect the school. He might think I was making his job harder, but not getting the local cops mad at us was part of that protection.

I gathered, from what I could overhear, that Miller was in Gareth's office. Gareth gave a quick set of directions, said, "Yes, we'll wait," and handed the phone back to me.

"Miller and Flynn are on their way," he said.

With a discouraged glance at Greenberg's vehicle, snuggled up to mine like a machine with sexual congress on its mind, he said to Amad, "Perhaps it would be wise if you positioned yourself around that curve and flagged him down, so we don't have another collision?"

Amad nodded, looking relieved to be getting away from us, and loped back to where the vehicles were parked.

"Too damned many cooks, Gareth," Greenberg muttered. "We could have handled this ourselves."

Right, I thought. You could have organized a search of the river if the footprints lead that way? Handled a crime scene if we had one? Coordinated a wider search if it turns out Heidi has left the campus? Destroyed your important on-going relationship with the local police? I held my tongue. I might have some suggestions about Greenberg in a one-to-one conversation later, but right now, handling the chief was Gareth's problem.

"I know it's frustrating, Stan," he said, "but the police are already involved. And good relations are important. I think you taught me that?" He dropped a firm hand on Greenberg's shoulder and squeezed. It was a guy thing. I don't think I've ever dropped a confidential hand on someone's shoulder and squeezed.

It worked. Greenberg smiled. "Too damned right," he said.

We stood in the damp and dripping clearing and waited impatiently for Miller and Flynn.

Soon there was the crunch and hiss of tires, the squeal of brakes that needed attention, and Miller and Flynn piled out of another SUV. Take the people away and it would have looked like four clandestine SUVs had sneaked off to the woods to party. Five, counting Amad's, which was parked farther into the clearing.

In his bulky coat, Flynn looked like a barrel on legs, but he moved with economical speed. Miller wore the unhappy face of man who resents being left out and I felt Gareth shift beside me, bracing for what might come. Nothing came, though, except a crisp, "Fill me in," directed at the security chief. Greenberg did an economical update. Miller said, "Wait here," and walked off, leaving Flynn with us like a German Shepherd on alert.

First, Miller examined the jacket, bending to examine it without disturbing how it lay. He even took out his phone and snapped some pictures. Then he went to the tracks. He studied them, crouched down and studied them some more, and then rose and returned to us. "At least two people, one of them with big feet, maybe male," he said. A modern day Natty Bumppo. "We're gonna follow them and see where they lead."

He studied our little group like a man choosing teams. "Amad, you found the coat?"

Amad nodded.

"You know this part of the campus well?"

Another nod.

"Okay. You come with me." He focused on the chief. "Greenberg, you come with us. The rest of you stay put."

Very diplomatic.

None of us wanted to stay put, but like good doobies, we did. Flynn's solid bulk and set face made anything but cooperation unthinkable.

My phone, like a cricket in August, was having a field day in my pocket. I had a business to run and a parent who'd recently been in crisis, so I stepped away from the group to check my messages. The instant I moved, Flynn stepped toward me. "Just checking my phone," I said, holding it up. He nodded and relaxed.

Well. Relaxed wasn't quite the term. No one here was relaxed. Just a slight softening in his rigid posture that I took for permission.

I walked maybe fifteen feet away, turned my back on them, and checked my messages. Andre, checking in. That one could wait until we were done here, though I sent him a quick text that I was tied up, Dad was home, and I'd call when I could. Two from Suzanne. They could also wait. A message from my mother, asking me to call. That one couldn't. I dialed and raised the phone to my ear.

"Don't panic," she said when she answered. "I just wanted you to know that your father is home and resting. He wants to go to the office. I won't let him. When you get a chance, we need to plan that shower." There was an actual giggle from my mother who never giggles. "Maybe we should make it joint shower."

Yeah. Right. I really, truly wanted to share a baby shower with Sonia. And I was so eager to plan my own shower. Thanks, but no. She wouldn't hear me, though, if I protested. At least it wasn't an emergency. I made a neutral sound she took as agreement, and she hung up. I was surprised by how relieved I felt, like someone had lifted a huge weight off my body.

Freed from the distraction of worry about my dad, I could bring all of my attention to the messy situation here, to a challenge that felt like trying to juggle slippery rocks. I stared out into the slushy clearing and then on into the woods. Black tree trunks, small evergreens trying to gain a foothold where the clearing would give them some light. Those hateful patches of lingering snow. And well beyond the open space, the black shape of a rock. It was pretty funny looking rock, though, with something white on top that seemed out of place. A mitten? Maybe Heidi had had white mittens and dropped one?

My well-honed ability to sense bad things clicked in. Without thinking, I started walking toward the rock.

"Hey!" Flynn said. "Where do you think you're going?"

God. He was such a cop.

"I think I see something." I didn't give him a chance to stop me, just kept heading toward that dark lump. My heart was pounding and my stomach twisted with anticipation. The closer I got, the less it looked like a rock and more like something I truly didn't want to see.

The thud of heavy feet said that Flynn was right behind me. I braced myself, expecting a restraining hand, maybe one that wasn't very gentle, but he surprised me. "What do you see?" he asked quietly, coming up beside me.

I paused and pointed. "Over there. That dark lump. The thing that doesn't quite look like a stump or a rock. With that white thing on top that looks like a mitten."

He squinted into the dark woods. "Yeah. I see what you mean. I'll check it out. You stay here."

I've been headstrong since I could walk, and despite my misadventures, I still was. With the perversity of someone who has seen far too many bad things and lacks the common sense to stay away, I followed him. The determined and resolute little girl I'd been had grown up into a determined and resolute adult. This was my find, even if I did not want to discover what I feared lay ahead. It wasn't voyeurism, it was experience. Cops keep things close, and whatever this was, Gareth and I needed to know.

I arrived a little behind Flynn, who moved with surprising speed. As I came up beside him, I saw blood on a ground that had been churned into a mess of snow, leaves, and sticks by the struggle that had taken place here. Too big to be Heidi. Too big, too male. But the man I'd first mistaken for a rock was very definitely dead. That white thing I'd taken for a mitten? It was his hand.

I'd been expecting to find Heidi. Expecting and dreading. That's what I'd braced for. But the shock of finding any body reverberated through me. I was having trouble catching my breath.

"Recognize him?" Flynn asked. His grip on my arm was firm and paternal, with that good cop's innate instinct for when people need support.

I couldn't see much and I didn't want to go closer. Even though the side of his head was bloody, I could at least tell that the dead man had short, light brown, close-cropped hair. Definitely not one of the students, though it could have been someone on the faculty. The blood-streaked face under the damaged head looked late twenties to early thirties. A big man, muscular, not heavy. He wore khakis and highly polished black shoes, and a dark green jacket open over a blood-spattered white shirt. A few feet away, a pair of glasses that had been lost in the struggle leaned against a rotting birch log.

I turned away, pressing my hands against my stomach, feeling strange and lightheaded. "I don't know him," I said. "I've never seen him before."

I waved a hand vaguely at Gareth, waiting impatiently with the security man who'd driven him while the rest of us had gone off on our separate quests. "Maybe Gareth does. Or Chief Greenberg."

"Come away now," Flynn said. He put a firm arm around my shoulders, turned me around, and steered me back toward Gareth. "This not a good sight for an expectant mother."

He sure had that right. I didn't think it was a good sight for anyone. Not even for Flynn, and he seemed tough as nails. I decided not to act macho, and accepted the comfort of that strong arm. Maybe pregnancy was making me soft.

I didn't know if babies reacted to maternal shock, but MOC had suddenly moved the evening acrobatic act up several hours. Probably mommies-to-be should be looking at kittens and lambs and baby ducks, inhaling a world of cute and warm and fuzzy. Not this. "Sorry, baby," I murmured, giving the little creature a reassuring pat. The acrobatics quieted.

Heidi's jacket here, signs of a struggle, a dead man, and those ominous tracks. *I am tired of questions*, I thought wearily, even as I wondered what it all meant.

As he led me back toward Gareth, firmly in the grip of an arm that felt like a warm log, I wondered who that poor murdered man might be. I never had seen him before, but I had a wild card idea, based on things we had heard in our interviews. An idea I definitely didn't want to have about something I wouldn't have seen if I weren't so stubborn. It was a long shot, but if my wild card idea was right, Heidi's situation might have just gotten far, far worse.

CHAPTER 19

Flynn handed me over to Gareth like I was a poor little woman in need of care and protection. Never mind that the poor little woman had found the body and it wasn't her first. He couldn't help it. They spend their lives serving and protecting and that is difficult to turn off. Right now, I didn't mind. He was right, standing in the cold and damp looking at a man who'd had the side of his head smashed wasn't good for MOC or for me.

"What is it?" Gareth asked.

"Body," Flynn said. A man of few words, he was already walking away, talking into his phone, no doubt contacting Miller and then making the calls that would summon the necessary crime scene personnel.

"Oh my God, Thea, how awful!" Gareth said, substituting his arm for Flynn's. He'd gone pale and could barely get out the essential question, "Is it Heidi?"

"No. It's a male," I said.

"What is going on here?"

There was so much despair in his voice I wished I could reassure him that everything would be fine. But obviously, very little was fine and things were growing less fine all the time. It took all my will power to keep from climbing in my car and getting out of Dodge. An escape made rather difficult by the way Chief Greenberg's car was snuggled up to my bumper and the proximity of my car to the one Gareth had arrived in. A literal example of no wiggle room.

I couldn't answer Gareth's question because I didn't know what was going on. How could I? I knew so little about the players in this situation, players Heidi's parents could have helped us learn about. Now there would be a million new things to deal with.

Gareth was my client and we would have to work together to manage this mess, but given how shattered he looked, my immediate job was to calm him down and help him through this. We consultants also have to serve and protect. I forced the image of headlines about a body on campus, angry and concerned parents demanding answers, and a mass exodus of students from my mind. At this point, they would likely wait until the end of the school year, and that gave us time to change their minds.

"I don't know what is going on here, Gareth. This situation leaps from crazy to crazier. But this isn't about your students and it's not about flaws in your campus community. It's about one girl who got pregnant before she came to Simmons, who is traumatized and emotionally unstable and making impulsive decisions. It's about the person who made her pregnant. About people who are trying to protect their secrets."

"Yes, yes, of course," he said impatiently. "But someone is dead, Thea. Who is it, and why here?"

He hesitated, grabbing a breath like a swimmer about to plunge deeply into an icy pool, and asked the question he didn't want to ask. "Did you recognize him? Just tell me. Is it Jaden? Is it Ronnie?"

His arm dropped, and he buried his face in his hands.

In that "oh, hell!" moment, I understood I hadn't given him adequate information. I'd known the body wasn't a student and without sharing that information had moved on to thinking about other matters. All I'd said was the victim was male and dead, so of course that's where his thoughts went. I wasn't doing a very good job of serving and protecting. Maybe because I was feeling pretty scattered myself. Guess I wasn't so rock-steady as I like to pretend.

Not here for myself. "It's not a student, Gareth. It's someone older. A man in his late twenties, maybe early thirties."

"Who then? Who is it?" he asked. There had been pain in his voice when he first called me about Heidi. Now he sounded ravaged. "So it's not The General?" And remembering our other missing man, "Or Ted Basham?"

"It isn't either of them. Too young. It's someone I've never seen before." Not that a dead stranger on campus was much help in the relief department. If he in fact was a stranger.

"This is beyond comprehension, Thea. And if that is Heidi's coat, what does it mean that it's here amidst a chaos of footsteps and a dead body? Where is Heidi? Was she even here and if so, why? Was she meeting someone? Do you suppose she saw something? Saw this happen? Do you suppose the killer has her?"

I saw a shudder go through his body. "That poor child. I'm supposed to keep her safe."

Hard to do when "that poor child" had chosen to run away, yet the responsibility still fell on him. It was an awful dilemma. How was he to reassure his community? Keep Heidi safe when he didn't know where she was and the other adults who ought to be responsible had just taken a powder?

Why was her jacket here, if that was her jacket? Had she been here with the man who lay over there, dead? Was he someone she trusted or someone trying to abduct her? Where was she now? Had she slipped out of her jacket in a struggle and run away? Or had someone taken her, perhaps the same someone who had killed that man? Miller the pathfinder thought he'd seen two sets of footprints leading away.

My stomach twisted as I imagined that poor, vulnerable girl in the clutches of a murderer, while another possibility I didn't want to consider surfaced like a message in a

Magic 8 Ball—what if Heidi *had* done this? Confronted the man who'd made her pregnant and struck out at him, then fled in panic when she saw what she had done?

Andre's voice in my head reminded me to slow down and not let my assumptions get ahead of the facts. Unfortunately, we had no facts.

Sorting this scene out would fall to Miller and Flynn.

Meanwhile, my mind was racing, trying to form a strategy to protect the school's reputation. A way to find Heidi. To find out who was responsible for her pregnancy, the question that lay at the heart of all of this.

The situation was overwhelming. We just didn't know enough. We needed to talk to Heidi's friends and ask them more questions. Do an internet search to test my suspicions about the identity of the dead man. Assuming they could be found, we, or Miller and Flynn, needed to ask General Norris, Mrs. Norris, and Ted Basham some hard questions. And I wanted to sit with Miller and Flynn again and test my ideas about the victim. Victims. By my count, we now had three—the dead man lying over there, Heidi Basham, and the tiny baby girl who'd been born into this horrible situation.

To answer my questions, I needed Miller and Flynn, but they would be tied up with this crime scene for hours. I also didn't want to forget about a piece of information one of the security guards had mentioned that might get lost in the midst of this—the find that had delayed Chief Greenberg's arrival. What had campus security found in one of the greenhouses that might relate to Heidi's disappearance?

It was like trying to think my way out of a tornado. Gareth and I were both good at managing difficult campus situations, but this went so far beyond the normal I wasn't sure what to do. I wanted to throw myself on the ground and beat my fists in frustration, like a toddler having a meltdown. I'd just found a man with his head bashed in. I was cold and in shock and utterly miserable. Wasn't I entitled to a meltdown?

Nope.

There wasn't time for misery or self-pity. Things had gotten seriously worse in terms of our campus crisis. What really gave me chills, though, was that Heidi was still missing, and might well be in the hands of someone who didn't have her best interests at heart.

I needed to help protect the school. I also wanted to find Heidi and protect her. That was my "Thea the Human Tow Truck," quality, the me that needed to protect the helpless and vulnerable. Which presented a dilemma if her interests and the school's diverged. Another part of me—Thea the I Don't Wanna—longed to declare this situation beyond EDGE's capabilities, and drive away, leaving it to someone else to sort out. I sure hoped my car was drivable. I was so done with dead bodies.

I looked around. Flynn was still over by the body, talking on his phone, and I could see Chief Greenberg, Sergeant Miller, and the security guard coming back toward us. Greenberg veered off and headed toward Flynn. Miller and the guard came to us.

"Gareth, the snow was so patchy those prints were hard to follow, but it looks like they may have gone right to the fence at the edge of the river. Whoever it was, they're long gone. We will have someone out with a dog, to see if we can learn more. We can use Heidi's coat as a scent object."

Then Miller focused on me. "Brian says you spotted the body?" he said.

I nodded.

"How in the heck did you do that?"

I repressed my initial, flippant, "Just luck, I suppose." There wasn't anything lucky about this. Besides, he couldn't know my history with dead bodies. I decided to deal straight. "I saw something white on a rock. I thought it might be a mitten, something Heidi had lost. A clue to a different trail, so I decided to check it out." I kept my eyes on the ground. "It was the man's hand. The dead man."

Saying that made me feel sick and MOC did a little flip in sympathy. I put my hand over what is currently—and repulsively—called a "baby bump" and turned away, watching Greenberg and Flynn's interaction. Greenberg appearing to try and muscle his way in, Flynn resisting. Then Greenberg headed back toward us, his body language saying he'd been dismissed.

"You're going to be around, right?" Miller said, staring at me. "We may want to speak with you again later. For now," he surveyed the line of cars, and frowned at the way Greenberg's was right on my bumper. "For now, we should get the unessential vehicles out of here to make way for the crime scene van. Chief Greenberg will stay with us. The rest of you can go."

Happy to be dismissed, I looked at Greenberg. "Maybe you could back your car up a little?"

I got a frown and a grunt, like moving was a massive inconvenience and my question was impertinent. "Oh, and before I forget, Chief Greenberg," I said, "was there anything to that student's find in the greenhouse that might be a clue to Heidi's disappearance?"

He frowned. "They found something they thought might be her purse. There was a purse, but there was nothing useful in it. No wallet, papers, ID, so who knows?"

Without more, he stomped away to move his vehicle.

A question to ask Bella. She would know what Heidi's purse looked like.

I took the risk of irritating him further by asking, "Where is that purse now?"

He threw up his hands. "I think someone took it to the office." He strode away, a very physical version of "we are done here."

Fine with me. I was done, too. With Greenberg.

Gareth conferred briefly with Miller, then said, "Meet back in my office, Thea?" And the party broke up. Party was never a more misused word.

On our way back to the cars, the security officer named Amad, who'd started this by finding Heidi's coat, came up beside me, and said, in a low voice, "Can you tell Mr. Wilson that there is maybe another set of tracks leading out of the picnic grove."

I would have said, "You should tell the police," but it was clear, from the anxious look he cast back toward Miller and Flynn, that doing that was outside his comfort zone, despite the nature of his job. "I'll tell him," I said. "When the police searched the area, I expect they'll find those tracks anyway."

"They are leading maybe back toward the buildings?" He hesitated. "I will tell Chief Greenberg as well, but he doesn't always listen to me."

I was not surprised.

I wanted to grab his arm, make him show me where they were, and follow them. I wanted desperately to find Heidi, even more so after Nina Smirnoff's cryptic remarks and what had just transpired. Anxiety gripped my stomach like the squeeze of a giant's hand. But while they'd been nice enough to work with, Miller and Flynn were now managing a crime scene. Bad enough I was the one who'd found the body; I knew from experience that any attempt to do further investigation on what was now their turf would not get a friendly response.

I also didn't have a lot of confidence in Greenberg's willingness to listen to Amad. Talking to Gareth was all I could do. "The police will probably find the footprints" I said again, because he still seemed so anxious.

He shrugged dismissively.

Between his thatch of curly dark hair and his dark beard, his face was hard to read. Was that skepticism or just dislike of the police? "Why wouldn't they find them?" Ah. Thea, the woman who is not a cop, acting like one.

"They are very hard to see, with the leaves and the sticks and all those patches of snow. Unless there is someone looking who knows what to look for."

"And that would be you?"

I thought that was a smile behind the beard. "I have tracked many people, Miss Thea. Many people."

How often people we might discount can surprise us. "But they will bring a dog," I said. "So the dog will find them."

Another shrug. "Yes, the dog will find those tracks if they let the dog find those tracks. Dogs, they are only as good as the people who handle them. I have seen much of this as well."

"You were a translator in Iraq," I said, thinking I meant far more than translator.

Another shrug. "And now I work here. These students, I like them very much. I was before someplace else and it was not so nice."

He had a story, I thought, and I had no time to learn it.

We arrived at the cars. Greenberg had grudgingly given me some room, so I turned around and headed back up the track. Gareth and his driver followed and Amad came last.

I parked, and to my surprise, Amad parked beside me.

"I must go back to work," he said, leaning out his window, "but there is one more thing. I found that other track, the single track, because I followed some small footprints. If you like, later I can show you."

He handed me a piece of a paper with a phone number on it. I thought about abandoning Gareth, grabbing Amad's arm, and going to check out those tracks.

But Gareth was waiting. There was much to be done. And Amad was already driving away.

CHAPTER 20

"We need to talk with Bella, Ronnie, and Jaden again," I said, when we were back in Gareth's office. "And Tiverton, of course."

He held out a hand to ward me off. "Let me get through my messages first. I still have a school to run and I'd like to spend a few minutes on something that isn't about Heidi. And drink some coffee. And eat something."

Without waiting for a reply, he shuffled the messages again, as though looking for some good news, then shoved them aside. "Thea, forgive me. You've just found that poor man lying there dead, and I'm not treating you with any consideration at all."

It's an odd thing about me. I can stare down bad guys, stumble over dead bodies, and handle other people's crises with calm competence, but when someone is kind to me, I fall apart. I dropped onto one of his comfortable couches, fumbled for a tissue in my pocket, and started to cry.

Poor Gareth, a kind man and a gentleman, he really didn't know what to do. I was supposed to be supporting him.

"I'm fine, truly fine," I said, as I soaked one tissue and reached for another. "Just give me a minute."

"Maybe a nice cup of tea?" he suggested.

Despite my tears, it made me smile. Tea for the horror of finding someone murdered was like sticking a Band-Aid on a broken leg. But where he came from, tea was comfort food. I swiped at my eyes and blew my nose. We had work to do and there was no time for a pity party. I might not want tea but I did need some food.

"Sandwiches?" I said. "And chocolate. This situation definitely calls for chocolate. What time is it, anyway?" Although it felt like we'd already put in an eighteen-hour day, my watch said it was only early afternoon. It seemed hours since we'd interviewed Ted Basham and Heidi's friends, and then been called to the clearing. I suppressed a light comment about how I preferred to avoid bodies before lunch. Neither of us felt light. The weight of this had settled on us like a dentist's lead apron.

He asked his assistant to organize some lunch and then returned to business. "You said you had an idea who that man…uh…the person who was killed…who he was?"

"Just a hunch," I said, "and I so hope I'm wrong."

I was torn as I pulled out my laptop, logged in, and typed in a name. I watched the results pop up, so badly not wanting my suspicions confirmed. The search led me, eventually, to a Facebook page, and to a sharp-faced man with military short brown hair, glasses, and an army uniform. He was a big man with broad shoulders and a petulant mouth. In some of the photos he was holding a serious-looking weapon.

I felt gut-punched.

"Oh, dammit, Gareth. I'm right. Look at this."

I put the laptop on his desk, the photo facing him. He studied it thoughtfully for a minute, sighed, and shook his head. "Sorry, Thea, maybe I'm being dense, but I have no idea who this is or what it has to do with Heidi or this school, or the man lying dead down there in our woods."

Oops. I'd skipped a step again. Gareth hadn't been there earlier when I interviewed Ted Basham about anyone who had been in and out of the house who might present a threat to Heidi. I knew Dee and Dum had been mentioned last night, but perhaps at that point Gareth was already tuning out. It was right after that that he and Basham had agreed to postpone discussion until morning.

"This is Lt. Alexander "Sandy" Crosby, one of the General's junior officers who, according to Ted Basham, were frequently in and out of the Norrises' house. The other one was Lt. Aaron Ramirez. One of Heidi's friends, I think it was Ronnie, mentioned them this morning. Heidi and her father referred to them as Dee and Dum."

"Crosby is the man who…he's the body down in our woods?"

"I think so."

"What do you think happened? What is that man doing here?"

I shook my head, unable to avoid another look at the man in the photo. "I really don't know. I can only speculate that General Norris must have brought him here for some reason. Unless he was the baby's father, and that's why he came. Heard the news, put two and two together, and hopped on a plane."

"But what was he doing in that clearing? Did Heidi arrange to meet him? Was she meeting someone else and he showed up? How does any of this even make any sense?" Gareth wondered. "And who killed him?"

He looked down at the messages on his desk, as though perhaps the answer was written there. "Could it have been Heidi?"

She was a big girl, I thought. We believed she'd been victimized, so could this be something she did out of shock, or outrage, or fear for her life? But what would this man, Lt. Crosby, be doing there? I couldn't imagine Heidi agreeing to meet him there.

"We don't have enough information to speculate," I said. "And there were tracks that suggested other people were there as well."

"It's a nightmare," he said.

We sat with that, ignoring our ringing and vibrating phones, feeling impotent as we pondered the answerless dilemma. Instead of trusting the school to help her, had Heidi called someone and arranged to meet that person down in the woods? If so, why would it be Crosby, unless Heidi had lied to her friends. Or her friends were lying to us about how much she disliked him. Now he was dead. We had no idea who had done it. And increasingly, no idea who the bad guys and good guys were. And Heidi was still missing. Our shared fear, one we didn't need to articulate, was that whoever had killed Crosby either had Heidi, or she was dead, too. Perhaps dumped into that cold spring river?

An abandoned baby and a mother in denial had seemed like crisis enough. That paled in the light of what we now knew. I wondered if we should tell Miller and Flynn about Crosby's identity and what we'd heard about his relationship to Heidi? If it was time to suggest dragging the river? If they were getting dogs out yet and what, if anything, that would tell them?

"Miller and Flynn probably know who he is by now," I said. "I'm sure he had ID. But they probably don't know his connection to Heidi."

"Neither do we, really," he said. "All we know is that he was known to her. He was a regular visitor to her home. And someone who, it is alleged, was in the habit of "accidentally" walking in on her. She didn't like him, so why would she call him? We don't know anything else about the nature of their relationship."

His hands curled into fists, a gesture of frustration, not potential violence. "Thea, we have got to find Heidi."

Easier said than done, or we would have found her by now. Her friends had searched, campus security had searched, and the police had searched. What more could we do? It was likely she wasn't on campus anymore.

Knowing that I sounded like a broken record, I said, "I know we've got other things to do. And I know you don't want to hear this, but we need to get Jaden, Bella, and Ronnie back here now, Gareth. One of them may know something that will help. Maybe something they don't even know they know. Or something they're hiding, still believing they're protecting her, like more information about their contacts with Heidi last night. And we haven't talked to Tiverton."

"After what's happened? We may well scare the heck out of them," he cautioned. "They're just kids, remember. We're supposed to be looking after them, not dragging them deeper into this."

He waved a hand at his paper-strewn desk. "We have a lot of other things to focus on right now. A lot of upset parents to deal with. Let's let the police do their job while we do ours."

I swallowed my protests—he was the client, so he called the shots—and bent to the jobs that needed our attention. My impatience to get out there and play Nancy Drew didn't help Simmons with its larger problems while staying here and doing damage control might.

Although we had little to tell them, the students couldn't be ignored. You can't keep something like a body and a swarm of police cars a secret on a boarding school campus. We planned another all school meeting for later in the day. Then we scheduled a meeting with the faculty to update them, and another with the school's PR director and his staff. At this point, damage control felt like sticking a lot of Band-Aids on a succession of broken legs, but we had to do it. We both hoped that by the time the meetings rolled around, someone—Miller or Flynn—would have further information for us. Or Heidi would have been found. Still, the possibility of very bad news hung over the room like a thick, dark cloud.

We were so immersed in our tasks that we were surprised when Gareth's assistant announced that Dr. Purcell was here. In our lurch from crisis to crisis, no one had thought to call her and cancel.

She sat quietly on the couch, exuding an enviable calm, as Gareth updated her on all that had happened since the previous day. She watched Gareth as the description of events unfolded. I watched her. There were definite reactions on her otherwise controlled face when he said

Heidi had run away in the night, aided by fellow students, the pill hidden under her pillow, and when he told her about finding the jacket in the woods and a man's battered body nearby.

When he was done, she said, "I need to think about this. Confidentiality can be quite a problem sometimes."

"What do you mean?" Gareth said. "You knew Heidi was planning to run away?"

She countered with a question of her own. "Do you genuinely believe Heidi is in danger?"

Despite how impressed I'd been by her insights yesterday, I thought this qualified as a dumbass question. Then I thought maybe it wasn't that she doubted us, but that for reasons related to deciding to break confidentiality, she needed someone in authority to confirm it.

Gareth seemed to have summoned a deeper level of solemnity as he answered. His voice was deeper, his already troubled face was etched with concern. In that moment, he looked ten years older. "We absolutely believe she's in danger, Dr. Purcell, if she's even still alive. A man who is possibly her abuser, a man we can assume came all the way from California, has just been found murdered in a wooded part of our campus. There are signs of a struggle. What we believe to be her coat is lying on the ground near the scene. And she's still missing."

He paused, and then qualified his statement, since we still had no idea, beyond our supposition, why Crosby had come. "I should say that we don't know whether this man—the man who has been killed—presented a threat to Heidi, as we assume to be the case, or came because he fathered the child, and had some less sinister motive. It is a muddle of questions with few answers. What is clear is that the homicide of someone she knew has occurred, Heidi has disappeared, and we have no idea whether her disappearance was of her own volition or at the hands of another."

He let that go a beat, to underscore the solemnity, then added, "Either way, she needs to be found, and we would appreciate anything you can tell us about her state of mind or intentions when you saw her yesterday."

Despite the seriousness and dark import of his words, Elaine Purcell didn't immediately respond. She stayed still and watchful. Then she said, "Neither you, nor this man, Lt. Crosby, are related to the girl. What about Heidi's parents? Where are they in all this?"

Gareth threw up his arms in a gesture of extreme frustration. "Missing. Both of them. The people who should be here offering support, concern, and insight, have vanished. Her mother and General Norris headed for the airport at four a.m. this morning, telling their innkeeper they planned to return to California. When we called to inform her about Heidi's disappearance, Mrs. Norris agreed to return. That was many hours ago. She has not appeared and is not responding to our calls."

Another baffled shrug. "Her father was here this morning, scheduled to meet with the police for questioning this afternoon. He is on crutches from an injury and said he was going back to my residence to rest. Instead, he got in his car and drove away. He, also, is not responding to us. At this point, all she has is us. As head of school, in the absence of her parents, I stand *in loco parentis* for this minor child. So yes, I can confirm that we believe Heidi is in grave danger. If you know anything that might help us find her, you should share it. I strongly believe that we are facing a potentially tragic situation here."

His shoulders slumped. There was a man on his campus with his head beaten in. The situation was already tragic. There was a tremble in his voice as he repeated, "If you know anything that might help us locate Heidi, you've got to tell us."

CHAPTER 21

Dr. Purcell studied her hands, knotted in her lap, then raised her head and looked at Gareth. She looked sad. "Ordinarily, I wouldn't tell you any of this. But since you believe that Heidi is at risk, which her disappearance and the murder of this man she knew back home definitely suggests may be the case, and since there are no parents available to give me permission to speak with you, I am going to deem you acting in place of a parent. Here is what I know. I am not sure how any of it may help."

She rubbed her forehead, as though making the decision to disclose Heidi's confidences was physically painful. "She told me that she had begged her mother to come alone. That if her stepfather came from California with her mother, if he approached her at all, she was going to run away. It's not...it's not that I didn't take her seriously, Dr. Wilson. Even in her fragile condition, she was very clear about that. I just thought that—"

She broke off, considering how to answer.

"I just thought I'd have more time to convince her of the folly of any impulsive decisions. I counseled her about not doing anything hasty. I reminded her that her body needed time to rest and recover. That she was awash with hormones from the pregnancy and delivery and she should not make any precipitous decisions. I told her that you, by which I meant the school, would ensure that her stepfather was kept away from her, and only her mother admitted. I also gave those instructions very clearly to the nurse at the infirmary—only her mother was to be admitted. And to ensure that Heidi would rest and not act precipitously, I gave her a sedative and left orders that she was to be given another when that one wore off."

She shook her head in a gesture of irritation at her flawed decision-making. "She seemed such a sweet, passive, agreeable girl. Confused and frightened, yes, baffled that she had been pregnant and that people wouldn't believe she was telling the truth when she said she didn't know. But she didn't strike me as impulsive or a risk taker. Nor did I take her dislike of her stepfather as a sign that he presented a danger to her. I expected when I returned to see her today that we would dig deeper into her concerns about her stepfather. And I would probe further about the circumstances of the pregnancy. I believed I was at the beginning of a potentially lengthy therapeutic relationship."

Again, she looked at Gareth. "Heidi was adamant that she would not return home to live with her mother, but whether that position was anything beyond a strong dislike of her stepfather, or whether the household presented a danger to her, I didn't have a chance to explore. I'm afraid we were focused in our conversation on issues surrounding her denial of her pregnancy and insistence that she has never had sex."

She considered, then added, "There was also the issue of not being believed by the community. That was of great concern to her. I assured her that we would find a way to help them understand how her denial could be genuine." She looked sadly at Gareth. "I'm not sure I convinced her on that score, though. I think someone must have said things, said directly to her or things she overheard, that were deeply upsetting."

"Dr. Purcell," I said, "is there anything you can recall from your conversation that might give us direction in our search for Heidi?"

"I'm afraid not. She mentioned her concerns about whether her friends would believe her several times. She shared her fears about being judged by the community. But nothing about any place, or any one, she might run to. It was more a matter of escaping from than running to."

"We understand," Gareth said. "You had little more than an hour. But we had to ask."

"There was a friend that she mentioned. A girl named Stephanie. They were friends back in California. She said she hoped Stephanie was all right. That's all she would say, though. I don't know if this girl—assuming you could locate her—could give you more information about Heidi or her situation."

I didn't either. My attempt to contact Stephanie Smirnoff had been a failure.

She gathered her things and stood. "I'm sorry, Dr. Wilson. I hope you find her. This is a terrible situation for everyone."

She was nearly at the door when she stopped and turned. "I have no idea how this might help. I took it as metaphorical. But at one point she said she just wished she could crawl into a safe, dark place where no one would think to look for her. And then, she almost smiled when she said that she actually knew of such a place."

And with a swish of heavy silk skirt, and a waft of the most subtle perfume, she was gone, leaving us with the awful image of a wounded and vulnerable child curled up in a hole somewhere like an animal gone to ground. The image was beyond depressing. How would we ever find this place, if it even existed? Was it somewhere on a campus that, theoretically, had been carefully searched? Still, meager comfort though it was, it was better to think of her in some secret hiding place than in the hands of whoever had killed Lt. Crosby. I'd managed campus deaths before, but this one felt overwhelming. We sat in a heavy silence, each trying to summon the energy to move on.

I was trying to decide, once again, whether my pride would let me cry "Uncle" and flee, when the door opened and Peggy appeared, pushing a cart of food, one of her hands clutching another thick wad of pink message slips.

She had a pleasant, transparent face that right now looked like she'd lost her last friend. "I'm so sorry to be bringing you more bad news, Gareth, but the manager at the Loverage House bar just called. They've got a man there, a bar patron, who has quickly and efficiently drunk himself into a near stupor. When they tried to roust him, he got belligerent, said he had plenty of reasons to get drunk, and said they could call you if they wanted to know why."

She hesitated before she finished delivering the bad news. "I'm afraid it's Heidi's father. Mr. Basham. They want to know if you will come and get him."

CHAPTER 22

Gareth looked at me bleakly as he sank wearily onto his chair, the sheaf of messages in his hand. The trolley with our lunch waited, ignored, by the window. "The sky is falling," he said. "How can so many things possibly go wrong? I can only imagine the harm that man can do, out there in a public place, drunk and babbling."

I shared his concern. A lazy, self-indulgent man like Basham, whose response to his only child's emergency and mysterious disappearance was to head to a bar, might say any damned thing that came to mind if he was drunk. We had to get him back here and under control as quickly as possible.

Gareth sprang to his feet, transformed into a man of action. He was half way to the door when he stopped. "Dammit, no. I haven't got the time," he said, shaking the sheaf of messages, then swept that hand toward his crowded desk. "There's all this waiting."

"Give me directions, and I'll go get him," I said. "Let me take Amad along as muscle, just in case he gives us any trouble."

"Amad?" he said, looking blank.

"The security guard who found Heidi's jacket," I reminded him. "A big guy, dark-skinned, strong. With an accent?"

"Oh. Right. Amad. The students really like him. He'd be good. Ex-military, I think." A half smile. "Sure. Yes. Go. Take him." He bent over the messages and started reading through them.

"Gareth?"

He looked up, surprised to still find me standing there.

"What are you waiting for?" he said. "This is an emergency."

"For directions to the bar. For you to call Amad, since you're his boss, not me. For a decision about whether we should take a Simmons security vehicle. For instructions about where to take him once we've extricated him from said bar."

He ran a hand over his face, his fingers rasping over his whiskers. "Am I losing it, Thea?" he asked.

"Just temporarily overwhelmed."

He picked up the phone, reached Amad, and told me, "He'll be at the front door in five minutes. Take Basham to my house. Uh." A pause. He'd just instructed me to take a reportedly belligerent drunk to the house where his wife and two small children lived. "Maybe Amad should stay with him, so he doesn't wander off."

He stared out into the dull gray day. "Loverage House is a colonial-era inn and restaurant. You go out the gate, turn right, and half a mile down, take a left onto Goodfellow Street. It winds a couple miles into the town center. Follow it to the town common, and it's at the end of the common. Big, sprawling gray building with parking at the back. You can't miss it. There's a back entrance that goes right to the bar."

He shook his head in wonderment at the mess we found ourselves in. "Next we'll get a call that Mrs. Norris has been in a traffic accident. Or that General Norris is brawling somewhere. My students are more mature than Heidi's parents. Who knows what goes wrong next?"

He left unsaid the possibility of bad news about Heidi.

I picked up my bag and coat and started for the door, hating to leave him just then. He still needed shoring up. There were a zillion things to be done. And as MOC reminded me with a sharp kick, there was the matter of food. I grabbed a cookie on my way out. Weren't oatmeal and raisins food?

Amad waited at the door in a silver Ford SUV with the engine running and the heat on. Almost May. There were patches of snow on the ground and we needed heat. This weather certainly proved that April was the cruelest month. Sometimes I wonder why we live in New England. I've heard the suggestion that it builds character, but by now, mine ought to be built. Seriously, universe, I would like the occasional break.

He came around to open my door for me, giving me a shy smile as I climbed in. "So now we are going to pick up a drunk?" he said.

"That's about the size of it. It's Heidi Basham's father, Ted. He seems to have gone into town and got himself pickled."

"Pickled?"

"Uh, intoxicated."

He drove us slowly through the campus, waving at several students that we passed, and out the gate where news vans lurked, turning right without being told. "This is all very sad for Heidi," he said.

"I just hope she's okay."

"I also."

"I wanted to follow those tracks," he said. "The ones I told you about. Before it got dark or the snow is all melted. But there are police everywhere, and we are also rather busy on the campus today. Heidi's friends are asking me what I know and if there is anywhere else that they should look."

He snapped on his turn signal. "When my shift is done, if she isn't found, I will go back out there. Try to follow those tracks. I am very worried about Heidi."

"You know Heidi?"

"Oh yes. This is Simmons, Miss Thea. It is a special place. The students here see those who work for them. We are not invisible, as in many places. And Heidi is very kind. She is sometimes asking me about where I am from. And about my family. I tell her that I have a small boy who loves to read, and she has given me some books. She is a very lovely and special girl, and I worry for her."

We turned left onto Goodfellow Street. Such an old-fashioned New England name. *Right about now,* I thought, as we drove past a row of stately white homes set back from the road behind genuine white picket fences, *we could use some good fellows.* Amad seemed like a good fellow.

For a moment, staring out at houses that could be called homes, where people lived lives without crisis and drama and bodies, my "I don't wanna" was ascendant, instead of my perpetual sense of duty. I wished we could drive forever. I could admire yards, and the bravery of bright yellow daffodils undaunted by the snow. I could imagine living in one of these appealing houses, and staring out at my own yard through tall glass windows. I can get kind of maudlin when I'm tired, and I badly wanted a house.

Amad rescued me from my pity party. "Excuse me, Miss Thea," he said, "but what are we to do with this pickled gentleman once we have captured him?"

I must have been punchy from lack of sleep, because his question made me laugh out loud. It felt good, in the midst of this awful situation, to laugh.

"We're to take him to the headmaster's house, where you are to stand guard so he doesn't escape."

"This is true?" he said. "How am I to restrain him?"

Gareth and I hadn't discussed that, so I said, "I don't know, Amad. All I know is that if he wanders around in an intoxicated state and shoots his mouth off, he could make Simmons's situation much worse. We have better things to do with our time right now than worry about bad parents behaving badly."

"This is all very sad for Heidi," he repeated. "Well, I will do my best. Maybe he will be so drunk…pickled…that he will go to sleep." He laughed as he said "pickled," clearly delighted with the word.

We pulled up behind the inn and parked as close to the door as we could get. Amad switched off the engine. He unfastened his seatbelt, remaining seated in a very cop-like posture with his hands at ten and two, and said, "Now what do we do?"

Perhaps he, too, had wanted to take the journey but never arrive. "Fetch him," I said.

He didn't move, and I realized his dilemma. He was an Arab-looking man in a very white Massachusetts town, being asked to enter a very New England-y tavern and remove a drunken white guy who might make a scene. He had a uniform, but it carried no weight outside the campus, and we were living in an era where people were suspicious of Middle Eastern-looking folks. This town was better—or should have been—Simmons had an international population and they came into town to shop and eat, but he wasn't a student.

"Both of us. Together," I said. "I am not sending you in there alone."

His hands dropped from the wheel and he got out of the car.

Together, with me in the lead, we walked up the slippery brick walk to a shiny black door with a sign that read: Nathaniel Stow Tavern. I wondered if anywhere in the world there might be a place called the Rebecca Stow Tavern. But no. Women stayed home and tended the fire and made soap. Men went out to the tavern to drink.

I was still kind of punchy.

The black door opened to a small vestibule with benches on both sides, pegs on the wall for coats, and two of those pseudo-candlelight lanterns with flame-shaped bulbs that gave off a sickly kind of flickering yellow light. Beyond there was a larger room, lots of dark wood and slightly better lighting. The bar was a thick, heavily shellacked slab of pine. The tables were graced with red checked tablecloths and faux candles in crackled yellow glass and plenty of people were tucking into their lunches. The inviting aromas of their lunches made my stomach growl.

At the far end of the room was a big brick fireplace with a real fire, flanked by two high-backed settles fronted by low tables. On one of the tables were the remnants of several drinks and a lunch. The tables in that area, which should have been the most popular on a day as gray and damp as this, were empty. The reason was instantly clear.

One of the settles was occupied by a man whose posture was perfectly balanced between vertical and horizontal. Oblique, my brain supplied. He was singing a tuneless tune, and keeping time with one unsteady hand. Tucked into a voluminous overcoat, he looked like a pile of rumpled laundry. Or a bum.

The beefy man behind the bar was watching him warily. He turned when we came in, took in Amad's uniform, and said, "Simmons?"

Amad nodded.

The man shook his head and said, "He's all yours. Good luck."

"He paid his tab?" I asked.

"We're square. Just get him the hell…uh…heck out of here. Please. He's the maudlin, obnoxious kind. Keeps trying to talk to people about what a shit father he is."

I wanted to ask what else Basham had said, but this guy wanted Basham out right now, as did we. I looked over at the man on the settle. "We may need your help."

"Which will be gratefully given." His long-suffering smile was fleeting. "Tell Gareth the asshat didn't say anything too damaging."

Ah. Small towns.

I crossed the room with Amad and the bartender behind me and approached Ted Basham.

"We need you back at Simmons, Mr. Basham," I said in my best "don't mess with me" voice. "There have been developments."

"Wha...who? Have you? Found? Oh, God...what? Where am I?...How did I? I only meant to...My leg was hurting, see, and I..." A sloppy grin. "Just getting me some lunch."

A mostly liquid lunch. The shape of the glasses suggested martinis. The mess on the plate showed his sandwich had been more dissected than eaten.

His babble was a string of self-centered, "I" and "I" and "Me." Her friends said Heidi was a sweet and kind girl. Now that I'd met the parents, I couldn't help wondering how that miracle happened.

He stumbled to his feet, and Amad, moving with unexpected speed, handed him his crutch and took his free arm. The crutch was muddy and damp, like he'd been hiking in a swamp.

Fortunately, Basham was a docile drunk and came quietly. I went ahead to open the doors. Amad led Basham with a firm, "don't give me any crap" grip, and the bartender came behind just in case Basham hesitated. He hovered until we had Basham in the backseat, securely belted in, and the door shut. Then, with a wave and a muttered, "Thank God!" he turned and went back inside.

I climbed into the passenger seat, Amad got behind the wheel, and we headed back to Simmons with our prisoner.

Both Amad and I contemplated homicide several times on the short drive back to the campus. Amad had a pretty good poker face—or cop's face—and the disguise of a full beard, so his reaction didn't show there. I was reading the grip of his hands on the wheel.

It started before we were even out of the parking lot. That's when Basham started whining. Despite the way he slurred his words, I could understand most of what he said. If I thought I was having a pity party on the way to pick him up, I didn't know what a pity party was.

"Christ, I'm such an ass! Knew I never shoulda left her with them. Knew Norris couldn't be trusted," he said. "If I only coulda taken her, I woulda. But ya can't keep your kid...in a car trunk. Right?" He snuffled. "You gotta...buh...lieve...me. Love my little girl. Do anything...for her. Did something for her."

It was such an odd statement. I wondered what he thought he'd done for Heidi.

A police officer is not supposed to question a suspect when the person is intoxicated. It might make the statements inadmissible. Or so I've heard. But despite the accusations sometimes hurled at me, I was not a cop. I did a cop-like thing, though, kicking myself for not doing it earlier. I got out my phone and started recording the conversation.

"What do you mean 'Norris couldn't be trusted'?" I asked. I asked it in a sweetly conversation voice, not the "come with me or else" voice I'd used in the bar.

"You know. Treated her like shit but kept staring at her like a man isn't supposed to look at kid." Basham fumbled with the controls on the door. "Mind if I roll down the window. It's hot back here."

Amad lowered the window slightly.

"Thanks." Basham sucked in air loudly and exhaled a breath so redolent of alcohol I wondered, briefly, if babies could be affected by second-hand alcohol.

"At the time that you and your wife were separating and custody was being decided, did you suspect that General Norris had an inappropriate interest in your daughter?"

"Oh, yeah. I sure did."

Beside me, Amad's hands took a death grip on the wheel.

"Yet you left her with them, knowing your ex-wife would be unlikely to protect Heidi?"

"Feel awful about it." Another big inhale and boozy exhale. "But Heidi said she could take care of herself. Heidi's always...pretty mature for her age." He stumbled over the word 'mature' but I thought that was what he said.

I tried to keep anger from my voice as I said, "How old was Heidi when you left?"

"Thirteen. Fourteen. Ya know, I lose track sometimes. The years fly past. Busy with the band. Man's work...important, right? Remember when she was just…little bitty thing, learning to walk with that prosthesis." The word 'prosthesis' nearly floored him. "Hardly held her back at all. 'Course, Lorena found it repulsive. She hated helping Heidi put it on. Hated getting her fitted for bigger ones as she grew. Heidi such a cute lil' thing. 'Cept for this. Lorena so mean. Mean to me, too. Said my fault…baby wasn't perfect."

And Heidi still kept hoping her mother would love her. The sadness of it stabbed me like a dagger.

We slowed at a crosswalk to let a speed-walking pod of senior citizens cross. They wore brightly colored sweats and chattered merrily as they anything but speed-walked across the street. I put a cautioning hand on Amad's arm, and saw his death grip on the wheel slacken.

"Do you believe General Norris is the father of Heidi's baby?"

"Nah. Figure that asshole Norris too smart for that. He'd use precaution, ya know?"

Kill. Him. I was going to kill this man if we didn't get back to Simmons soon. I tried to repress my anger and consider what other questions I should ask while he was too impaired to be cautious. "So, not The General. Who, then?"

"Told you this morning. Dee or Dum—horny guys, wouldn't care what they nailed. Or Dennis because he's just mean enough to do that. Or what's his name. Music guy. Name doesn't begin…letter D. Bill. Will. Better if it was Dill."

Basham began to sing.

Amad squeezed so hard I thought the steering wheel would crack.

"I thought Will, the music teacher, was her friend?"

"Is. Very. Good. Friend. I think. Was friend. Not anymore."

"Why isn't he her friend anymore?"

A delighted, demonic cackle from the backseat. "'Cuz he's out of the picture."

CHAPTER 23

W e were back at Simmons, the turn onto the campus just ahead, but this was no time to stop. It would be far better to keep driving and keep Basham talking and see what else he would say. I didn't want to tip Basham off, though, by saying something to Amad. Basham had gone back to singing one of his tuneless tunes, and probably wouldn't notice if we missed the turn.

I didn't have to say anything. Amad sailed past the entrance without a word.

"When you saw her yesterday, did Heidi say anything about her baby's father?"

A sound that was sort of grunt and sort of laugh. "You forget. My daughter has never had sex and never had a baby."

"You don't believe her?"

"Well, I do. And I don't. Innocent. Naïve. Could of…not…understood." He yawned. "Feeling very tired," he said. "Re…covering. Accident, ya know? Be good to lie down a bit. We almost there?"

Like a little kid on a car trip. "You said it could be Dee or Dum or the music teacher, Will. But now you say Will is out of the picture. Is that because things have been said that make you believe he's not the father?"

"Nope." He said it smugly, in an "I know something you don't know" tone, and yawned again.

We were on the verge of losing him. "You think he *is* the father?"

"It doesn't matter now, does it?"

"Why not, Ted?"

"Told you. Out of the picture. Told him. Stay away. My little girl, right?"

He wasn't going to make things any clearer. "So we should focus on Dee or Dum?"

Another smug "Nope." Then, "Dee is out of the picture, too. For…" A hesitation so long I thought he'd gone to sleep, but apparently he was just organizing his words, because eventually he said, "for a different reason. Man's gotta do…my little girl 'n all that."

He trailed off and went silent. When I looked back, his eyes were closed.

We were losing him. As weariness and his last drink overtook him, he was morphing into the stupidly wily, game-playing, maudlin drunk. We'd probably lost our moment. I looked at Amad, who gave a slight shake of his head. I didn't know if he meant "give up" or whether he wanted to ask a question himself.

He turned onto a side road and drove more slowly. "Mr. Basham, your daughter Heidi cared very much for this music teacher, this man named Will?"

Basham made an affirmative sound.

"So if he is, as you say, 'out of the picture,' this will make her very sad, yes?"

Another affirmative sound.

"And this man cares for your daughter, just as she cares for him? Is this right?"

A slurred "right" from the back seat.

"So why, if I may ask, are you pleased he is out of the picture at a time when Heidi needs people who care about her most?"

Basham was silent. I held my breath, wondering if he would reply. There were sounds of him moving around on the seat, and some sighs.

Finally he said, "Oh shit. I don't know. I thought I was doing the best thing for Heidi. Her dad and all that."

"And what thing was that?" Amad again.

He seemed to be doing a good job of getting responses from Basham, so I let him take the lead. Maybe, as intoxication crept over him, Basham stopped responding to the female voice, a ploy he'd likely mastered dealing with his ex-wife.

We slowed to pass a woman walking her dog. Dark clothes, wooded area, dark dog, walking with her back to traffic. Some people, I am convinced, either have a death wish or are totally oblivious of their surroundings.

I was so busy being judgmental I almost missed Basham's reply.

"I told the damned fool not to come. Stay away from…Heidi. My daughter. Not his."

It wasn't what I was expecting. "You knew William McKenzie was coming here?" I said.

"Yup."

"How? Heidi told you?"

"Nope."

He sure liked saying "Nope." I hoped that wasn't all he planned to say. Amad and I held our breaths in sync, like we'd been doing this for years, waiting.

"It was that boy. He told me."

This was like pulling teeth. "What boy?"

"That one who is Heidi's friend. The one who called me."

I racked my brain, trying to recall which of Heidi's friends had called her father. Bella had. And one of the boys. "Was it Ronnie? Or Jaden?"

Silence. Some rustling. An extremely loud yawn.

Come on, I thought. Answer the question before you fall asleep.

"Ronnie."

"And Ronnie told you that he'd also called Will McKenzie?"

"That...Heidi...called him. Well, damn! I wasn't gonna have my place ush...uh...surped...by some goddamned music...musician. I'm uh goddamned father, aren't I."

Biologically. Jeez. First his disappearance and now this. But he had been calling her. I was in an emotional rocking chair, swayed back and forth as the conversation progressed. My initial impression had been of a loving but ineffectual father who'd tried to come through when his daughter needed him. Now I wasn't sure what to think. This sounded more like a pissing contest.

Evidently, neither was Amad. "Mr. Basham," he said. "Are you telling us you came here not because Heidi needed you but because she called Mr. McKenzie instead of you?"

"Nope."

"Then why did you come?"

"Friends...girl with that squeaky little voice...and that boy. Thought. Ought to be family here. Said Heidi had asked for me. I think. Uh. Dunno." A little chuckle. "I am family. Sorta. I guess. Got turfed out, but...Then Lorena's bitchy little sister said what kind of a father was I anyway and did I want the goddamn general handling things instead. That..." A long pause while he assembled his words. "Got me. Don't wanna goddamned General Norris acting like father to my girl. Not the way he wants to act like a father. Is there uh..." Another pause while Basham sorted his words. "Funny father like funny uncle?"

He laughed hysterically at his own joke. "Heidi already...hash...uh...has...funny uncle. Not really funny though."

I was still struggling to square the father who called often, the one his daughter confided in, with this guy, who seemed to be saying he'd come partly because people told him he should, and partly because he was engaged in a "who has the right" contest with General Norris and his ex-wife. And the music teacher. I asked for some clarity.

"So, Ted…you said you talk to Heidi often on the phone. That the two of you are close, right? So why would you hesitate about coming if she needed you?"

I sensed Amad didn't like my question and was about to intervene, but Basham answered before he could. "Phone…is…easy."

"Heidi didn't want General Norris to come, right?"

"Ri…"

"Do you know if he brought Dee or Dum with him?"

Probably I was jumping the gun. Asking the question without laying any groundwork first. Amad thought so. He shot me a disapproving look.

"Dunno," Basham said. "Dunno whether Dee came because…general asked…or just such a suck up. He's…" There was rustling in the back as Basham rearranged himself of the seat. "…not okay. Not near my daughter. Not…a problem anymore." More rustling, then Basham said, "Oops. Not meant to say that." He fell silent. Then, "You're not the cops anyway, are you?"

"No. We work for the school, Ted."

"Good. So forget what…I said. K?"

"I think I have taken a wrong turn," Amad said. "Excuse me while I turn us around." He pulled into what looked like the entrance to a small park, but didn't reverse and change direction.

"Mr. Basham," he said, "do you know where your daughter is?"

Basham didn't reply.

"Were you involved in her disappearance?"

"Not really," Basham said.

Not really? I clenched my hands together to keep from turning around and whacking him. Whacking is not part of my job, and is normally frowned upon in independent school circles.

"What does that mean, please?"

"I was going to meet her. Down by the river. Take her away somewhere. My daughter. My baby. Then her goddamned mother and that jerk showed up with Dee trailing behind them like a little poop. I guess I was upset. There was a struggle. Heidi ran. And I left."

I had one more question. Well. No. I had dozens of questions, but this was about getting a clearer picture of who was in the picnic grove. "What about William McKenzie? Was he there?"

"Not for long."

"Was Heidi involved in what happened to Lt. Crosby? Uh…to Dee?"

He heaved a huge sigh, then uttered his favorite word. "Nope."

"Someone hit him. Crosby, I mean. Was that you?"

He yawned. "That…is all…I am going to say. Maybe…already…said too much. Can we go now, please? I'm badly…need nap."

He didn't wait to reach Gareth's house. Only a moment later, the car was filled with bubbling snores.

Amad headed back to Simmons.

"It is all very unclear," Amad said. "He must be questioned again when he is sober. But somehow he is involved in what happened where we found that body and Heidi's coat."

I absolutely agreed. Questioned for sure, and not by me. If my own interviews with Basham were any guide, whoever questioned him would have a job of it.

I was racking my brain, trying to recall if his crutch was wet and muddy when he was in Gareth's office this morning. If he seemed unsurprised by her disappearance when we went to the infirmary early this morning after learning that Heidi was missing. I just didn't know. He only had one crutch with him. Was there a second one somewhere that might show evidence of a struggle? Did I remember correctly that when he first appeared in Gareth's office, he had had two?

Why had everyone been down there in the picnic grove last night? I could imagine Heidi, in the midst of her distress, asking her father for help leaving Simmons, where she felt judged, or to escape from The General, who she believed presented a threat. He was a wimp, but pretty much all she had. But then why had General and Mrs. Norris shown up in such an obscure place? How could they have known? And why Dee? Uh, Lt. Sandy Crosby? Was there more information available from the innkeeper about the Norrises' coming and goings?

Too many questions on too many fronts. It all made my head hurt. Those questions needed answers and sorting it out would need staff. This was a job for supercops, not for a mere consultant.

As the landscape flew past, I puzzled about the timeline. When had all of this taken place? If what he was saying was true, how had Basham gotten out of Gareth's house without anyone noticing? What the heck had happened in that clearing? Had Basham assaulted Lt. Crosby or had someone else? What the heck did he mean by "I was upset" and "there was a struggle? Was there some disturbing significance to his remark "my daughter. My baby?"

And why, in the midst of all he'd said, had there not been a single word of concern about his daughter? Because he was so self-involved? Or because he had her hidden somewhere and knew she was safe?

What a sordid mess.

CHAPTER 24

It took two of us to wrestle our nearly comatose passenger out of the vehicle and up the three steps into Gareth's guest wing. A guest wing with its own entrance that made it clear Basham's nocturnal escape—assuming he was telling the truth—was far easier than I'd imagined. We half carried him into the guestroom, pulled off his overcoat and shoes, and covered him with a fluffy duvet. He didn't rouse enough to say thanks, just rolled onto his side, burrowed into the pillows, and completed his journey to dreamland.

I took a quick look around, but didn't see another crutch anywhere, and if there were dirty or bloody clothes somewhere, they weren't visible. Plenty of other tossed clothing and papers were strewn about, though, and there was a half empty bottle of Scotch on the bedside table. He really hadn't needed to go out and get himself drunk in town. He could have done it right here.

It was a beautiful room, cozy and inviting, done in rich forest green and burgundy, with a gas fireplace and comfy armchair beside it. All of which, given the careless mess he'd made, seemed completely lost on Ted Basham.

We stepped outside and Amad said, "I will drive you back to the Administration Building, then come back here to keep an eye on Mr. Basham."

As he drove, Amad said, "What are you thinking about this, Miss Thea?"

"I am thinking that this is a job for the police and that Basham's crutches have suddenly become objects of great interest." I sighed. "I am wondering how did everyone know that Heidi would be down there in the picnic woods?"

"These are good questions," he said. "And what about this person called 'Dee?' Is he the one that has been found dead?"

I sighed again. I was very tired. A meal and a nap would be awfully welcome. "I believe that Dee, or Lt. Sandy Crosby, is the victim down there in the woods. He works for General Norris, but there is no logical reason for him to be here."

"How it is they say? The plot thickens? Is that it?"

"That's it, Amad."

I was sure we had more things to discuss, but he had to get back to guarding Basham, who had proved himself utterly untrustworthy, and I had to get back to Gareth. "Thanks for coming along," I said. "I could never have done this without you."

"I cannot say 'my pleasure' as this is not a pleasant business, but I do think that together we got some most disturbing information from Heidi's father. Will you be sharing it with Dr. Wilson, or should I pass it along to Chief Greenberg?"

I could tell passing information to the chief was not a possibility that appealed to him. Just from my brief contact with the man, I knew he'd likely be dismissive. Anyway, I was the one who'd recorded it.

"I'll tell Gareth."

"Thank you," he said.

I longed to stay in the warm car and be driven about, free from the tasks of parsing Basham's ramblings and helping

Gareth handle his crisis. When Amad stopped, though, I hopped out, and he drove away. I headed for Gareth's office, and the sandwiches I hoped were not too stale.

The food trolley was untouched. I didn't know if Gareth had been too busy to eat, or had politely waited for me. "Eat something," I muttered as I fell on a slightly dried out tuna sandwich. The first half disappeared quickly. There wasn't time for the kind of ladylike eating that my mother had raised me to do. It was more like Andre's cop-practical "eat when you can."

Gareth shook his head. "I can't eat," he said. He was practically tearing his hair out as he waited for my report. I gave it between bites and sips of lukewarm coffee. The half sandwich kept hunger at bay for a moment, while we caught up, but I needed to eat more. MOC was hungry. And there were lovely cookies, too.

"He was pretty fuzzy on details…slurred speech and a lot of rambling, but it sounded like he was there in the picnic grove with Heidi last night, that The General was there, too, and that Basham may have tangled with Lt. Crosby."

Gareth was staring at me like I'd taken leave of my senses. "Impossible. He's fantasizing," he said. "Basham was in my house, asleep, all night."

"He was in the guest wing, wasn't he?"

Gareth nodded.

"And doesn't it have a private entrance?"

Another nod.

"So it is possible that he slipped out, whatever took place down there happened, and then he slipped back in?"

Gareth threw up his hands in a gesture of surrender. "Possible," he said. "So are we to think that Basham arranged this with Heidi when he visited her? That that scheme was what led to her asking Jaden to tamper with the alarm?"

"Or they arranged it in a phone call. But what was Heidi's mother doing there? And The General? Even if Heidi wanted to get away from Simmons, she would never make a plan that involved him."

"Unless in her emotional state, she confided the plan to her mother, who swore not to involve General Norris and went back on her word. Or unless everything we've been told, and everything we think we know about Heidi is untrue. Which I would need a lot more evidence to believe. And how would we get that?"

I brushed crumbs off my face and the front of my sweater, feeling fearfully far from sartorial splendor. "Talk to…"

"Dammit, Thea. I know we have to talk to her friends." His hands clenched. "I am trying to run a school committed to openness, honesty, and responsibility, yet I am forced to deal with a set of parents who wouldn't know the truth if it bit them."

I started to speak but he cut me off. "A man has been murdered. Much as I dislike doing so, we have to tell Miller and Flynn about your conversation with Ted Basham." He went behind his desk and threw himself into his chair. I half-expected the chair would crumple under his weight, but it was a sturdy oak and leather number more than half a century old. A chair as rugged and sturdy as Gareth himself. It only tilted and groaned.

He waved a fistful of pink message slips. "With all this damned interviewing, when do I get time to run the school?"

"Bit by bit," I said.

"Which bit shall we start with?" he said. "Miller and Flynn?"

I nodded.

He was reaching for the phone and I was reaching for the second half of my sandwich when there was knock on the door and his assistant stuck her head in.

"There are four students out here who insist on speaking with you, Dr. Wilson. They say they won't leave until they do."

CHAPTER 25

Gareth spread his hands in a gesture of resignation. He was supposed to be in charge, but circumstances were out of his control today. "Give us a minute," he said, "and then send them in."

I stared regretfully at the sandwich I'd been about to eat. Better to get this interview over with first. MOC didn't think that was a good idea, though, and gave me a couple of vigorous kicks to underscore the point. Mothers-to-be are supposed to pay attention to nutrition, and I've always been awful about eating regular meals. Obviously, this child was well aware of that.

I sent a quick text to Miller, saying we had some information to share. I wanted to offload my memories of the conversation with Basham while it was still fresh, though I expected he and Flynn would still be tied up at the scene. Then the students came in.

Interview was absolutely the wrong word for what happened next. It was an invasion. We'd barely had time to draw a breath before there was a knock on the door and Bella, Jaden, Ronnie, and a girl I hadn't met, I assumed she was probably Tiverton, tumbled into the room, a jumble of voices filled with urgency and demands. Four distressed teenagers can create a lot of commotion. From the cacophony, the words "Heidi," "body," and "alive?" were clearest.

Gareth simply stood and held up his hand—the school meeting signal for coming to order.

Distraught as they all were, it worked. All four fell silent, waiting for him to speak.

"Let's all sit down," he gestured toward his two big couches, "and talk about this." He remained standing until they were all seated, then he and I sat. He took a moment to reintroduce me and remind them why I was there, and then went immediately to their most urgent question.

"Yes, there was a body found down by the river, but it is not Heidi. She is still missing, and we still need your help to find her."

"Whose body is it then?" Ronnie asked.

"What about her stepfather? Did you ask him where she is?" Jaden interrupted, not having focused on Ronnie's question. "She was so afraid of him, and so worried about him coming here. And if she didn't know about this pregnancy, who better to be the cause than someone right there in the house and already acting like some skeevy, child-molesting creep. We told you how he acted."

There was a chorus of yesses as the others leaned in, waiting for his answer, the body, for the moment, overshadowed by what he had to say.

"Her stepfather has gone back to California," Gareth said.

"How do you know?" Ronnie said, which was a very good question.

"Her mother and stepfather were staying at the same inn that I am," I said. "They left early this morning. I saw them get in their car, and the innkeeper said they were going to the airport."

Did a culture of truth-telling mean we had to tell them we now wondered if his departure had really happened?

"How could they do that?" Bella said, her delicate face tight with outrage. "It's her mother's job to be here looking after her. Why, I'll bet she hasn't even seen the baby yet, and that baby is her granddaughter."

"She's a sorry excuse for mother," the girl named Tiverton said. "We're a better family to Heidi than she is."

"Yeah. Where's her mom in all this?" Ronnie said, voicing the group's outrage. "Did she book it for California as well? She's never been willing to step up for Heidi."

"Mrs. Norris was contacted about Heidi's disappearance before she got on a plane. She's supposed to come back here," I said, "to help us deal with Heidi's disappearance." It felt like a dumb thing to say since she'd never appeared.

"I'll bet he didn't go back to California at all. I'll bet he took her," Ronnie said. "I mean, who had more motive to want to shut her up?"

He looked around at the others, who murmured their concurrence.

"Probably they both took her. Heidi says her mother always puts him first."

"I hope not," Bella said quietly. Her voice was so small and soft I thought none of the others had heard it, but they fell silent, waiting for her to finish speaking. It was such a Simmons thing—this respect for each other's voices.

"How would we know they really left, Dr. Wilson?" Bella asked. "I mean, this is so suspicious, Heidi and her parents both disappearing around the same time. Is there a way to know?"

Honesty was the campus rule. Much as he might have liked to dissemble, Gareth answered. "We don't know if they left, or if Heidi is with them, Bella." He leaned forward, his hands knotted, his face betraying his anxiety. "We're still sorting this out. When I spoke with her mother this morning, she said General Norris was flying back to California, and she was returning to Simmons to help us deal with Heidi's disappearance. Only the police have the resources to check and see if one, or both of them, got on a plane, but they are tied up right now, investigating that…uh…body down in the picnic grove."

He looked at me, perhaps hoping to be rescued, but I didn't have anything to offer, so he took a breath and carried on. "Whatever the status of her mother and stepfather, it would be very helpful to us, in finding Heidi, if we could get the deepest possible understanding of her, her relationships, fears, concerns about people who might have posed a threat to her—anything you know about her circumstances before she came to Simmons. For example, do you know why Heidi was so distressed that her stepfather was coming. Or who she might call for help."

But Ronnie wasn't done. "I bet they grabbed her, or tricked her into meeting them by saying they'd help her, and now she's in their clutches. Or else they…"

He stumbled to a stop, not wanting to finish the thought. "What about her useless father? Where is he in all this? I saw him driving away this morning, and I haven't seen that fancy red Beamer coming back."

This was a far less confident and bombastic Ronnie than the boy we'd seen earlier. Watching him, I realized something I'd missed before. While Ronnie might try to wear the guise of "just a friend," he was in love with Heidi. It was also clear that the others knew this, and respected it.

"Headmaster," the girl named Tiverton interrupted. "Before we talk about Heidi, do you know who it was…the person who was killed?"

Tiverton was a tall, athletic Latina dressed in yoga pants and a plaid flannel shirt open over a tank top, with hair even wilder than mine. She was gorgeous and tough and owned her height and strength and kickass figure with an easy comfort. It was utterly un-PC of me, but I couldn't avoid thinking that a photo of the four of them would have made a perfect cover for the school's marketing materials. They were diversity personified. They would also have been great co-stars of a teen superhero series. Imagining teen superheroes sure beat what we were doing here.

"Yes, Dr. Wilson," Jaden said quietly. "Since you want our help 'finding' Heidi, can you tell us who was killed?"

I hadn't noticed it before, because he was so nervous, but there was a quiet authority in Jaden's calm voice. Evidently the others recognized it, because they all fell silent and waited for Gareth's response. All of them had authority and agency, as great superheroes should. It looked like Heidi had been wise—and lucky—in her choice of friends. These four absolutely had her back.

"We don't have any official confirmation of his identity," Gareth said. "It was a male, maybe late twenties to early thirties."

"Official confirmation?" Ronnie scoffed. "Come on, Headmaster. We're her best friends, and we're concerned. What Tivvy asked is whether *you* know who he is. Like if it's her stepfather or her dad or whatever. Do you? 'Cuz if you do, you need to tell us."

Boy, a culture of honesty could be such a bitch.

Gareth rubbed his eyes wearily. He looked exhausted. He needed to drink that restorative cup of tea we'd discussed earlier and feed that big, athletic body. He was running on fumes.

"We think we do," he said, "and if we're right, it's a very peculiar thing. One we can't easily explain and one that we fear will make Heidi even more distressed than she already is."

He stared out the window, but I knew he was really viewing an internal picture of Heidi's face when she learned the troubling news. Unless Heidi had been in that clearing, as her father's drunken rambles suggested, and already knew. In which case, she was even more badly in need of comfort and safety than ever. Dammit! We needed to know what had happened down there last night, and all the players who could tell us were either dodging us or passed out.

"Headmaster," Bella's shy voice chimed in, "we know this is hard for you, just like it is for us. We're not here to attack you or make unreasonable demands. We aren't here to accuse you of anything. We're here because our friend is in trouble. She's missing and we want to help you find her. We want to comfort her and let her know that she's believed and cared about. Which, because of how her parents behave, isn't easy for her to accept. So please be honest with us about what you know. And let us help you if we can."

The other three, in their individual ways, seconded Bella's statement.

The air in the room shimmered with tension. The clock on the wall said that Gareth had to be at a meeting in twenty minutes. Before that, he and I needed to talk and, if possible, update Miller and Flynn.

Gareth looked at the four of them. I knew what he was thinking—that the news they insisted he deliver would amp up their anxiety about Heidi. But honesty was the rule they'd all agreed to live by, so he took a deep breath, let it slowly out, and said, "I truly wish I didn't have to tell you this, because it's very bad news indeed. We believe the person who was killed is a man named Lt. Alexander Crosby. He went by Sandy, and we believe Heidi's father, and quite possibly Heidi herself, referred to him as Dee and another of General Norris's aides, as Dum."

Their reactions were as individual as they were. "Oh dear. No!" Bella said, looking stricken. "Why would he be here? He's definitely not her friend."

Ronnie didn't speak, but his big fists curled like he wanted to punch something.

Jaden studied his shoes, and Tiverton said, "Are you sure? Because how would you know that it's him? It's not like he's been here to visit Heidi or anything. He's just a slimeball perv, and one of the reasons Heidi wanted to come here. You've never seen him, so—"

"So yes, we can't be certain," Gareth agreed. "But Ms. Kozak saw him, his…uh…the victim. We've looked him up on the internet, and from his photographs, it does appear Crosby is the person who was attacked…and it is his body that is down there in our assembly clearing. His death that the police are now investigating."

Bella's voice came from behind two small hands clasped over her face. "This will be too terrible for Heidi. If you hate someone, and wish them dead, and then…" Her hands dropped. "But where is she? What's happened to Heidi? If

Dee was here, she's got even more reason to flee. Does that mean Dum is here, too? I mean, they'd only come if her stepfather wanted them here. There's no other reason."

Her words accelerated. "Was she there? Does she know that he…that Dee has been killed? Have the police taken her? Has the killer taken her? How can something like this happen here, where we're supposed to be safe?"

It was the central question for everyone on the Simmons campus.

Jaden moved closer and put an arm around her shoulders.

There was silence, and then Ronnie repeated Bella's question. "Was Heidi there? Down in the picnic grove? Did she see what happened?" He popped to his feet. "Headmaster, have they taken her?"

Gareth drooped like someone had drained a few pints of his blood as his four students stared at him, waiting for answers he didn't have.

All he could do was take refuge in honesty. "We don't know if Heidi was there. Our security staff found a pale blue jacket we presume to be hers. There are tracks in the remnants of snow, and the police will have the dogs out searching for anything which might provide some answers. In the meantime, we hope for the best, assume she's still all right, just hiding somewhere, and put our heads together to come up with places we might look, and anyone we should talk to who might have ideas about where she's gone."

There was a moment of silence, like at a church service after the benediction, and then everyone started talking at once.

This time, it was my turn to stand and hold up my hand for silence. "We want, and need, to hear what you have to say, but while we talk, Dr. Wilson and I need to eat. This day started very early for us."

They looked at me blankly.

I pointed to the trolley with the sandwiches, tea, and coffee. "Maybe you'd like some cookies?" I said, reluctantly offering the plate.

In my experience, while adults may lose their appetites under stress, teenagers need to snack. It worked. They fell on the cookies like they'd been starving in the wilderness, while Gareth shot me a grateful look and took a sandwich.

As we ate, the four of them provided what more they could about Heidi's home situation, and naming three of the same four possible suspects Ted Basham had. Beyond that, they didn't have too much to offer. None of them knew of any day students who were close enough to Heidi to have picked her up and spirited her away, nor of anyone in the area to whom Heidi might have turned for help if she was desperate to leave the Simmons campus.

It was then that I asked my last question, the one meant for closure, to dismiss them. I wasn't hoping for an answer. "Thinking beyond Simmons," I said, "is there anyone from back home she might have called on? A close friend or close friend's parent, perhaps?" I was thinking about Stephanie, who'd also left for boarding school, or her mother who had tangled with General Norris.

They did mention Stephanie, and Bella said she could probably find Stephanie's contact information. She thought Heidi had it somewhere on her desk. "They don't talk much, but I know they were close."

The only other person they could think of was her music teacher back in California, William McKenzie, and they all thought it highly unlikely, even though Heidi had called him, that he could have come. He wasn't a rich man, they said, and was hardly likely to jump on a plane and get tangled up in the mess that was going on here.

"He is nice, though," Bella said. "He sends her things, and when he calls, he makes her laugh."

I didn't mention that Ted Basham had suggested McKenzie might be here or that he'd done something to sever his daughter's connection to her music teacher. His ramblings had been too vague.

Their revelations, unenlightening as they were, involved a great deal of consultation and discussion among the four of them. Before I could ask my question about someplace on campus where Heidi might be hiding, based on the comment Dr. Purcell had made, Gareth looked at his watch and announced we had to get to a meeting.

Ronnie repeated what was obviously his greatest concern, "You need to find out if The General really left, because if he didn't, he's where to look for Heidi."

We would ask that, of course, as soon as we could talk with Miller and Flynn.

Ronnie's statement ended the meeting. Before they left, I asked about caves or holes or hiding places, but they had no ideas. The four of them trooped out, leaving me with a host of unanswered questions and the disappointed sense of someone whose eagerly-anticipated ice cream cone has fallen on the sidewalk.

Despite their willingness to help, I still thought there were things they weren't saying. We'd learned little. Heidi was still missing and so was her mother. Her stepfather's whereabouts were unknown. We still had a murdered man on campus. The situation was a private school's worst nightmare.

CHAPTER 26

W hat do you say to an anxious student body when all you have is a deepening crisis and a huge dearth of information? Or, in the current parlance, a big nothingburger? Tell the truth as we knew it, complete with our unanswered questions. That's what Gareth did.

It was both painful to watch—because I knew how much he wished he could give them better information—and impressive, because his finest leadership abilities came out when he spoke. He was open and eloquent, and in such evident distress at the situation, and at their distress, that he convinced the majority of them of the complexity of the situation and the need for patience while he sought answers. He acknowledged their right to be scared. He joined them in their concern and frustration about what was happening on their campus.

In all my years at schools, I had never had a principal, superintendent, dean, or headmaster who exhibited so much leadership, honesty, and compassion. I was reminded of how utterly unsuited I would be to his job. I also felt our vast to-do list growing tentacles that wrapped me in anxiety and despair. At the top of that list? We had to update the Simmons parents about the situation as soon as possible. An on-campus homicide, even if the victim was a stranger to the community, couldn't be ignored. It would be all over the news.

Then we needed to have a sit-down with Miller and Flynn, share what we'd learned about their victim and from Basham's babbling, and hopefully get more information from them. We needed this murder solved and Heidi found so that Simmons could return to some kind of normal. I had such a knot in my stomach about Heidi and all the unknowns it was difficult to breathe.

Gareth was coming to the end of his Q&A session—mostly Q and little A—when there was a reprise of yesterday's dramatic interruption. This time, the person who burst in demanding answers and an immediate interview with Gareth was not Heidi's mother but her father.

If her fellow students had had any doubts about why Heidi had needed to escape her parents and find refuge at Simmons, yesterday's entrance by Mrs. Norris, and now this one by Ted Basham, set them to rest.

When he made his dramatic entrance into Gareth's office, challenging the Norrises' attempt to keep him in the dark about Heidi's situation, Basham's unkempt look had had a deliberateness about it. An artsy, "I just threw this together" assemblage of carefully curated garments that was rather attractive. Today, uncombed, unshaven, and in clothes he'd slept in, the look was grad student laundry basket. His face was still creased from sleep, and quite possibly, as his staggering gait down the aisle suggested, he was not fully recovered from his recent drunkenness. He stood out in this room full of fresh-faced youth like a worm on a flower.

"Headmaster," he bellowed, "I've been entrapped by your underlings. We need to speak at once."

Though "entrapped by your underlings" was a hell of a phrase, this particular underling didn't like it much at all.

"As you can see, Mr. Basham, we are in the middle of a meeting here. Please go and wait for me in my office," Gareth said.

"I'll wait right here," Basham said, thumping with his crutch for emphasis.

"Suit yourself," Gareth said. He shot me a "do something" look and went on with what he'd been saying.

Basham stayed, swaying and occasionally banging his crutch. The students who were near him were frightened. *Where was Amad*, I wondered? He'd seemed capable and responsible dealing with the intruder in Heidi's room, and on our mission to extricate Basham from the bar, so how had he let Basham escape? I tried to get a better look at Basham's crutch. Had he done something to Amad?

Whatever had happened, we needed security here now. I had no qualms about having Basham removed by force, if necessary, and I'd bet Gareth wouldn't, either. Heidi's family had caused enough disruption.

I slipped out to the hall and dialed Amad's number.

"Security. This is Amad," he said.

"It's Thea. I'm in the assembly room and Ted Basham is here making a scene. What happened?" I tried hard not to yell.

"He is there?" Amad sounded astonished.

"You were supposed to be watching him."

"I am so sorry, Miss Thea. I was called away by Chief Greenberg. He had some questions he wanted to ask me about that body in the picnic grove. He said he would have someone else take my place."

I wondered if that someone had actually shown up or if Greenberg had even followed through. Was someone from security lying bludgeoned on the floor in Gareth's guest wing or had Basham been left unguarded?

"We can figure out what happened later. Can you come right away, please, and bring someone to help you?"

"I am on my way," he said.

I debated calling Chief Greenberg and alerting him about Basham's escape. Instead, I put my phone away, wondering whether to go back inside or stay out here. We were lurching from crisis to crisis today like Frankenstein's monster. Triaging what to do next was a challenge. Then I thought about Gareth's wife and small children and the fact that they'd been left unprotected. I got the phone back out.

Greenberg's "Hello," was every bit as charming as I'd expected. "It's Thea Kozak," I said, "Gareth's consultant. Mr. Basham is in the assembly hall, making a scene. Someone was supposed to be watching him at the headmaster's house. I'm concerned that whoever that was, or Gareth's family, might have suffered some harm."

It took a lot of self-control to utter the nearly neutral "might have suffered some harm" when I wanted to scream at him to get over there and check things out.

His "Oh, shit, I forgot," was far from reassuring.

"I have Amad and another of your men responding to the assembly hall," I said. "Maybe you could have someone check on Mrs. Wilson and the children?"

"*You* have people responding?" he said. "Who made you the fucking boss around here?"

Yup. Charming. Deciding to leave musing about what the job of a "fucking boss" might entail for another day, I pushed the button that ended the call. True, it had been a hard few days here on the Simmons campus. The near death of a premature baby and the actual death of a stranger were definitely stressful to deal with. But as chief, it was his *job* to deal with these things and still keep the campus running. Evidently grace under pressure wasn't in his skill set. No wonder Amad had been reluctant to share information with the man.

There was the commotion of heavy, hurrying feet and Amad and the man who had driven Gareth down to the picnic grove came into the hall. I gestured toward the central doors. "He's just inside there. And be careful. He's got his crutch."

"We're supposed to be worried about an old guy on crutches?" the other guard said.

Amad rolled his eyes and gave me a "see what I have to deal with?" look.

"The students are already upset, particularly those sitting near Mr. Basham. Please get him out of there with a minimum of disruption if you can."

The guard, whose name tag read, "Lewiston," headed toward the door without consulting Amad.

"Maybe you want to make a plan?" I told his retreating back.

Definitely the chief's man. He didn't slow, or turn, or show any sign he'd heard me.

"I should go and help him," Amad said.

"You have pepper spray?" I said.

"Sure." He patted his hip.

"Don't be afraid to use it."

Before he could get to the door, though, there was a roar, and a crash, and Lewiston nearly flew through the door. Right on his tail was Basham, flinging himself through the door, swinging his crutch wildly, losing his balance, and then weaving like a cartoon character before finally falling with a thump on his ass. The crutch landed a few feet away, and Amad quickly confiscated it.

Staring at Lewiston, who was bleeding from where Basham had whacked him with the crutch, and Basham himself sitting in stunned surprise on the floor, I wondered how any right-thinking parent could possibly consider sending a beloved child to this school, no matter how appealing its community values were.

"You have a car outside?" I asked.

Amad nodded.

I didn't suppose they had a jail cell at the security office, but I couldn't think where else they might take him. Definitely not back to Gareth's house. Nor to his office. There wasn't time to consult the chief. Any minute the students would come pouring out. "Can you take him back to the security office and keep an eye on him until the headmaster can deal with him?"

Lewiston looked dubious. "The chief doesn't like…" he began.

I ran out of sweetness and light. "Never mind what the chief likes. This is an emergency, okay? Take him there now and tell Greenberg you're to keep him there and wait for a call from Dr. Wilson."

Amad handed me the crutch and bent to grab Basham's arm. I glared at Lewiston, who seemed to be waiting for word from on high, until he grabbed the other arm and Basham was led away. I didn't offer to follow with the crutch. Yes, I had probably overstepped my bounds, and no, I wasn't sorry.

I heard a car door open and shut, then tire sounds as they drove away. I quickly stashed Basham's crutch in a closet, and waited for the assembly to end.

CHAPTER 27

S oon the doors burst open and a flood of students poured out. It was a while before Gareth emerged, and when he did, he was surrounded by students still pelting him with questions. He held up his hand for silence, said, "I'll meet you back at the office," to me, and lowered his hand. It was like he was conducting an orchestra. When the hand came down, the student volume rose again until it filled the hall.

I retrieved the crutch and headed back to his office. The weather had shifted again, and the air that rolled toward me had softened, bringing with it the scents of spring. I walked slowly back to the Administration Building, watching a patch of blue sky and sun poke its way through the clouds. That touch of blue lifted my spirits a bit, as did a walk in the fresh spring air. I walked slowly, unwilling to have this peaceful solitude end. When I got to Gareth's office, I would be plunged back into a morass of confusion and unanswered questions.

My phone buzzed as I walked. Hoping it was Andre, I pulled it out and checked the number. It was one I didn't recognize, but it had a Massachusetts area code, so I answered.

"We're in the headmaster's office," Miller said, "where the heck is he? Where are you?"

I guess no one was all sweetness and light today. "We're on our way back from an assembly. We'll be there in a few minutes."

"Better be," he muttered. "I've got a murder to investigate. Unless you've got something useful to share, I've got no time for this."

Maybe I only imagined it, but I could almost hear him biting his tongue to hold back a string of obscenities. I couldn't blame him. He had a ridiculous mess on his hands just like we did.

Reluctantly, I said goodbye to skies of blue and accelerated my pace, nearly decapitating an exiting student with the crutch as I flew through the door. I apologized and thumped my way up the stairs. I know crutches are supposed to be helpful devices, but right now, the one I was carrying was anything but. Sure. I know. We're not supposed to be carrying them. Crutches are supposed to help carry us.

Miller and Flynn were perched on opposite couches, looking like they were vying for who was most miserable. Their feet were wet and muddy and their shoulders slumped with weariness. I looked at the food trolley. Not much. Two stale sandwiches, two cookies. The coffee pot was empty.

"I could ring for some coffee, if you'd like," I offered.

"That would be great," Flynn said.

Miller only grunted. He was staring at the crutch. "You hurt yourself?" he asked.

"It's Ted Basham's," I said. "He was a bit inebriated and using it inappropriately, so I confiscated it."

"Sounds like there's a story there," Flynn said.

"There is." I parked the crutch and reached for Gareth's phone. "Which I'll tell right after I order some coffee," I said. "It's quite a story. Or part of a story. More in your line than mine."

The way Miller shook his head, I wondered if he still suspected I was some kind of private detective. If so, he was going to be disappointed. I was just a tired and frustrated consultant who couldn't get her work done because new emergencies, like the many heads of a hydra, kept cropping up.

Gareth's assistant was happy to get coffee, and offered more cookies and sandwiches, to which I readily agreed. A steady diet of sandwiches would not be my first choice, but any food was better than no food. MOC agreed.

"And a pot of tea," she said, "Gareth's running himself ragged today."

It was an excellent idea. A nice bracing cup of tea was just what Gareth needed. Or a couple nice bracing Scotches and a break in the action.

I dumped my briefcase on a chair and hung my coat on Gareth's coatrack. I knew they were anxious to get whatever we had to offer and move on. I wasn't sure that I should do that before Gareth joined us, but before I could decide, he rushed through the door, shutting it quickly behind him like he was being chased by something dangerous.

"Another reporter somehow sneaked onto campus," he said, lurching for the phone. "I have to call Security."

Miller tapped the notebook he was holding on his thigh and looked at Flynn. "Seems like we're a pretty low priority around here," he said.

As Gareth muttered, "Get someone over here now!" into the phone, I got out my phone and leaned toward the waiting detectives.

"The man who was murdered," I began.

"Lt. Alexander Crosby," Miller said. "You know him?"

I shook my head. "No. But Heidi knew him. He worked with her stepfather, General Norris. According to her friends, he's one of the reasons she wanted to come to Simmons."

Into the phone, Garth said, "No. No. Don't bring him here, I don't care what he says. Just hang onto him. I'll deal with him when I'm done with my current emergency." He put down the phone with a bit too much force and I guessed Chief Greenberg had been his usual pleasant self. I hoped, when things returned to normal, he'd be showing Greenberg the door.

"I should back up," I said. "This morning, when we were talking with Heidi's friends, they mentioned that there were a couple of young officers who worked for The General who were frequent visitors at the Norrises' house. Heidi's father referred to them as 'Dee and Dum.' Evidently, The General and these two men were in the habit of walking in on Heidi unannounced—her mother reportedly refused to let her have a lock on her door—and it was their intrusions on her privacy, in part, and her mother's unwillingness to protect her, that fueled her decision to come to Simmons."

"Interesting," Flynn said, with a weary smile. "You don't happen to have her hidden away somewhere, do you?"

"I don't," I said, "but the more I hear, the more I wish I did. Or hope she's safe with someone who can protect her."

Miller grunted. "So, aside from confirming a connection between Heidi Basham and our victim, was there something else you wanted to share?"

"I do. I have an audio recording on my phone that you need to hear."

Miller looked at Gareth. "Have you heard this?"

"I have," Gareth said. "Let me give you the background. After we all met with Mr. Basham this morning, he said he was going back to my house to rest, and we agreed we would confer again later in the day. He never returned to my house. A few hours ago, the school received a call from the manager at the Nathaniel Stow Tavern informing us that Mr. Basham was there. He was quite intoxicated and making a scene, and they asked if we would please send someone to pick him up. I sent Thea…Ms. Kozak…and one of our security guards to collect him. This recording was made on the drive back to Simmons. The male voice is one of our security employees, Mr. Dalmar Amad."

Miller looked at me. "You're not a cop, huh?"

I handed him my phone. "If I were a cop, I couldn't have made this recording."

We smiled at each other.

"I did ask him if it was okay, and he agreed."

There was silence in the room as the detectives listened to my recording. Twice.

"It doesn't take that long to get from The Tavern back to here," Flynn said.

"Mr. Amad missed the turn."

Flynn nodded. "He asks good questions, your Mr. Amad, as do you, Ms. Consultant."

I said thank you.

"Where's Mr. Basham now?" Miller asked, his eyes fixed on the crutch. "And is that his crutch?"

Gareth said, "At security, with Chief Greenberg."

I said, "Yes, that's his crutch. I don't remember if he had two of them, but if so, it may be at the headmaster's house in the guest suite."

Miller and Flynn looked at each other and headed for the door.

"My phone," I said, holding out my hand. "I'll send you the recording, but I need this phone."

"*We* need this phone," Miller said.

Oh crap. I was in no mood to play the phone game with a couple detectives. Been there. Done that. Everything I need to do my job is on my phone, plus it's how I contact my family and Andre. My father's condition was still uncertain. Miller was not walking off with it.

"I'm sorry," I said, planting myself firmly between Miller and the door. "My father's just had a heart attack. We're waiting to see if he'll be okay and this is my link to my family. So either I can send that recording to your phone, which is the simplest solution, or we can both go to the nearest phone store where I can buy a new phone and we can wait while I have all of my contacts and data transferred to it. I absolutely respect the work you have to do, and I am doing everything I can to assist you—I believe the recording is evidence of that. I ask that you respect my work, as well."

I hated confrontations, but I wasn't letting my phone disappear into his pocket, his car, his evidence files. A mean cop will run right over a request like that. I know. I've dealt with them. I didn't think Miller was that type, but he probably didn't like having me call his bluff.

There was that tense moment while Miller and I glared at each other. It was fine with me if he won the glaring contest. Just so long as I kept my phone. Then he said, "All right. Send it," and we went through the ritual of connecting our phones.

They would have left then, but the coffee and sandwiches arrived and Miller and Flynn weren't fools. Hot coffee and food were what they needed, so they sat back down.

As they fell upon the food, Gareth said, "Shall I let Chief Greenberg know you're coming?"

I thought we all knew the answer to that, and Miller confirmed it, "No. I think we'll just show up."

And then, because I'd been moving too fast to think clearly, I remembered some things that Heidi's friends had said. The only things that might be useful to the detectives were these: If Dee had come east for some reason related to General Norris's business, business presumably involving Heidi, had Dum come as well, and was he still around? Could he have taken Heidi? Did he still present a threat to her?

The matter of whether Norris had gotten on a plane was something these guys could check, so I asked them about that. "Have you been able to establish whether General Norris, or both the Norrises, flew home today?"

Miller looked like he was considering whether to answer my question when Flynn said, "There's no record of either of them taking a flight today."

I realized, when he said that, how much I'd been hoping the Norrises were gone. Their continued presence seemed like very bad news for Heidi.

"So where on earth are they?" Gareth said. "Do you think…" A pause while he considered how to word his question. "…that Heidi is with them?" The phrase "perhaps unwillingly" was implicit in his question. Violence had occurred down in that clearing last night. If Heidi had been there, and seen what happened, she was either involved or at risk.

"That's the big question, isn't it?" Miller said. "Maybe things will be clearer after we've spoken with Mr. Basham."

I bit my lip to keep from saying "good luck with that." Miller and Flynn were far more formidable opponents than Amad and I, though I sensed that Amad could be a plenty tough and effective interviewer if he was allowed to be.

The only other thing I thought they ought to know about was William McKenzie, and though I shared his name and his connection to Heidi, I thought it was a long shot.

After decimating the offered food, they departed with Basham's crutch in tow and quiet descended on the office.

Gareth said, "Now what?"

He wasn't referring to our work. After the events of the day, we were both expecting another shoe, or perhaps a whole bushel of shoes, to drop.

Minutes later, as we were tackling our message to parents, an unexpected shoe dropped through Gareth's door.

CHAPTER 28

Lorena Norris didn't look much like the elegant, perfectly coiffed woman who had disrupted a school meeting the day before. She looked like something the cat had dragged in. Her uncombed hair was plastered to her head. Her clothes were wet and muddy and she wasn't wearing a coat. She hadn't lost her attitude, though. She swept through the door like a queen and headed for one of Gareth's couches, declaring, "Before I return to that chintz abomination we stayed in last night, Headmaster, I could really use a drink."

I headed her off. "A moment, Mrs. Norris," I said. "Let me find something to cover a chair. You wouldn't want your damp clothes to ruin this lovely furniture."

Gareth looked at me, both of us wondering what was going on and how long she intended to stay. The day had been a constant series of disruptions and we had work to do. We were also wondering why she was dirty and disheveled. I would have thought she never appeared in public looking this unkempt.

She sniffed, and, as a mind-reader, I knew she was thinking that she didn't care what she ruined, but she hesitated, and that gave Gareth time to whip a green nylon poncho off his coatrack and spread it over a chair. She staggered across the room and dropped into it, staring around in confusion as though, despite her confident entrance, she wasn't sure where she was. Then she slipped her feet out of her shoes and curled her legs up beside her in the chair. "Scotch, Headmaster. Please."

At least she said please. But something about her demeanor wasn't right. So not right that I got my phone out again. Before I started to record, I hesitated. I'm not a cop, so I can do things like this. I am a person with a conscience, so I felt guilty taking advantage of someone who might not be entirely herself. Then I thought about what she'd done—or let be done—to her daughter. I started recording.

"We rather expected you this morning, Mrs. Norris," Gareth said. "After we spoke on the phone about Heidi's disappearance."

She waved a hand airily. "Afraid I was delayed a bit. Had to see my husband off and all that." She touched her head, as though she was trying to remember something.

Gareth fixed her drink and handed it to her.

When she reached for it, I saw that there was blood on the hand that had just touched her head. Now wrapped around the glass, it was smearing the crystal with reddish streaks.

I watched her closely as I asked my questions. "You and your husband left your inn and headed for the airport very early this morning, didn't you?" I said.

She nodded. "We were anxious to be away. General Norris had pressing business back in California."

"But when Dr. Wilson called you, you agreed that you would come back here to Simmons and help us deal with your daughter's disappearance."

"Did I? Such a busy time. I'm afraid I don't recall…"

"And now it is late afternoon," I interrupted. "When you spoke with Dr. Wilson on the phone, you said you would be here this morning. Where have you been for the past ten hours, Mrs. Norris?"

"Oh, don't be silly." She waved the glass for emphasis and liquid sloshed onto her hands and her clothes. "I came straight from the airport."

By way of where, New York City?

"Did you come in a taxi?"

She looked at me, puzzled. "The General drove me, of course."

"You just told us that he got on a plane to fly back to California."

"Oh dear." She took a bracing slug of her drink. "I seem to be confused."

Something was definitely wrong. I stepped closer, studying her face and her head. Some of what was slicking down her hair was definitely blood but I couldn't gauge the extent of any wound. Was it serious enough to make her lose track of time and become incoherent? We had little idea of her normal state, beyond self-centered and imperious, to compare this to.

"Gareth, I think we should call an ambulance," I said. "Mrs. Norris is injured."

"I am just fine," she declared. "And I am not fond of hospitals."

But we could see that she was far from fine.

"Maybe we should call Miller and Flynn," he said softly. I nodded, and he stepped out of the room to make that call. We didn't want to spook her. Who knew how she might react?

"Even if you can't tell me where you've been all day, do you remember how you got here just now?" I asked.

Mrs. Norris pondered about my question. "Escaped," she said finally. "I wanted to tell someone about...about The General's aide. About that poor man that got his head bashed in. Dum. No. Uh. Dee. Lt. Crosby. Such a nice boy. My ex-husband calls them Dee and Dum, you see. His aides. The General's aides, I mean, not my ex-husband's. If they were Ted's aides, they'd be nubile twenty-somethings with skirts up to their crotches and tops down to..." Here she fumbled, then gave up. "I had to escape, you see, because The General didn't want me to talk to anyone about what happened. He said not to be stupid or I'd get him in trouble."

I took a chance on my next question. "Why would your husband be in trouble?"

"Oh, you know. That whole business with Heidi." She rolled her eyes. "You see, I really don't want to talk about that."

I wanted to pursue the matter, but she was getting agitated and I knew she would resist me, so despite our desperate need to know the details of what happened in the picnic grove, and learn where Heidi was, and possibly even learn something about the baby's conception, I went back to questions about her timeline. Probably Miller would think I was poaching on his turf, but she was here, and somewhat talkative. I didn't want to let the moment pass.

"When you left the inn where you were staying very early this morning, Mrs. Norris, did you go to the airport?"

She looked at me blankly. "The General was going to take a plane. And then…" She sipped her drink. "You know, I can't remember much about what happened next."

"You got in your rental car. Did you go to the airport?"

"Yes. To the airport. Then we took a taxi to a hotel. Kind of a downmarket place. Not at all what I'm used to. Nor what my husband would normally choose."

She put a finger on her lips. "But I am not supposed to talk about that."

"Where is The General now?"

"At the hotel?" She giggled. "No. He's probably out looking for me and swearing like a sailor because I escaped. I was worried about Lt. Crosby, you see. If he was all right. People kept hitting him, you see."

People? Did she mean more than one? Obviously, she had been there last night. I would have to probe carefully to get the story without spooking her. Each in their own ways, Ted Basham and his ex-wife were giving us information we weren't meant to have.

Gareth slipped quietly back into the room and stayed by the door, learning against the wall.

"You escaped from your husband because he didn't want you to disclose his role in what happened down there in the woods last night?" I asked.

She nodded. "He was in the bathroom and Dum was out getting us lunch and I just slipped away. Then Dum…Lt. Ramirez saw me and chased me, and that's when I fell down and hit my head, at least, I think that's what happened. Maybe Ramirez hit me? Anyway, I hid in some bushes because I didn't want him to find me. Lt. Ramirez is not the nice man he wants people to think he is. It all has to do with my difficult daughter, you know. The General says not, but I wonder if he and Lt. Crosby did something…"

She stopped. "Oh, but The General says we will not speak about that."

She looked down at the delicate shoes she'd abandoned on the rug. "I was trying to walk here, but I wasn't feeling so well, so I called an Uber."

"Can you tell us what happened to Lt. Crosby?"

"Sandy?" Another giggle. "He got hurt. Ted went after him. I remember that. But Ted, you know. Such a wimp. He ran away. Then someone else hit him? Sandy, I mean, not Ted. It wouldn't bother me if someone hit Ted."

She tapped her forehead and sipped her drink and I tried not to yell at her.

"I forget," she said. "It was dark and very confusing and everyone was fighting and Heidi kept screaming. She was very angry with me for bringing her stepfather. I was supposed to go alone. I offered to help her leave Simmons until things settled down, find a quiet place to stay off-campus, which she was eager to do, and Heidi said she'd meet me if I came alone. Of course General Norris wouldn't let me go to a place like that by myself. Certainly not in the middle of the night."

Lorena Norris sighed. "She's always been so unreasonable where The General is concerned."

She gave us a look, which I presumed was supposed to convey what a caring and protective man her husband was. "You know what's odd?" she said brightly. "What's odd is that Ted was there. What was he doing there, do you suppose? I cannot imagine Heidi would have asked him for help. We all know how he is."

Or we were learning.

"So where is Heidi now, Mrs. Norris. Is she with The General?"

"Oh, don't be silly. Heidi hates my husband. I already told you that. She says he watches her. She says his behavior is inappropriate. Of course she's not with him."

I wanted to whack her, but somebody already had. "Then where is she?"

She gave a careless shrug. "Oh, she ran off somewhere. She's such a willful girl. Maybe..." Another shrug. "Maybe The General is still looking for her? I only hope Lt. Ramirez is more helpful than Lt. Crosby. Sandy. He does upset Heidi, though."

Gareth and I exchanged looks. Though neither of them had intended to be cooperative, we'd learned a lot from Ted Basham during his mutterings on the ride back to Simmons. Now we were getting information from Mrs. Norris. Everything her parents said and did deepened our concern for Heidi, and our understanding of why she'd needed to come here. Not wanted. Needed.

Mrs. Norris looked around the room again, as though she still wasn't sure where she was. "I came to get my daughter. Heidi. Have to take her back to California, where we can keep an eye on her. Really. Having a baby at her age. So irresponsible. I really didn't want children, you know. But Ted did, and then of course he was too busy to raise her. I was right, of course. She's been nothing but trouble."

A pause. A sip. "So, Dr. Wilson, do you know where Heidi is?"

"Don't you? She was down there in the woods with you last night."

She pondered on that for a while. "Down in the woods? What woods? I don't understand. Why would I have been in some woods at night?"

She cautiously fingered a fold of her dirty silk skirt. "Is that how I got so dirty?"

I wondered if her injury might have come from Basham's crutch. "Where Lt. Crosby was killed," I reminded her.

"Sandy? He's dead. Oh, that's so sad. How did it happen?"

She gave us a perfectly innocent look and finished her drink. "I think I want to go back to the inn now and get out of these clothes. It would be so kind if you would drive me, Dr. Wilson, but if you can't, will you call me a cab, please?"

"Mrs. Norris," Gareth said, "we haven't discussed your daughter yet, which is, I presume, your reason for being here. We're concerned about her whereabouts, and then there's the matter of the baby."

"Heidi? Oh, don't worry about her. We wanted her to come with us, but she ran off with that man while everyone was fighting. I'm sure she's fine. She's always been very good at taking care of herself. As for that baby, it is no concern of mine. I don't like babies."

Gareth and I exchanged looks again.

"What man would that be?" he asked.

"Oh, you know, Dr. Wilson. That silly old music teacher who has such a crush on her. I thought she'd left all that behind, but now he's appeared out of nowhere, supporting her in her ridiculous defiance, and believing all that nonsense about Crosby and Ramirez and The General, and now Heidi refuses to come back to California with us."

So William McKenzie had come.

The plot had now thickened beyond any hope of comprehension, and we were no closer to finding Heidi.

She was staring sadly into her empty glass. We left her to it and stepped back. "Are they coming?" I said in a low voice.

"Any minute," he said. "Flynn is. Miller is still trying to get a coherent story from Ted Basham."

"Good luck with that," I said.

I would be so glad to hand this mess over to Detective Flynn. Except that we still needed to find Heidi, and a new wrinkle—that she might be with William McKenzie—had developed in that area. If Heidi was with him, an adult with access to cars, taxis, hotels, or even planes, she could be anywhere. Could we count on him to understand why Heidi shouldn't run away? Would there be any way to reach him to even make the argument?

Gareth, having the same thoughts, shook his head.

We stood waiting, silent, hoping for the sound of steps in the hall and a knock on the door. A moment later it came, in the form of a visibly angry Flynn. He swept into the room like an avenging angel, and, ignoring us, crossed the floor until he stood directly in front of Lorena Norris.

She gazed at him blankly. "Are you my cab driver?" she asked.

"Lorena Norris?"

"Yes?"

"Detective Brian Flynn, Mather police. I am arresting you as an accessory to the murder of Lt. Alexander Crosby."

"Oh, don't be silly," she said. "If Sandy's dead, I didn't kill him. My husband did."

CHAPTER 29

—————◆—————

"Which husband?" I'd only meant to think the question, but it popped out before I could censor it. I guess I was more tired than I realized. MOC's growing presence was definitely making itself felt.

Gareth and Flynn were staring at me. Mrs. Norris didn't seem to have heard. She was brushing at some dirt on her skirt. Then she looked at me and smiled, and said, brightly, "Both of them."

"If you will come with me, please," Flynn told her.

"We're at the inn just down the road," she said. "I assume you know where that is?"

"Excuse me," Flynn told her, coming back to us and gesturing for us to follow him out into the hall. When the door had closed behind us, he said, "What the hell is going on? What is the matter with that woman?"

"Blow to the head, we think," Gareth said. "There's blood in her hair, and she seems very disoriented."

"Why the hell didn't you tell us that over the phone?"

Gareth spread his hands in a helpless gesture. "Because Lt. Miller didn't give me a chance to. Because he said you'd be right over and then hung up on me." He took a breath and then said, "It is not my fault, nor the fault of the

Simmons School, that Heidi Basham has the misfortune to have impossible parents."

He looked at me. "Thea, do you think we should play Detective Flynn the conversation you've been recording?"

Before I could answer, Flynn gave me a dirty look. "You and your goddamned phone again? It's a damned good thing you aren't a detective, because you'd be bounced out on your ass for this."

Right now, though I'd never tell him, being bounced out on my ass and letting the police deal with this three-ring circus would be just fine. Except I couldn't abandon Gareth.

"I know it's not admissible, Detective," I said. "Given her impaired state. But I thought it might be our only chance to get some answers, so I took it."

He held out his hand. "Give me the damned phone."

"I called for an ambulance," Gareth said.

Flynn looked torn. Calling an ambulance was the right thing to do. Police have an obligation to look after people, even their suspects, if someone is injured. But even though he'd be walking on eggshells in an effort not to taint anything he learned, he still wanted a chance to speak with Mrs. Norris without the presence, and kerfuffle, of medical personnel.

He sighed, fiddled with my phone, and my discombobulated conversation with Mrs. Norris began.

He listened all the way through, shook his head, and handed it back to me. "Gad, Kozak," he said. "You are a piece of work. Your husband teach you how to break the rules?"

I didn't give his question the dignity of a response. Nor did I tell him that plenty of cops—too many cops—as well as some bad guys, had honed my interview techniques. And my opinion that lots of cops know how to break rules, or at least bend them creatively.

It's hard to make anyone believe that I truly do *not* want to mix it up with bad guys. It's just part of the job I do. The part my partner, Suzanne, doesn't believe is necessary.

Maybe next time, she could jump in as a school's troubleshooter when something awful happens on a campus. Maybe her tidy suits and ladylike ways would work wonders with cops and bad guys. Maybe sweet smiles and a soft voice were the answer to finding Heidi.

He got out his own phone. "Okay. Do that thing you did with Miller's phone and send me that interview."

I had just finished and put my phone away when a commotion down the hall signaled the arrival of the ambulance crew. Usually you get the ambulance, EMTs, sometimes another car full of medical professionals, and often a fire truck as well. We got the works.

"This will help us keep the campus calm and running smoothly," Gareth muttered. "Will this never stop? This…uh…how do you Americans say it? A dog and pony show?"

"We're doing okay," I said, though I didn't believe it. I'd read somewhere that if you think and act positively, positivity will follow. Don't believe everything you read.

As we reentered Gareth's office, Flynn was on his phone, updating Miller. I caught the words "total clusterfuck," a marvelously evocative term, and not much more as the commotion of helping professionals arrived to take Mrs. Norris in hand. Gareth gave them a quick update and motioned to Mrs. Norris, who appeared to be watching her own hand moving through the air with the wonder of a small child.

Were we ever going to catch a break?

When the commotion, Flynn, and a loudly complaining Mrs. Norris, had departed and the office door was shut again, Gareth and I sat on the sofas and stared at each other in despair. Before our conversation began, he said, "Excuse me. I need a moment," and headed, I presumed, for the facilities. I needed a trip there myself, but first I had to check my phone.

Two from Suzanne. Important, but not first priority. A couple other client matters I could deal with quickly. Nothing from my mother, which made my breathing easier.

And an exuberant message from Andre. "I've finally found our house! Call me."

I called him.

"You may hate me for this," he said when he answered. "But I've gone ahead and made an offer."

I ought to have been mad. This was a decision we were supposed to make together. But I did not want to be bringing MOC home from the hospital to our rented apartment, and real estate deals took time. "Tell me about it," I said.

"Better than that. Check your e-mail. I've sent you a dozen pictures. It's perfect. It has a yard, and a workshop, and a perfect kitchen, and a master with a Jacuzzi, and—"

I couldn't check my email while we were talking, but his enthusiasm was infectious. "I'll look. This is exciting."

"You'll love it," he said. "So how are things going there?"

"To use a word I just overheard the local cops use, it's a clusterfuck."

"That bad?"

"That bad. I wish you were here. Everything is such a mess. The girl is still missing. Both her parents were evidently at the scene when the stepfather's aide was killed last night, and both of them are as narcissistic and looney as can be. The father dealt with his daughter's disappearance by going into town, getting drunk, and making such a scene the bar called and asked us to please come fetch him.

"The stepfather, who was supposed to be flying back to California this morning, never got on a plane and now he's missing. The mother says he took her to a seedy hotel and tried to lock her up to keep her out of the way, but she escaped. And then the mother, after being missing for most of the day, turned up with a head wound and an incoherent story both about her whereabouts today and about what happened last night. She says the girl, Heidi, has run away with her music teacher. No. Wait. That's not right. She fled the scene of the murder with a man her mother claims is her fiftyish music teacher from back in California."

"You think this music teacher is the baby daddy?"

"I think he's her knight in shining armor. Though honestly, at this point I don't know. And with all this chaos going on, plus a murder investigation, Gareth and I have had no time to deal with campus issue and the parents. It just keeps getting worse."

He said, "You want to quit and come home, don't you? But you can't because the school needs you." My husband is a perceptive fellow.

"Got it in one."

"You're not a quitter, though sometimes…" He abandoned his sentence. "Wish I could help."

"Me, too."

"You taking care of MOC?" I detected a protective papa bear growl in his voice.

"I'm trying. This kid has a thing about regular meals."

"Unlike mama. And your dad? Is he okay?"

"No relapse so far. He must be doing okay, mom is back to talking about a baby shower. A joint baby shower."

"You and Sonia together?" He knew how I'd hate that.

"That's her plan. Well. Her plan is that there should be a double shower and I should plan it."

"Unfortunately for your mother, you and I are going to be terribly busy moving into our new home."

"So sad," I agreed.

I realized I wasn't upset that Andre had gone ahead and made a decision about the house without me. I trusted his judgment. We'd looked at dozens of houses together. Plus, the word "home" resonated in such a positive way. I really wanted a home. I didn't get to dwell on the possibilities, though. Andre was still focused on the issue that had brought me here.

"How are you going to find your mystery girl?"

"Or her mystery companion? I have a few ideas. If we can get access to her cell phone records, there is probably a record of calls to him. By 'we' I guess I mean Sgt. Miller and Detective Flynn. Though I would much rather find her myself. They're so pissed off at this point they might not handle her very gently."

Was I remembering that one of her friends might have called William McKenzie and might have the number or was that Heidi herself? It was hard to sort things out when new troubles just kept happening. "I think one of her friends might have his number. And if we can contact him and convince him Heidi is in danger, and that she'll do better with the police if she stops hiding, then he'll be reasonable about bringing her back."

"You hope."

Andre was even more cynical about human behavior than I was. He had a lot more experience. But from all we'd heard, William McKenzie was a caring and responsible adult. His goal, again if everything we'd heard was true, was to protect Heidi from her obviously irresponsible, and quite possibly dangerous, family. I told Andre all that.

"But it's all speculation at this point," I said. "Getting straight answers from anyone is almost impossible. Her parents are competitive, self-involved liars who are more interested in who can best the other than in their daughter's welfare. Her friends are more forthcoming, but they're into that 'friendship trumps all' secrecy adolescents embrace, and there isn't anyone who seems to care that there's a helpless infant involved."

I thought I heard him growl. We are both very protective of children.

"You hope you'll find the girl before Miller and Flynn do because you don't entirely trust them not to be bullies. Are they bullies?"

"Just because I know some of the world's greatest cops doesn't mean..." I started.

"I think they're pretty good guys," he said.

Our words crossed. I laughed. He laughed. I didn't even ask why he thought that. Cops have such an old boy's network.

He said, "Come home to me," and I kind of melted, because that's what he does to me. "Or," he added. "I will come and get you."

I wouldn't mind that at all. "Go right ahead," I said, and we disconnected.

Gareth had entered so quietly I hadn't heard him come in. "Glad you can find something to smile about," he said.

"My husband just bought a house."

"Right," he said. "Do you get to live in it?"

"That's the plan."

"Well, we've got forty calls from parents, wanting an update on the situation here, and I expect more will follow. What do we do now?"

I wanted to look at the house pictures Andre had sent. Instead, I put my phone away and gave my attention to Simmons and its troubles.

CHAPTER 30

W ith help from the school's PR person, we slogged through another version of the message to be shared with parents who called, and a letter to be e-mailed to all of the students' families and posted on the school's website. I thought it was a pretty effective message, acknowledging their concerns and explaining that while a victim of violence had been found on the campus and police were investigating, that person was not a student or faculty member nor in any other way connected to the campus community. We then put the message in the context of the school's fifty years of principled service to the education of its students, and the fact that this event was rare not only in the context of the Simmons School history but that Simmons had a reputation for being extremely safe and caring within the private school world generally.

By the time we were done, darkness had fallen, rain had returned, and Gareth confessed himself "knackered."

"I need to go home and hug my wife and kids," he said. "What else do we need to do right now?"

"Nothing that can't wait. Take a break. We can meet again later, if you want, or in the morning."

There was a silence between us, as we remembered how last night had gone and reflected on our unspoken fears that something awful would happen again tonight. He might nestle into the bosom of his family and I might get some badly needed sleep, but neither of us would rest easy until Heidi was found, Lt. Crosby's killer was identified and arrested, and order was restored to the Simmons campus.

"Will Mr. Basham likely be returned to us by the police?" he said. "I confess I'm not keen on having him back in my house after all that's happened."

I didn't blame him. Nor did I have an answer about what Miller and Flynn might be up to, and neither of us was inclined to call them. Not after our last tangle with Flynn. They were probably up to their ears in trying to make sense of what Basham and Mrs. Norris had to tell them anyway. Neither of Heidi's parents was an easy interview. Then, if what Mrs. Basham had said just before the ambulance hauled her off was true, they would be out looking for General Norris.

Gareth was eager to be with his family. I was imagining a delicious bacon cheeseburger, a hot bath, and a long chat with Andre about the house, but there was one stone I needed to turn first. "Before you go, can you arrange for me to speak with Ronnie Entwhistle again?"

"Just Ronnie? Not the four of them?"

"If I'm remembering correctly, Ted Basham said Ronnie is the one who told him that William McKenzie knew about Heidi's situation. That Heidi had called him and he might be coming to help her. That was when Basham got into his "I'm the dad" thing and declared he'd sent McKenzie on his way. Since Mrs. Norris said Heidi left the picnic grove with McKenzie, McKenzie is our best chance for finding Heidi. To do that, we need his phone number. I'm hoping Ronnie might have it, and I'm thinking that he might be more forthcoming if I see him by himself."

"It's a good thought," Gareth agreed, "but I'm concerned about putting any of them through further questioning just now. They're very young and the whole business has been quite traumatic. I'm sure they're blaming themselves for all this. Jaden because of his fiddle with the infirmary door,

Ronnie because he fancies himself in love with Heidi, Bella for not being a better roommate, and Tiverton—well, you met her. She likes to fix things. She's a rescuer, and she hasn't been able to rescue Heidi."

I was impressed with his knowledge of his students. I'd known plenty of headmasters and deans at other schools who barely knew their school's populations. Still, I needed to talk to Ronnie sooner rather than later. My energy was ebbing. "I think Ronnie can handle a few more questions, but if you think that's too much, just call and ask him if he has a way to contact William McKenzie."

"I can do that." Gareth picked up the phone.

I could guess from what I overheard that Ronnie didn't want to see us and knew of no way to contact McKenzie. It disappointed me that Gareth didn't push harder, but they were his students and his job was to protect them. It also disappointed me that I wouldn't get a chance to observe Ronnie's demeanor when I asked my questions.

When Gareth disconnected and apologized, I didn't press it. I had one more iron in the fire. One I was deliberately not sharing with my client. He needed to go home to his family undisturbed by the details of my next venture.

He gathered his things and headed for the door, saying, "Let's both hope tonight is more peaceful than last."

I agreed, though I was still waiting for another shoe to drop. But if our experience was any guide, it might be that we were dealing with a centipede that dropped its shoes at random, and anything might happen.

As soon as the door shut behind him, I called Amad and asked if he could meet me. I said I'd catch him up on the details when we met. He was off work in fifteen minutes, he said, and would meet me in the parking lot outside.

Then I sat back down on one of Gareth's very comfortable couches and pulled up the pictures Andre had sent. It wasn't what I was expecting. Until a murder made it impossible, the house we'd thought would be our dream house was new and modern and on a street lined with similar houses. This looked more like his grandfather's farmhouse. On a country road, separated from neighbors by wide lawns dotted with substantial trees. It had a large barn that served as garage, and, I guessed, the space that would be his workshop.

I got nervous. I am a suburban type, while Andre is more rural. Would this really be *our* dream house, or just his?

I scrolled on. There was the big front porch we wanted—the one where I would be able to hang my wicker porch swing. A wide front hall with polished old pine boards. Sitting rooms to the left and right. I scrolled on to the kitchen. I don't get to cook as much as I'd like, but my dream kitchen needed to be big and bright. I didn't care so much about fancy appliances like a six-burner stove, but I affirmatively disliked stainless steel.

I held my breath and scrolled to the kitchen. This one had tall, glass-fronted cupboards, a large center island, and a window over the sink that looked out over what would be my yard. No stainless steel. The room needed paint and the appliances needed to be replaced. Otherwise, it was perfect.

Time was running out, so I zipped past the dining room and found the master bedroom and bath. Once again—perfect. How had he found this place, when we'd been looking for nearly a year and only once came close? And why hadn't he photographed the baby's room?

It didn't matter. If all went well, we were going to have a home.

I put the phone away and grabbed my coat.

Amad was waiting by my car, which I now noticed was parked in a very dark corner of the lot. I must have been awfully distracted when I parked, because I am easily spooked by dark parking lots at night. Normally, since I never know how long my days will be, I try to park close to the buildings or where there's a light.

When we were near enough to speak, he said, "So, Miss Thea, are we going to look for Heidi now?"

"We are. I hope you have some ideas, because I have none."

Amad had been my only idea. A man who could track in the desert seemed like an excellent ally under these circumstances.

Talking quietly, in case someone passed by, I filled him in on the afternoon's revelations, in particular what Mrs. Norris had said about Heidi running away with William McKenzie. "If she left with him, he may have a car, and then we have no way of locating him. I tried to get his phone number from one of Heidi's friends, but he claimed not to have it."

"That would be Ronnie?" Amad said. "The big, angry boy who is in love with her? It is okay, Miss Thea. I have that number."

Did Chief Greenberg have any idea what a treasure he had here? I doubted it. If I ran this place, we'd be waving goodbye to Greenberg's departing back and Amad would head security. Although Lewiston, and perhaps others, wouldn't like it.

"So, what do we do?" I asked. "Call first or search first?"

I wanted to ask what had happened with Ted Basham, but that would have to wait. We needed to keep our focus on finding Heidi.

"Search first," he said. "Those tracks led toward the outbuildings where we store old furniture, and equipment for the gardens."

"Weren't those buildings already searched?"

Amad's response was somewhere between a laugh and a snort. "And how carefully do you suppose they did that? A bunch of damp, dark buildings with cobwebs, truck tires, a tractor and…" He hesitated. "I think the word is clutter?"

"The word might be clutter. Okay. Let's go there."

"You may want this," he said, offering me a flashlight.

I smiled and pulled out my own mini Maglite, another gift from my cautious husband. I carry pepper spray and a flashlight with me always. At home, I had the mother of all flashlights, also chosen by Andre, perfect for blinding or bashing bad guys. I knew. I'd tried it out. This was the more ladylike traveling version.

Amad smiled. "That will do."

Despite the drizzle and damp, we passed dozens of students heading out to dinner. It seemed like every one of them knew Amad, and greeted him by name. It was a Simmons thing, but it was also an Amad thing. This man and this place suited one another.

Toward the back of the dorm buildings, where the road curved away into some trees, there was a lone figure hunched on a bench. Everything about his posture said despair. As we got closer, I could see that it was Jaden. He looked up, appeared to recognize us, then bent his head again. But while he might want to ignore us, we weren't about to ignore him. We sat down on either side of him.

Since he knew the students so well, I let Amad take the lead.

"So, this does not look good, Jaden," he said. "Why are you sitting out here in the wet?"

Without looking up, Jaden said, "I'm a liar and a bad friend."

"In what way are you these things?" Amad asked. His voice was soft and unthreatening.

"I didn't tell Ms. Kozak and Dr. Wilson what I knew. Everything I knew. If I had, maybe that man wouldn't have been killed in the picnic grove, Heidi wouldn't have run away, and my school wouldn't be in this awful mess."

"Why didn't you tell?" Amad asked.

"Because it wasn't my secret to share." He threw a quick glance at me. "I know you said that sometimes to keep people safe, we have to tell their secrets. But this was such an awful secret. I thought it was up to her whether she wanted to share it. I didn't realize she would be in danger."

It was damp and cold out here, and we were on a mission, but I stilled my impatience. What I hoped Jaden was about to tell us was very important.

Amad was taking it slowly, letting Jaden tell the story in his own way. Good that he was doing the interviewing, because I was so impatient I might have blown it. Jaden had already had two chances to tell us what he knew. I wondered whether what he'd held back had put Heidi in greater jeopardy and that was the cause of his despair.

"This is something Heidi told you?" Amad asked.

"Yeah. I mean like last night, when I went to see her at the infirmary. I mean, when I saw her there. When she asked me to fix the door. But it's…just because she told me doesn't mean that she wasn't telling the truth. I mean the truth about not having sex and not knowing she was pregnant. I guess. I mean, what she said was…"

Jaden had been trying to hold himself together. Now he started to cry. Crying in front of Amad might be okay. He was known, he was there to protect them and keep them safe, and he gave off a reassuring vibe. I was a stranger. And a woman. I stayed very still and tried to be invisible, resigning myself to the fact that this was going to take time, while Amad produced a handkerchief and handed it to Jaden.

Dark was coming in fast now, the way it does in the shoulder seasons. It seems like in summer and in winter, the light gradually fades out. In spring and fall, it comes on surprisingly fast. Darkness would make our search much harder. But this moment was important. I thought about the phone in my pocket, and how it liked to ring at inconvenient times. I hadn't put it on vibrate after my conversation with Andre. *Please,* I thought, *don't let Suzanne call me for an update.*

"I just hate that this happened to her," Jaden mumbled through the cloth pressed to his face. "It is so ugly."

He fell silent.

"Take your time, Jaden," Amad said. "It is hard to share ugly things about people we love. I know that. But what you have to say, it is important for protecting Heidi if danger is still out there, and maybe important for helping her to stay at Simmons, when we know this is a good place for her."

Thank goodness it was Amad, and not Chief Greenberg or even Miller and Flynn doing this interview.

"Would they really send her away?" Jaden asked.

This time I did speak. "Her mother wants to take her home," I said. "And if she has violated the school's rules, or the police decide to charge her with a crime, Dr. Wilson may have to. That's why it is so important to be able to explain her actions and show she's not a liar. And we still need to protect her from…"

I hesitated. The truth was that while we suspected her stepfather's involvement in some way, and that of his two aides, we had nothing to support that except her friends' stories of how things had been in the household. I thought Jaden was about to give us more substantive information, but we had to keep reminding him why betraying Heidi's confidence was so important. "From the person responsible for this pregnancy."

"Persons," Jaden said.

I wasn't about to correct him to say only one person had caused the pregnancy. There might have been more than one person involved, if there had been a sexual assault.

My stomach clenched in anticipation of what we might be about to hear. Footsteps crunched on the path, and the three of us fell silent, waiting tensely as a figure holding a flashlight appeared from around the curve. A burly man in a Simmons security uniform. He and Amad exchanged greetings and he crunched away.

"Persons, Jaden?" Amad nudged.

Jaden sighed. "I wish I didn't have to…Heidi will never forgive me for telling you this. It is so personal."

Another silence.

Sitting close to the boy on this small bench, I could feel his entire body gathering to tell us the story he didn't want to tell. At last he said, "It was The General's two aides. The ones Heidi's dad calls Dee and Dum. What they called their last chance before she left for Simmons. They put something in her drink, so she doesn't remember it well. But she knows her mother was out, and believes The General knew it was happening and didn't do anything to help her."

CHAPTER 31

A *date rape drug*, I thought. No wonder she didn't know she'd had sex. She hadn't, in any meaningful sense of the word. She'd been drugged and raped and her vile stepfather, he of the dismissive "she's not my daughter" and the claim that she had likely gotten pregnant "in the usual way" remarks, had let it happen. I wanted to strangle General Norris with my bare hands. A hiss of indrawn breath suggested Amad shared the sentiment.

Had her mother known?

No wonder Heidi had been so adamant that she didn't want her stepfather around. How terrified she must have been when, in desperation, she had asked her mother for help and her mother had appeared with The General and at least one of his aides. Her rapist and his enabler.

"Heidi had no memory of ever having had sex," I said. "Do you know whether she's remembered something or whether she was told about this incident?"

Even as I asked, I wondered who would have told her. Not even someone as insensitive as Mrs. Norris was unlikely to have done so, since it put her own husband in jeopardy. Not impossible, though, since back in Gareth's office she'd seemed to implicate her husband in a murder. Maybe her friend Stephanie? Maybe Stephanie had somehow been involved? Her mother's comments suggested something had happened that Stephanie also wanted to get away from.

"She says she remembered something," Jaden said. "Just some vague images that came back to her. She says she must have been repressing them because they were too awful to remember. And once they started coming, she remembered more. I don't understand, though, why she would ask her mother for help, when her mother let this happen."

"Maybe Heidi couldn't think of anyone else to ask?" Amad suggested.

"It was her mother that she'd have to go back to if she left Simmons," I said. "Maybe she hoped her mother would come through for her this time—help her negotiate with the police and how to stay here. Help her make decisions about the baby."

I wondered why, if she was trying to make a connection with her mother, she'd also asked her father to the meeting? Was he there as insurance? Was it possible that in the midst of her post-delivery trauma, Heidi had still deliberately engineered a confrontation with both of her parents, hoping they'd step up for her? Or to challenge them with their joint negligence and the damage they'd done before departing in the company of her music teacher? If so, she'd likely not anticipated the presence of The General and Lt. Crosby. There was no way to know until we spoke with her.

That confrontation must have been terrifying for her.

Mrs. Norris had been so proud of bringing her husband against her daughter's wishes because, as a woman, she needed protection. But had she known that Dee, and possibly also Dum, would be there, too? And how had the mysterious William McKenzie gotten involved?

So many questions and the only person who could answer them was still missing.

"Her mother is a monster," Jaden said. "And poor Heidi just kept hoping and hoping that her mother would change and act like a loving mother."

He sighed. "If I had to guess, I'd say she asked her father for help, and her father said something to her mother just because he can't help being provocative. I don't know why Mr. McKenzie was there. Maybe Ronnie does."

He checked his phone for the time, and sighed again. "I have to get to dinner, and then I've got a study group. Are you guys going to find Heidi? Will you make sure she's all right? Will you let me know when you find her?"

I was struggling to find an equivocal answer when Amad said, "Yes. We will find her, Jaden, and yes, we will keep her safe." Saying what he knew Jaden needed to hear. "Miss Thea will call you when we find her."

I was grateful that he'd answered. I can be a bit too righteous about telling the truth, although under duress, I've told some whoppers in my day. Always in the service of defeating bad guys or protecting the innocent, of course.

I put Jaden's number in my phone.

Before he left, Jaden asked me a question. "If there's anything else we need you to know, about finding Heidi, how do we reach you?"

I gave him my phone number, and added, "And I'm staying at the Caleb Strong Inn."

We stood together, watching Jaden walk away, his shoulders bent like he carried the weight of the world. Carrying the weight of a friend's terrible confidence was burden enough.

"We must be getting on," Amad said. "I must get home so my wife can go to work."

I followed him down the dark path to a cluster of unlit, deserted-looking buildings. When he stopped outside the first one, facing what looked like a big barn door, I said, "How do we do this?"

"We look," he said. "One building at a time. And hope that we will find her here."

And so we looked. Together. It might have been more efficient to do it separately, but he knew the buildings. And while I am as brave as can be, my personal history with bad guys has made me cautious, and MOC was making me more cautious still. Risks I might have taken by myself, I now would avoid.

As we moved among the clutter of machinery, tools, and supplies, I stayed back and watched Amad work, his eyes and his light constantly searching for signs of recent occupation. Could somewhere in one of these buildings have been the place that Heidi had referred to as the space she could crawl into and disappear?

There were four buildings and they took a long time to search. Careful as Amad was, I was the one who found it. Just a small hatch that I opened without expecting anything only to find it was the opening to what must have been a grain storage bin. It was musty, and empty, but the dust on the floor was disturbed by numerous footsteps, and a small, colorful backpack rested against the wall.

"She was here," I said, picking up the pack.

But though the contents definitely belonged to a woman—or a girl—there was nothing personal and no clues to where she had gone.

"How odd that she's left it behind," I said.

"It looks like she—well, they…" Amad used his light to show me footprints made by two different people, "left in a hurry."

That was all we found, and though Amad searched the area around the buildings, there were no clues about where they had gone.

In the end, we stood discouraged and empty-handed in the dark yard between the buildings. Dusty, dirty, and decked with sticky cobwebs.

"I am so sorry, Miss Thea," Amad said. "She was here. Now she is gone. She was here with another person. A man, I would guess. But I do not know where else to look, and I must be going home now."

"I understand."

I could only speculate about where Heidi and McKenzie might have gone, and no idea how they had left the campus without being seen.

"I'm sorry," he repeated. "Now I will walk you back. Simmons is a very safe place, but there are bad people coming from outside."

I was glad to have him walk me back. Before we set out, I remembered something else. "Amad, you said you have William McKenzie's phone number. Can you give it to me?"

"Of course."

I put the number in my phone, and then he walked me back to my car. I had to assume that hiding in one of those decrepit buildings was what Heidi had meant by a place she could crawl into and be safe.

The campus was eerily quiet. No one was out, and I was wondering if something had happened while we were doing our search, something that had called the community together, when Amad said, "They are all studying. That is why it is so quiet."

I watched him get into a weary little Corolla and drive away, wishing he didn't have to go. He might have had some thoughts about how to persuade McKenzie to trust us.

Then I got into my own car, started the engine, and just sat, holding my phone in my hand, wondering what the best way to approach William McKenzie was.

Maybe a cheeseburger would make things clearer. It might not have fine cuisine, but I bet that the inn we'd visited earlier on our mission to retrieve Ted Basham might have a good one.

I put the car in gear, and like a hungry Neanderthal in search of a woolly mammoth, I crept into town to bag a burger.

CHAPTER 32

I t was on the late side of the dinner hour, and I was tempted to snag one of the settles by the fire. They were tainted by the memory of Ted Basham and his disturbing confidences, though, so I picked a table in a quiet corner, gave my order, and got out my phone. Don't get me wrong—I hate being tied to a phone. Many days, I want to toss it off a bridge to sleep with the fishes, but I am a slave of duty, and often, duty contacts me via this buzzy little device.

Even as I sat there staring at it, the darned thing came awake in my hand and requested my attention. "Ms. Kozak? It's your innkeeper at the Caleb Strong Inn, Austin Palmer? I was just checking that you would be returning to us tonight? I'm afraid we've got rather a full house."

"I am returning to you, Mr. Palmer, just as soon as I finish my dinner. Unless some other catastrophe occurs between now and then."

"Very good," he said, "I shall look forward to seeing you."

Despite his politeness, he sounded frazzled. Maybe it was just the condition of the world these days. Or maybe, if she hadn't been detained by the police, the addlepated Mrs. Norris had returned, forgetting that she'd checked out. It was unsympathetic of me, since Mr. Palmer had been kind, but as long as I got my bath and some sleep, I didn't care what else was going on.

My burger arrived and I fell on it with gusto. A few stale sandwiches and some coffee just didn't do it for me. I try to do the salads and fish and chicken thing, but sometimes a person just needs to eat a good burger. Or steak. Or chocolate cake. I was tempted to ask for the menu back, to see if they had chocolate cake, but I was tired, and a bath and a chat with Andre beckoned.

Austin Palmer hasn't been kidding. There was only one parking spot left in the lot, and due to some very bad parking by a suspiciously familiar red BMW, I could barely squeeze the Jeep in. I was just coming in, happily anticipating my chat with Andre, when Ted Basham, thumping along on one crutch, lurched out of the breakfast room—now the room the inn advertised as its sherry and dessert room—and planted himself in my path. "You bitch!" he said, in what was definitely not an indoor voice. "You turned me in to the cops!"

It is something I discovered investigating my sister Carrie's murder, and have rediscovered during my illustrious career protecting independent schools—when men don't get their own way, they almost instantly revert to the "B" word. It helps to remember that the word is an acronym: Babe in Total Charge of Herself. I smiled at the glaring, crutch-wielding fellow, and said in my sweetest indoor voice, "Excuse me, but you are blocking the way to my room."

"I'll block you right in the head," the charming fellow responded, and by then, a very distraught-looking Austin Palmer had appeared from the bowels of the house, clutching a tea towel.

Now I knew what Palmer's phone call had really been about.

"Mr. Basham," he said, in tones that were both firm and polite, "I must ask you to be considerate of your fellow guests."

Under the circumstances, I had to work hard not to burst out laughing.

"Thank you, Mr. Palmer, and excuse me, Mr. Basham, but I am going upstairs now. As for turning you in to the police, threatening to strike a pregnant woman with a crutch might merit another visit from them. I should think you'd prefer to avoid that?" Clearly, Gareth's speech patterns were rubbing off on me.

Basham grudgingly moved enough to let me squeeze past, and I headed for the stairs. I resisted the temptation to whack Basham with my briefcase—a briefcase which has done yeoman service against bad guys in the past—and the even greater temptation to stop and inspect the dessert selections. Might there be chocolate cake? I have a sweet tooth as big as a tusk. But discretion is the better part of valor. Basham was gunning—or crutching—for me, so escape was in order.

As I passed the parlor, I noticed a familiar figure occupying the sofa facing the door. Mrs. Norris, cleaned up nicely and in jeans and a clingy white top was bent intently over her phone. I didn't know whether the new outfit meant she'd been shopping or that The General had reappeared with their luggage. I'd been right, her draperies did mask a dynamite body. It was her character that wasn't attractive. I was confused though. Hadn't Flynn said he was arresting her? Maybe this town had a rather porous jail.

I wondered if Basham knew she was there? Or was Basham here because he couldn't resist getting in his ex-wife's face?

The only thing that would have completed the picture was if Mr. Palmer had Heidi and William McKenzie also stashed somewhere around the premises.

I didn't pause to chat but hurried upstairs, eager to close my door on this nuthouse as soon as possible. Neither of Heidi's parents had anything to recommend them and if

The General sneaked in to join them, we'd maybe have a murderer in the house as well.

I dropped my briefcase and got out my phone, settling back against the vast array of pillows on my king-sized bed. King-sized beds seem silly to me. Andre and I sleep so entwined we could make do with a twin. I wished Andre were here to share this bed. It was very soft and wonderful.

I made a couple quick calls about clients, a longer call to Suzanne to update her about Simmons and discuss some simmering projects and our urgent need to hire new staff. Then I was ready for Andre. He didn't answer. I figured he was in the shower, so I left a voicemail saying I was in Room 12 and had a comfy king-sized bed and I wished he was here.

I wanted my delicious bath, but I didn't want to miss his call, so I waited, poking ineffectually at some paperwork and then staring into space as I tried to figure out some strategy that would let us find Heidi and restore order at Simmons. I wanted to call William McKenzie, but I didn't want to spook him. Even when I'd worked out a strategy and made the call, I went straight to voicemail. There was no way I could leave what I needed to say in a message, so I hit "end" and called Andre again.

Still no answer.

I decided I'd waited long enough. It was bath time. I was just getting clean underwear and the inn's plush spa robe when someone knocked on my door. I wasn't sure if I should answer. What if Ted Basham was there, and forced his way into my room? This was an inn, so there wasn't a peephole in the sturdy wooden door.

Exercising discretion again, I called, "Who is it?"

"Austin Palmer."

I opened the door and my innkeeper was standing there, holding a tray. He smiled a little shyly. "I thought you might be reluctant to come downstairs again, so I brought you some dessert."

My hero.

I smiled as he set the tray on a small table by the fireplace. Yes. There was chocolate cake.

"I thought General and Mrs. Norris checked out this morning," I said.

"They did. You saw them go. Evidently, she forgot. She was delivered here not long ago by a police car. She tried to go to her room, realized she didn't have a key, then pitched a royal fit when I reminded her that she'd checked out. An even bigger fit when I said I couldn't give her a room unless she paid in advance. I wasn't going through a repeat of their arguments early this morning."

"Did she have any luggage with her?"

"Just a couple of bags from a local store and one from CVS."

So, as far as we knew, The General was still among the missing.

"What about Mr. Basham?"

"Oh. His arrival brought real fireworks. The school called to reserve a room for him—I gather he was staying with the headmaster and it wasn't working out—and he showed up shortly after I'd taken Mrs. Norris to her room. I was just checking him in and he was being very impatient about it because the machine was slow when Mrs. Norris came down to ask for something."

He hesitated. "Demand something, I mean. A nail file, maybe? When she saw him, she started yelling. He yelled back, and I was forced to raise my voice to get them under control."

He swept a hand across his brow. "I do not like to raise my voice."

"You've had a hard day," I said. "Starting very early this morning. I've only met Mr. Basham and Mrs. Norris briefly, but my sense is that their relationship is pretty toxic."

"I can bear witness to that," Palmer said. "There's one further complication…"

He didn't get to finish before there was another knock on the door. A rather heavy fisted knock. I had visions of

Miller and Flynn, coming for a cozy visit, or Ted Basham, swinging his crutch.

"Who is it?" I asked.

"The man of your dreams," a voice said. And of course, it was.

I let Andre in, introduced to him Austin Palmer, and Palmer excused himself. "Mr. Lemieux, can I bring you something? Sherry? Coffee? Some dessert?"

Bless his handsome heart, the man of my dreams didn't correct poor Austin Palmer and say, "Detective Lemieux," something he is known to do. Nice of him, since Palmer had already had a very bad day. But my guy is a professional reader of people.

"Coffee and chocolate cake would be great," Andre said, grinning at me and looking past me at the bed. "We are both very fond of chocolate cake."

It was true. Andre and I liked to have bed picnics, where we spread everything out on a picnic towel, climbed under the covers, and snacked while we watched old movies. Chocolate cake was an essential part of those picnics. Alcohol usually was, too, but for MOC's sake, I was abstaining.

"I'll just be a moment," Palmer said, and left us.

"I am insanely glad to see you," I said.

He stopped whatever else I might have said with a kiss.

Andre and I have spent the years since we met doing a dance called "Don't rescue the little woman. She wants to rescue herself." Sometimes, the little woman had needed rescuing. Sometimes, she'd even rescued him. But tonight, I was delighted to see him. He probably hadn't come to rescue me. More likely, he'd been lonely, I wasn't that far away, and the man loves to drive. But if he had come to the rescue, I was more than willing to be rescued. Maybe I'd proved whatever I needed to prove. Maybe I was grateful for a sounding board who was neither an anxious client nor a skeptical local cop.

Maybe I just loved my husband.

Oh. God. That was so sappy.

There was a tap on the door, and once again Austin
Palmer entered with a tray. He set Andre's coffee and cake
down beside my plate of desserts, and turned to go. Then
he hesitated. "There's something…"

Another hesitation. "That is, there's another guest here.
Two guests actually. Who can't be allowed to meet some
of our other guests. That is…maybe I shouldn't even be
telling you this. Only you work for the school and I know
you are concerned about that girl's welfare. And quite
honestly, I don't know what to do. They were already here
when Mrs. Norris arrived. And then Mr. Basham. It really
is…"

He shrugged and spread his arms in despair. "Just a
nightmare. I've run this place for a dozen years and never
had anything like this."

He'd said, "they," so I braced myself. Either General
Norris and Lt. Ramirez were hidden somewhere in the
building, or it was Heidi and William McKenzie.

I went for the second possibility. "Heidi Basham and
William McKenzie?" I asked. It was so improbable it had
to be true.

"Yes. Oh yes, indeed. They've gone out, I sent them
down the back stairs, but when they come back, I fear all
hell is going to break out. And we've got other guests."

Andre was looking at me, waiting for an explanation. As
quickly as I could, I brought him up to speed.

Austin Palmer waited until I finished. "Maybe you can
head them off," he said. "Or sneak them in. Or
something?" He ended on a pleading note.

Maybe I, or we, could. If we knew where they had gone.
If we could do it without arousing the wrath of Miller and
Flynn. "Do you know where they've gone?" I asked,
hoping Palmer's talkativeness had gained him this
information. They might even have asked for directions.

"To the hospital. To see the baby."

"How long ago did they leave?"

"Maybe an hour ago. She slept most of the day, poor thing. At least that's what Mr. McKenzie said. He seems like a very nice man."

Another time, I might find Austin Palmer's gossiping troublesome, but he'd been an invaluable help in this case.

If we hurried, we might get to the hospital while they were still there. It looked like coffee and cake would be postponed.

CHAPTER 33

A fter Palmer had departed, Andre looked ruefully at the
cake. "I'm guessing you want to try and find this
girl."

I nodded.

"Can I drink my coffee first?"

I nodded again. I wanted to stay in, eat cake, and snuggle
up with this guy while he told me all about how he'd found
the house of our dreams. Instead, I quickly used the
bathroom. I combed a few clinging cobwebs from my
adventures in dark and dirty barns out of my hair while he
drank his coffee, then I grabbed my coat and followed him
out the door.

"I'll drive," he said.

I didn't argue.

"The local cops going to be pissed if you don't tell them
where to find this girl?" he said.

"Heidi Basham," I said. "Yes. But I really don't know
whether she'll be there or not. Or whether they already
have some kind of alert to let them know if she shows up
there. Maybe, since she allegedly abandoned the baby, they
didn't anticipate she might show up. Or whether the
hospital refused to let her see the baby and she's already on

her way back here. And local cops have got a murder to investigate."

"Which she may be involved in?"

"Or a witness to."

"Tell me what you know about this girl."

"It's a long story."

He was fiddling with his phone, finding directions. He seemed to fiddle for a long time before he set it down and Siri began telling him what to do. "We've got some time. So tell."

I told. The initial event. The psychiatrist's thoughts. The stories her friends told—initially and during subsequent contacts about Heidi's vulnerability, the presence of Crosby and Ramirez in the house, and her mother's inaction. The ridiculous rivalry between Heidi's parents that didn't show any concern about their daughter. The initial call to the picnic grove after finding Heidi's coat, my finding the body of a man we later identified as Lt. Alexander Crosby, and the incoherent versions of the events given in subsequent interviews by Ted Basham and his ex-wife.

I described our retrieval of the drunk Basham—with a quick aside about Amad—and Basham's subsequent disruption of the school meeting. The arrival of Mrs. Norris in a bedraggled condition and her story about escaping from her husband and her accusing her husband of murder. Told him about Jaden's painful and reluctant revelations about Heidi's drugged rape. Amad's and my fruitless search for Heidi on the campus. The possibility that she was with her music teacher, who had come from California to rescue her.

"Why the music teacher, if he isn't the baby daddy?"

"I think he's her knight in shining armor, come to her rescue because everyone else who ought to be helping her is pathetic, irresponsible, and self-involved."

"The poor girl," he said.

Then, after navigating a snarl of Boston drivers, "And that poor baby. What will become of her?"

"So far, neither of the girl's parents has shown any concern for the baby. Mrs. Norris proclaimed herself too young to be a grandmother and said the baby wasn't her problem. The dad, who's kind of a past-it Peter Pan, can't even care for his daughter, never mind an infant."

"Tell me about Sgt. Miller and Detective Flynn."

"Like you said, I think they're pretty good guys. Good interviewers. Impatient, as you'd expect. You've talked to them, haven't you?"

He made an affirmative sound.

"And of course, since I'd recorded Basham and Mrs. Norris, they kept trying to take my phone," I said. "I am tired of cops trying to take my phone."

"Maybe you should start carrying a 'drop phone' the way cops used to carry 'drop guns.' Make your recordings on a burner that you can hand over and go on with business as usual."

"In the future, Lemieux, I'll add a burner phone to the list that includes pepper spray and a flashlight. But the conversations I recorded with a drunk Ted Basham and a disoriented Mrs. Norris were on my real phone. They badly wanted the phone."

I stared out the window. "I wasn't giving it up. You're in my phone. Our house pictures are in my phone. My work is in my phone."

I was going to say my life was in my phone, but in truth, my life—Andre and MOC—were right here in the car with me.

"Your training officer should be shot," he said. "Don't you know that's all inadmissible?"

"Sure. But I'm not a cop, Detective Lemieux," I said. "Just a consultant. Even though Sgt. Miller doesn't quite believe that. I still wanted to make a record of what they were saying. Now, can we talk about something else, please? Something that isn't related to the rape of a child."

I shuddered as I said the words, realizing how horrifyingly true they were. "I want to know how you found that house."

I waited while the GPS chirped out a series of directions.

"The house? Guy at work," Andre said. "His brother had been out to a domestic at the house. Third time cops have been out there. I guess they did a lot of the renovations themselves—part of their dream of living in an old farmhouse in the country—and the process was ruining their relationship. Next day, the cop is gassing up his cruiser and sees a big moving van go by. Just out of curiosity, he follows it and yup, it goes right to that house. He decides to check it out, just to be sure one of them hasn't killed the other and is now heading for points unknown. Couple comes to the door, all smiles, says they've learned their lesson. They ran out of money, decided to finish the work themselves, and discovered home renovation is not for them. They think they can save their marriage if they get rid of the house. They ask if he knows of anyone who'd want to buy it, because they are in a real hurry to leave it behind. Guy says his brother knows someone—that would be me. I get the call, go look at it, and boom! We got a house."

"So much for realtors."

"Yeah. You wanna buy a house? Call a cop."

"As a marketing tactic, I doubt that it will fly."

"Worked for us."

There was a moment while he considered what to say next, then added, "There is still a lot of work that needs to be done. I only sent you pictures of the good parts. MOC's room needs...uh...a ceiling?"

"But you like that sort of thing. And you've got your dad, and your brothers."

"But will you be okay, living in a construction site?"

"We'll have to see about that. As long as it has a working kitchen and that beautiful tub, I should be okay. Just don't expect much help from me. Experience to date says I'm not very handy."

He flipped on his blinker and turned into a road that led to a parking garage. Parked, backing in the way cops do to be ready for quick escapes, and we headed for the hospital.

"Don't get nervous or anything," he said, "but we were followed."

I rolled my eyes. "Nervous? I've got a big tough cop with me. Probably we're being followed by more big tough cops."

He rolled his eyes. "We'll see."

I hoped it was just Miller, or Flynn, or some of their people. I wasn't in the mood for a confrontation with bad guys. I never have been, yet bad guys have a way of appearing in my life.

When we asked for the neonatal ICU, we got a dubious look from the woman at the information desk, and a rude glance at my rounding midsection. I was on the verge of huffily saying it wasn't for me when Andre showed his badge and we were on our way.

"I know you hate hospitals," he said, "but we're on a mission here."

I'd never been to a neonatal ICU, but I knew they were scary places. Doubly scary if you are a pregnant woman who has already lost one baby.

The man who reads minds put an arm around me and said, "You're okay."

Heidi Basham was sitting in a rocking chair, holding a tiny bundle with a little pink cap on its head. She wore a beatific Madonna smile as she bent over her daughter. It instantly brought tears to my eyes. The man watching her through the glass with a smile of his own had to be William McKenzie. He started when he saw us, his eyes darting like he was looking for an escape route.

Because I see him through the eyes of love, I forget what a formidable figure Andre can be—all six foot plus of him, broad and muscled and bristling with what the cops call "command presence." He looks at you and you want to confess every misdeed you've ever done. Well. Other people do. I don't. I've seen the guy in a teeny red Speedo. He looks at me and I get other ideas.

"Relax, Mr. McKenzie. We aren't here to arrest you," Andre said. "We've been looking for Heidi."

He nodded toward the girl and the baby. "I guess we've found her."

"Poor girl's scared to death that the school will throw her out. She can't go back to her mother's house," McKenzie said. "And she can't live with her father. He's a useless charmer who thinks he's a good dad. We just didn't know what to do. She's a wreck. I thought maybe seeing the baby would help."

He studied Andre. "You're a cop, right?"

Andre agreed that he was.

"And you're William McKenzie," I said. "You came all the way from California to do what? How do you plan to protect her from them?"

McKenzie shrugged. "I guess I haven't thought that through yet. Heidi needed help. She was afraid her mother would bring her stepfather, and that her stepfather would bring her rapists. And they would do whatever was necessary to keep her from revealing what they did. She begged her mother not to bring him. But her mother has never done anything Heidi asked. That hasn't changed."

"Does her mother know about the assault?"

McKenzie shrugged. "Not unless her husband told her. Heidi didn't know about it herself. Or have any memory of it. Or however you describe the aftermath of a date rape drug. But I think her mother knew something had happened. Even after Heidi was accepted, she was on the fence about Heidi going to Simmons—the expense and all—and suddenly it was a done deal."

McKenzie's clothes were rumpled and dusty, like he'd come straight for a plane and then spent some time in that dirty grain bin. He had flyaway curly hair and the vague blue eyes of a dreamer. A knight not in shining armor but in loosely woven hemp.

"Look," he said, "I know her abandoning the baby looks bad. But she honestly didn't know she'd had a baby. Not until she went to the hospital. And then bits of memory started coming back and she began to realize what had happened. What was done to her. And then she was panicked. She'd asked her mother for help. Then she asked her father for help. And she asked me for help. She had no idea what she was stirring up."

Another look at Andre, as though he was the one to be convinced. "If she needs corroboration, her friend Stephanie can provide it."

Despite her protective mother, it sounded like Stephanie and Heidi were still in touch. "We'll need to talk to Stephanie," I said. "Her information will be helpful in ensuring that Heidi isn't charged with a crime. I tried to reach her earlier but her mother stonewalled me."

McKenzie nodded. "Stephanie's a victim, too," he said. "Please tell me you're not here to arrest Heidi? She really didn't know she'd had a baby." His dreamer's eyes pleaded with us.

I wanted to say "save it," because in many ways, assisting Heidi to run away could have made things much worse. Instead, I explained. "We're not the cops," I said. "I work for Simmons."

A quick look at Andre. "What are you trying to pull here?" McKenzie said. "He's a cop. He said he was a cop."

"He's such a truth-telling boy scout, isn't he?"

He gave me a puzzled look and turned back to look at Heidi, peaceful in her rocking chair. "She's an amazing girl. A real survivor. She's survived a birth defect, and her toxic parents, and a nasty divorce and a perverted stepfather. She'll weather this, too, if she can stay at Simmons."

"Helping her stay at Simmons is what I'm all about," I said. "Gareth is in her corner and will keep her at school if he can. But she has to stop running and hiding and tell her story to the local cops."

And spend months in therapy, I thought, as the ugly memories surface.

"And who is going to protect her from Norris and his little toadies?" He looked at me, and then at Andre. "You two?"

I thought he was in the clearing last night with Heidi. Had he not seen what happened to Crosby? Had she seen it? Questions to be answered later. I bit back several retorts and merely nodded. "Why didn't you and Heidi go to the police?" I asked.

"Heidi didn't want to. She didn't think anyone would believe her. She's just a young girl who's been traumatized. She's scared."

"You said Stephanie can corroborate..." I stopped. "You're here as the grownup, right?"

He nodded.

"So why are you taking orders from a frightened and distraught sixteen-year-old girl instead of taking sensible steps to protect her?"

"She's very mature for her age."

"Excuse me, Mr. McKenzie, but when you talk like that, you sound like her pathetic man-child of a father. You can't protect her by hiding her. How does that help her return to Simmons? Or were you planning on hiding her forever?"

McKenzie didn't like that very much. "Look, I'm the only..."

A nurse approached the glass and glared at us, a finger to her lips. We were disturbing the babies. Heidi didn't seem to have noticed. She was smiling and rocking and holding her daughter.

Andre was watching the corridor expectantly. I wondered if he knew who we were expecting, or if he was simply prepared for whatever came. Ever since he'd said we were followed, my anxiety level had been amping up.

McKenzie's freaking knight in shining armor crossed with California hippie avatar wasn't helping. In a clinch, he was more likely to need looking after than to be useful. He was watching Heidi with a goofy smile that made me think he was imagining the three of them returning to California, becoming a little family, and making music together happily ever after.

I suppressed my urge to whack him upside the head and say "get real." He'd come when Heidi needed someone.

I shifted my attention back to the corridor. My money was on The General and his remaining minion. If it was them, Andre would have to do double duty. I'd mixed it up with bad guys before, but now that MOC was with me, I wasn't about to.

If it turned out to be Miller and Flynn, come to snatch up Heidi, I didn't know what I would do. I was supposed to be the rescuer. I had no idea how I would do that here, but I'd have to do something. That toddler's "I don't wanna" melt-down was looking very appealing again, but I'd criticized McKenzie for not acting like a grownup, so I couldn't take that route. Heidi was the child. I was the grownup. Somehow, I wanted to come out of this with Heidi safe, not in custody, and as soon as it was practical, headed back to Simmons.

Seconds felt like hours as I waited for something to happen. Shootout at the O.K. Corral was one thing. Shootout at the neonatal care unit quite another. I had crazy visions of a Matrix-style, slo-mo conflict, all done silently so as not to disturb the babies.

With McKenzie pressed up against the glass, watching Heidi like a kid at an aquarium, I stepped back and whispered to Andre, "I'm scared."

"Don't be. Everything is going to be okay. Trust me."

I did trust him. Of course I did. I just didn't trust anyone else involved this so eloquently named "clusterfuck."

It might be perfectly descriptive, but I needed to excise that vulgar word from my vocabulary.

I looked at Heidi again, watching her trace her daughter's tiny face with a fingertip. Mothering had to be instinctive for her. She couldn't have learned that from her own mother, the woman who hadn't wanted a baby. Who had blamed her husband when the baby wasn't perfect. Her mother—many mothers—would have been repelled and repulsed by a child that represented a horrible assault. I thought about how her friends had described her. Calm. Generous. Loving. I momentarily forgot about whoever was coming and joined McKenzie in watching a miracle.

It always happens in the moment when you let your guard down. I was watching a courageous girl and beautiful motherhood as General Norris and Lt. Aaron Ramirez burst off the elevator and stormed down the corridor, guns drawn.

What the hell were they thinking? Were they planning to burst into the nursery and grab Heidi, here in front of all these people and undoubtedly recorded by hospital security cameras as well?

Andre stepped forward to block them, and my heart seized with fear. He was strong and competent and fearless. But he was one to their two, and they were also presumably strong, competent, and fearless.

And armed.

CHAPTER 34

I stepped back away from Andre so that I couldn't be grabbed and used as a shield, while McKenzie turned and stared at the approaching duo, frozen in mid-turn.

The commotion made Heidi look up, and she jumped from the chair, holding her daughter protectively against her chest, her eyes fixed on General Norris and Lt. Ramirez, terrified, yet making a visible effort not to scream and frighten the babies.

A nurse stepped protectively in front of her while another put an arm around her and urged her toward a door.

Heidi stared at the two men like a deer trapped in headlights. She couldn't move.

Andre faced them, his hands up in a calming gesture. "Let's put those guns away, gentlemen, shall we? There are babies here."

Without responding, General Norris nodded at Ramirez, who tried to open the door of the nursery. It was locked.

"Shall I shoot the lock, sir?" he asked.

What was wrong with these people? These were tiny, fragile, newborn babies, and he wanted to fire a gun? What if it ricocheted? What if it went through the door and hit a baby, or the brave nurse who was now standing protectively on the other side of that door?

Why didn't Andre do something?

In another second, I had my answer. Moving as quietly and efficiently as a swarm of black ants, a Boston Police SWAT team appeared. It was impressive. Terrifying. Like something from a movie.

Seconds later, as Norris and Ramirez were being secured, General Norris loudly protesting his rank and his innocence, Miller and Flynn appeared.

"My hero," I murmured, linking my arm through Andre's. "Did you know about all this?"

"Sorta," he said.

I am not a cop. I don't see the mysterious things going on around me that he does. Well, not always, anyway. Once again, my training officer has fallen down on the job. I am not sufficiently observant. Had we been a strange caravan, moving through the night? First us, then Norris and Ramirez, then Miller and Flynn, on their radio, frantically organizing this? Was that why Andre, who normally drives like a bat out of hell, had taken his time on our journey? I thought it was because of Boston traffic.

William McKenzie still stood frozen, wearing the bewildered look of a man tapped to appear in a movie without being told what his role was. No. That was unfair. He might have been unfit for the lead role he'd cast himself in, but he *had* come when Heidi needed him, and she had definitely needed someone last night. He'd had a minor part, and he'd performed well.

In my pocket, my phone buzzed. My mother. I hoped she was only calling to talk about details for the shower, but I needed to be sure there wasn't a new crisis with my father. I answered.

"I've got some great ideas for that shower," she began.

"Is Dad okay?"

"Yes, dear. Of course. Otherwise I would have called you."

Yeah. Right. Like she did when he had his heart attack. "Sorry, Mom. I can't talk right now. There's a SWAT team here and some bad guys are getting arrested. I'll call you tomorrow."

I pushed end, leaving her to speculate about what I meant. Time enough for that tomorrow, when I could explain how we'd be busy with the new house. When I might have the patience for one of her rants about how other people didn't get into these messes and I needed to change my life and find a safer, more lucrative career.

Before they departed with their prisoners, Miller conferred briefly with Andre, thanking him for the heads up, and patted me on the shoulder. "Good work, Kozak," he said. "Now take that girl back to the Caleb Strong Inn, and don't lose her again before we can talk to her."

As if I was the one who lost her before, or the one in charge of her now.

"Before you go," I said. "What about Heidi? Will she be charged? Because you know that she's a victim here, just as much as that baby she's holding."

"We know," Miller said. "Her friend Stephanie called us and told us what happened. As much as she can remember, anyway. I assume we have you to thank for that, too?"

He looked beat, and grumpy, and already anticipating the long night of interviews and investigation that lay ahead. "We'll still need to talk with her, of course."

"Of course."

His smile was fleeting, but genuine, as he added, "Any time you want a job…"

"She's already got too many jobs," Andre said, wrapping his arms protectively around me. He and Miller and Flynn exchanged those cop looks that a civilian like me will never fully understand. Like they communicated on a different frequency.

"You're a lucky guy, Lemieux," Flynn said.

Then he and Miller marched off, surrounded by the fierce black ants, the general still protesting loudly. Through the glass, I could see Heidi standing behind the babies, holding her daughter, hope and wonder on her face as she watched General Norris and Lt. Ramirez being led away.

I looked at Andre. This part was over, a new phase of issues to be managed just beginning.

There was so much more that lay ahead. Updating Gareth. Getting Heidi safely back to the Caleb Stow, recovered and interviewed, and then reintegrated into the Simmons community. Gareth and Dr. Purcell would have the difficult task of helping her through the trauma she'd faced, and supporting her through police interviews and whatever criminal trials lay ahead. Helping her make good decisions about her daughter's future.

I was far from done, too. Gareth and I still had much work to do to reassure the Simmons parents and get things on campus back to normal.

Suzanne and I had new staff to hire and train. A zillion clients waited for my attention.

In my personal world, there was my mother to placate. A shower to be planned. My father to worry about. And all the challenges of our new, unfinished house. For once, something to look forward instead of dread. But, as Scarlett O'Hara reminds us in *Gone with the Wind*, tomorrow is another day. First, there would be chocolate cake.

EPILOGUE

Of course, sorting things out for Heidi, and for Simmons, was far from a piece of cake. Nothing ever is.

Heidi was able to stay at Simmons, and opted, with the support of her good friends, to share the reason for her pregnancy and why she hadn't known about it, which meant sharing the ugly story of her assault. In true Simmons fashion, the community came together to support her. It was a support she badly needed as her parents and stepfather went through their various legal processes.

Heidi's openness, and the community's acceptance of the situation, also made communicating with the Simmons parents easier. It took time, and several letters to parents and the parents of prospective students, but finally it was done without a significant impact on the incoming class.

Gareth thought the school was stronger than before.

Heidi's friend Stephanie had been there that night. She'd also been given a spiked drink but it had made her sick, and she had stumbled home in a dazed and confused state, too impaired to help her friend. Her mother had been out, and when she had confided the event to her mother the next morning, they had decided to wait and see how Heidi was. When Heidi seemed undisturbed and had no memory of the events, they had made the wrong-headed decision not to tell her what had happened or go to the police. Fleeing from the ugliness across the street had spurred Stephanie's departure for boarding school. Now she—and her mother—were wracked with guilt about what they had let Heidi go through, and how they'd let her rapists go free.

Spring came and students poured out of their dorms like creatures emerging from hibernation to turn their faces to the sun. Despite the grim days Gareth and I had spent doing urgent damage control, the warmth, and the sea of smiling students, comforted us as we wrapped up our business. I prepared to head back to Maine, to my next challenge—our house.

As I'd seen when Andre and I were at the hospital, Heidi had strong mothering instincts toward her daughter. After careful consideration, though, she decided that she wasn't ready for motherhood. The solution was an open adoption by a couple she already knew—Ruthie and Joel Ivens. In some places, the idea of a young mother giving up her baby to a couple who lived in the same dorm might have seemed crazy. At Simmons, it seemed reasonable. Indeed, Grace Ivens would grow up surrounded by love in a community that was delighted to welcome the little girl to their midst.

The model of a community being open-minded and accepting of each other also became a message for me. Much as I'd protested about having to plan a baby shower, never mind share it with my unpleasant sister-in-law Sonia, the Simmons model changed my thinking. This wasn't just about me. Mom and Dad were going to be wonderful grandparents, and Michael and Sonia's baby would be MOC's cousin. I didn't want to introduce our baby into a family riddled with strife and conflict. So when my mother called again to talk about plans, I swallowed my negative thoughts and plunged in.

The result was that Andre and I had a truckload of darling baby things, enough stuffed animals for triplets, and, as yet, no place to put a baby. But just as I'd swung into gear to plan that shower, Andre and his father were full speed ahead to finish the nursery so MOC didn't start life in a dresser drawer. Family rumor had it that Andre *had* spent his first month in a drawer, and he claimed it had scarred him for life.

The month after Simmons, I also took care of something to make my work life easier. I hired new staff. One more full time person, and a part-timer, to help us be more responsive to our client's needs. In the midst of our hiring, a miracle happened. My former secretary, Sarah, who used to read my mind and manage my life *and* my mother, finally left her abusive husband and moved to Maine. Just, as she put it, "so I could get my old job back."

After a few years of over-burdened dashes from one crisis to another, I found I was looking forward to coming to work.

The commute to work was longer, but it was on pleasant country roads, and I could already tell that I was going to become addicted to the farm stand and garden center I passed every day.

MOC kicked liked a soccer forward. Andre was singing while he worked. Reports were that Heidi and little Grace were thriving. And I was thinking about shucking "Thea the Great and Terrible" for good.

But maybe I've been a human tow truck too long. Someone will break down on my watch. I'm sure of it. And I will have to help.

Turn the page for an excerpt from

DEATH
COMES
KNOCKING

A Thea Kozak Mystery

Book 10

Kate Flora

I knew most people would think the soft gray green we'd chosen an odd color for a baby's room, but it was peaceful and soothing. The baby I was carrying was an acrobat. A night owl. A perpetual motion machine. I didn't yet know whether when MOC—our abbreviation for Mason, Oliver, or Claudine—appeared Andre and I would have a son or a daughter. What I did know was that whoever we met in the delivery room, the child would need peace and soothing. Or we would.

I was prying the lid off the paint can and wondering whether it was safe for a woman shaped like a whale to climb up the stepladder when the doorbell rang. I hesitated before heading for the stairs. We didn't know many people in our new town, which meant it was likely one of Andre's siblings. I like them well enough. They're family, after all, but they have a different sense of time from mine. Their visits go on too long and they're sense of personal boundaries seems nonexistent. I wasn't keen on a discussion of my girth, or my birth plans, or whether I was planning to breast feed, never mind whether MOC would be baptized.

Still, family is family so I headed downstairs. The woman I found on my doorstep was no one I'd ever seen before. I'd remember her if I had. She was absolutely stunning. She had long, straight black hair and piercing blue eyes and alabaster skin. She was wearing bright red lipstick and a dress that looked like she'd stolen it from gypsies—a multicolored extravaganza that screamed exuberance. I've never in my life owned something that bold. Tall women with big chests tend to try and minimize their physical footprint.

She smiled at me and held out a hand. "Hi, I'm Jessica." She gestured back toward the street. "I've just moved into the cottage."

It was only when she turned sideways and gestured that I realized the crazy dress was hiding a pregnancy about as advanced as mine.

"Thea," I said. "Come in. Welcome to the Whales Club. Would you like some tea? Or coffee? And I've got some lovely Finnish coffee bread."

"I would love some coffee," she said, following me into the house, "but I've given it up. Do you have any herbal tea?"

I did. Andre calls it 'gerbil tea' and says it tastes like a cup full of straw, but I've grown rather fond of it since I've cut down on coffee. Anyway, hibiscus and berry didn't taste like straw. In the kitchen, I put the kettle on, got out the bread, and sliced it. For a woman who often forgot to eat and usually had an empty refrigerator, I was becoming awfully domestic. Maybe having a house was changing me.

Jessica took a chair and studied my kitchen. "Wow. This is lovely. I've always wanted a place with tall glass cabinets like this."

"Me, too," I agreed. "So you've moved into the cottage. It looks really cute from the outside. Is it nice inside, too?"

She hesitated before answering, then said, "It needs some work. Well, a lot of work. But it will be nice when that's done."

We chatted, in the way women do, comparing our baby's antics and what we surmised about their personalities. As our talk went on, I realized that while she was a pleasant conversationalist, whenever I asked about her background, or why she'd moved to Addison, or any question that might have given me insight into who she was, she deflected the conversation to a different subject. After a pleasant hour, I realize that she knew a lot about me, and about all I knew about her was that her name was Jessica and she was expecting a baby girl. There had been no mention of husband, boyfriend, or significant other.

Her deflections were skillful. So skillful that I wondered if maybe she was hiding something. For all her attempts to appear casual and easy, once or twice, when Andre's dad and his cousin, who were working out on the barn, roared up the driveway in a truck, or dropped something with a clang, she was instantly alert and on the edge of her chair.

"My father-in-law and a friend," I told her. "They're fixing up the barn so we can put the cars there in the winter. And so Andre—my husband—can have a workshop out there. He loves to make things. He's made a beautiful cradle for MOC."

"Mock?" she said. "Is that what you're going to name your baby?"

"It's a nickname. Short for Mason, Oliver or Claudine."

"It will stick, you know."

"I know. What about your baby. Do have a name?"

Jessica smiled and patted her roundness. "Amaryllis. Amy for short. Her dad picked it out."

Then she went silent, her small teeth biting her lip, like she'd said something she hadn't meant to say.

"What does her dad do?" I asked. I didn't want to say 'your husband' because she wasn't wearing ring.

"Oh," she said, giving little Amaryllis another pat, "he's not in the picture."

I've been reading people for a long time, and it was clear to me that his absence wasn't her choice, and that it was very likely that his absence was permanent. I changed the subject. "I'm a consultant to independent schools. Private schools," I said. "My partner and I run EDGE Consulting. Right now, I'm working from home. Actually, yesterday they threw me out of the office and told me not to come back until Monday."

I looked over at the clock on the wall. In fifteen minutes, I would be calling in and Sarah, my secretary, would be updating me on all the crises that needed my attention. "Do you work?"

Yes. Rude question. But I was too curious to hold it back.

Jessica smiled. "I'm a consultant, too. To . . .uh . . . it's a government job. I just need to get the cable people out to get the cottage updated."

She'd almost given something away, though I had no idea what. I wasn't going to learn it any time soon, though, because she was on her feet and heading quickly for the door, saying, "Thanks for the tea."

I had no idea what I'd done to upset her, but she was definitely done here. So much for another new mother in the neighborhood. Maybe she was just shy or had something in the oven that would burn. So I tossed out, "I'm going shopping on Saturday to get some baby stuff. Want to come along?"

She hesitated a moment, like it was a big decision, then said, "Sure. I'd like that."

"Pick you up at ten?"

She looked down at her wrist, where there was no watch. "Sure. Ten. That would be great." And she was gone.

I stood in the doorway and watched her trot down the rolling green lawn, hesitating at the road and looking around her like she was afraid of hidden bad guys. She was definitely afraid of something. Then she hurried across and disappeared behind the hedge that shielded the cottage from the street.

———◆———

DEATH COMES KNOCKING

available in print and ebook

THE
THEA KOZAK MYSTERY
SERIES

Chosen for Death
Death in a Funhouse Mirror
Death at the Wheel
An Educated Death
Death in Paradise
Liberty or Death
Stalking Death
Death Warmed Over
Schooled in Death
Death Comes Knocking

Kate Flora's fascination with people's criminal tendencies began in the Maine attorney general's office. Deadbeat dads, people who hurt their kids, and employers' discrimination aroused her curiosity about human behavior. The author of nineteen books and more than twenty short stories, Flora's been a finalist for the Edgar, Agatha, Anthony, and Derringer awards. She won the Public Safety Writers Association award for nonfiction and twice won the Maine Literary Award for crime fiction. Her latest fiction is ***Schooled in Death***, her 9th Thea Kozak mystery. Her latest nonfiction is ***Shots Fired: The misconceptions, misunderstandings, and myths about police shootings*** with retired Portland Assistant Chief Joseph K. Loughlin. Flora divides her time between Massachusetts and Maine, and between cooking and gardening and obsessive writing.

CPSIA information can be obtained
at www.ICGtesting.com
Printed in the USA
LVHW031325240121
677344LV00002B/284